SECRETLY

[4 Books in 1]

Everything Changed When She Saw Him… The Latest Mind-Boggling Adult Collection to Release Stress and Anxiety after a Busy Day's Work

Amira Red

Table of Contents

5 stories: In-Depth Sex Stories for Lonely Men

6 stories: Taboo Stories of Forced Sex

5 stories: In-Depth Sex Stories for Lonely Men

Amira Red

Table of Contents

THE SWAP

Jim and Karen lived a few doors away from their best friends Peter and Wendy. All were in their mid-thirties and had known each other since college and had spent many holidays and social events together since then.

One Friday night, they found themselves in a group of eight at a wine tasting with several neighbors from the immediate area.

The wine had loosened a few tongues, and some of the questions became quite personal.

"You four are out with other people, that makes a change," came a comment referring to Jim, Karen, Peter and Wendy.

"We mix in larger groups, go out as a couple, as individuals, but as a group of four we have many common interests," Karen explained.

"Is one of those common interests a bit of bartering?" asked Matt, who talked about a bottle of wine over his limit and a big mouth at the best of times.

The group groaned in embarrassment, although secretly many would have liked to know the truth.

"There was nothing to report, no exchange of any kind," Peter offered.

All this had put a damper on the party and our four left early and went to Jim and Karen.

Jim put a bottle of wine and four glasses on the coffee table.

"We've all had enough wine, but just in case..."

They were all quiet for a while because the wine tasting had been disappointing.

"We gave them more ammunition when we left, now they imagine us all naked and lying in a heap on the carpet," Wendy remarked.

"You cannot control what other people imagine," said Peter.

"I can't blame them, I know what I would think if I were outside the group," Jim said.

"Are we all as pure as the driven snow, does anyone here want to confess that they have thoughts about another person in the group?

They were quiet for a while, then Karen spoke up.

"Remember that holiday in Scotland, it was Edinburgh, an Indian and a Chinese restaurant had been recommended, but we couldn't agree on where to eat. I took Peter and Jim to Chinese, and Wendy went to Indian.

"I reached for the soy sauce and rubbed my arm against Peter's arm, I held his arm and slowly pulled him away. That set me on fire, I think if we hadn't agreed to regroup later, I might have apologised by taking off my panties.

That was a wild thing to do by group standards. Not to be outdone was Wendy had a story to tell.

"We were on this cruise in the Mediterranean, and I hurt my foot. It was splinted in hospital, which made walking in the old cities quite a challenge. The three of them kept holding a hand or an elbow to give me support. I loved holding hands with Jim, I wore the splint and bandages longer than necessary.

Peter was next: "My weakness is to mentally undress Karen. In the unlikely event that I ever see her breasts or pussy, I wonder if they will look the way I imagine them to.

"That's no secret," Wendy said, "I often wonder if your intense looks will set her clothes on fire.

"That just leaves me," said Jim, "I keep dreaming of being shipwrecked with Wendy on a small tropical island. We never get over the problem of sand in our genitals."

"We are not quite as tense as we thought," commented Wendy.

The girls seem to like holding hands, it sounds very innocent, will someone change places?" Peter asked.

Peter and Karen made themselves comfortable on one two-seater, Jim and Wendy on the other.

They came closer and felt the warmth of their partner's thighs, held hands and talked quietly.

Peter and Karen's lips came closer and closer as they whispered. Jim and Wendy did the same. Each couple watched the other's progress. When the kissing began, there were no objections.

Karen climbed onto Peter's lap. Wendy immediately followed with Jim.

Karen opened her blouse: "You wanted to see if my breasts were the same as they appear in my dreams?

Peter reached for her and let go of her bra.

"In my dreams they were perfect, and they're even better in real life."

Jim was now kneeling on the floor in front of Wendy on the sofa with one hand on each thigh under her skirt, sucking on her nipples.

No one else dared to go on that evening, they ended the evening as if nothing extraordinary had happened, and Peter and Wendy set off for home.

They did not meet again until Sunday afternoon, when they went for a walk in the country and ended up at Peter and Wendy's house.

It was obvious that they needed a debriefing and a plan for the future, but they were all unusually reserved.

Jim broke the ice: "That was a great evening, my heart rate still hasn't normalized. Can I assume that we will all stay with our current loving spouses, with the possibility of further 'exchange' initiatives?

"Well said," Peter said.

The ladies both nodded in agreement and looked very pleased with themselves.

Peter and Jim decided to watch the rest of a game on TV, the ladies went into the kitchen to heat up some snacks and put on the coffee.

The game was over, the smell of coffee and food poured in from the kitchen.

Peter and Jim sat relaxed in their chairs, completely unprepared for their next surprise.

The ladies each came in with a tray of food and coffee - they only wore bras and panties.

"Remind me to tip the waitresses, Peter, lovely young girls," Jim asked.

"Peter has seen me naked on his bucket list, he's seen my breasts tonight, he might see my pussy. Karen explained.

"I suppose Jim and I will keep up with you - or go ahead," laughed Wendy.

Jim and Peter carried the trays back into the kitchen and put the dishes in the dishwasher.

When they returned to the family room they were presented with a wonderful sight. The ladies were naked and practicing dance steps to background music.

They asked the boys to sit down.

"Undress before you make yourself comfortable," Wendy demanded.

"Sorry, we're hopeless at dancing to stripper music and totally incompetent at lap dancing, but we'll do what we can," Karen explained.

"That's great, don't apologize," said Peter on behalf of the male audience.

Karen stood up on Peter's chair, lap dancing style, with one foot on each side of his thighs. That brought her pussy up to his face level.

"As beautiful as in your dreams?" she asked.

"Perfect." was all Peter could say.

"I wanted to split the lips of my pussy to show all my wealth, but I have to keep my balance, would you assist me, please?

Peter gently parted her pussy lips with his thumb and forefinger.

"I only have a tiny clitoris, maybe you can make it grow with your tongue," she invited.

Peter reached both hands, spread her pussy lips and tried to bury his face.

Jim and Wendy were at the same stage on the adjacent sofa.

The ladies changed their position and sat down on the boys' laps to kiss and touch each other.

"We can't leave you with angry erections," Wendy said, "I'll look for tissues and oils or lotions and hope that handwork is enough for the grand finale tonight.

Wendy instructed Jim to lie on his back on the floor and she overcame him in the style of 69, giving him a short lollipop before applying oil generously. He stuck one finger of one hand into her pussy and grabbed a breast with the other hand.

Karen had Peter on her hands and knees. She stood under him and turned down to suck his cock. Then she moved and positioned her breasts under his cock. Partly hand-fucked and partly tit-fucked, he made a deposit between her tits. Karen rubbed him against her skin and licked her fingers clean.

Jim and Karen went home, past the four neighbours who were also at the last party. They were standing in front of one of their houses, each with a glass of wine in his hand.

There were exchanged pleasantries, Jim and Karen felt suspicious.

"If they only knew what we've been up to lately," Karen laughed.

Within the group of four, nothing was said or discussed about the following weekend, except that they were to have lunch at a fish restaurant, followed by coffee and cake at Jim and Karen's place.

Maybe coffee and cake is a euphemism for coffee, cake, oral and vaginal sex?

In the middle of the afternoon Jim and Peter were in Jim's workshop when the ladies called them into the house. Wendy took Jim's hand; Karen took Peter and they went upstairs to the second and third bedrooms.

Wendy and Jim undressed quickly, he put his arms around her, grabbed her bottom and was up and in her before she reached the mattress. It lasted less than a minute.

"She laughed, "You have to catch the bus?

"Without that I would have been bursting at the seams, now I'll do anything you want, at your service.

"I'll finish off with a back and front massage with two fingers in the pussy and French kissing, then I'll ride you cowgirl. After that we will cuddle and sleep until we are hungry enough to go downstairs at six or seven.

Peter and Karen had a different approach. They kissed and cuddled on the bed before they undressed.

"Karen asked: 'Kiss and lick me from top to toe with special attention to my tits and pussy. If you do a good job, I'll do something similar to you. Then we'll decide whether we'll fuck first and then take a nap or take the nap first and then fuck before we go down for dinner.

That night, everyone agreed that they were anxious to fuck their spouses when they returned to their own beds, but they admitted they would fall asleep before anything happened.

SWIMMING AND SWAPPING

Angus and Sophia had been in their house for fifteen years. Angus was an avid do-it-yourselfer, and since Sophia was busy with the design and gardens, they had the house in good condition.

Their new neighbor's Bruno and Amelia were younger and they had bought a house at a bargain price that had not changed much since the 1970s. They worked hard to catch up with the furniture and improve their skills.

Many conversations took place over the fence, especially on weekends.

On one Saturday the residents on both sides of the fence were very busy until they stopped at about 5 pm.

Angus' last words were: "Skinny dipping our pool 8 pm sharp".

"You and your big mouth and your strange sense of humor, they may never speak to us again," Sophia lamented.

"Whenever we use our pool, it's usually just after dusk because you like the lights - and we go in naked so we don't have to rinse our bathers or destroy them with the chlorine.

"Yes, but we have no company and we invite them to be naked."

"A quick look at Amelia's tits would be better than a five-star movie."

"They're probably no prettier than mine."

"Probably not, but variety is the spice of life, and it could be detail, firmness, nipple length, colouring or something interesting.

"Angus, I think you're getting worse as you get older.

Around 8pm, Angus and Sophia were swimming naked in their pool and thought it highly unlikely they'd have company - until Bruno and Amelia walked in and had nothing on unless you count the two curled up towels Bruno was wearing

The visitors ran wildly towards the pool, shouting 'Good evening' as they bombed into the water.

"Do you often have lean dip evenings here," Amelia asked.

"Just us, never in company before, I thought Angus might have offended you, what about you, are you regulars in the nude bathing scene?

"Twice before, when we went to a mixed onsen in Japan, Bruno was disappointed because the ladies had such small tits, even if they were more to his taste, he couldn't have seen them through the steam.

"Another time, we jumped into a pond beside Ben Nevis in Scotland. Although it was the middle of summer, it was so cold that we couldn't find Bruno's penis or my nipples for an age afterwards.

"I have to thank you both for lending me tools, recommending craftsmen and advising me on do-it-yourself," said Amelia.

"Why change the subject, I enjoyed the tits and the nude swimming," Angus said, getting a serious look from Sophia.

They stayed in the water for an hour and Sophia suggested they have coffee on the terrace.

"You both reflect us in some way, the men have a strange sense of humour and we are all quite frank," commented Sophia.

"You can't argue with that," said Amelia, "it feels as if we've known you for years.

"You both, how shall I put it, come over here naked in response to something that could have been a joke, that's very daring, lead an exciting social life,"

Angus asked.

"Do we get along with other people, is that what you want to say?" asked Bruno.

"That's none of our business, we're just talking," Angus replied, sounding apologetic.

"We have swum naked with other people, two, now three times. Twice we've been to parties that were about gentle swapping. We didn't go back to reach higher levels of swapping.

"I'm curious, what exactly is soft-swapping?"

Partners are swapped to kiss. Normally, on this level, everyone is in the same room. Depending on the group, the rules may allow touching above the waist, under or over the clothes".

"Sounds like harmless fun," Angus said, "I'm ready when the rest of you are ready too.

"I think we must discuss this Angus," Sophia said sternly.

"We've just done that. All those in favour, raise your hand."

Three and a half votes in favor, counting a somewhat weak arm rising from Sophia.

The girls went into the house to freshen up and came back in underpants.

"Topless smooching, here we come," said an excited Bruno.

They started with the men sitting on patio chairs, with one girl on each lap. For greater comfort, they went on couches and lay down horizontally.

Within thirty minutes, they all emerged to get some air. After a very exhausting day they were tired and waking up on a cramped couch would not lead to a productive Sunday.

Amelia asked Sophia how she was feeling.

"I've always been a bit of a prude. A few hours ago I would have divorced Angus because he agreed to a gentle swing, he almost got kicked out because he invited you to swim naked. My attitude changes from minute to minute.

"It has to do with the feeling that we have known you for years and like and respect you both so much that the whole process is accelerated and exciting.

"Now I wonder what would give me more pleasure, a good hard fuck with Bruno or watching Angus fuck Amelia - but not tonight, I'm knackered."

"Well, same time, same place, same order of undress, tomorrow?" Bruno asked.

"Will I see you for coffee sometime during the day to plan the evening?" Angus suggested.

There was a lot of excitement in the air the following day at the morning coffee.

"Shall we swap places after our swim tonight?" Bruno asked.

"Shall we all continue with kissing and touching above the waist? asked Angus.

Four hands were raised very quickly.

"That's the tricky part, do we add oral sex on women, blowjobs, vaginal sex as a gradual process or do we jump ahead with our feet.

"All this," they shouted in unison.

Do we really have to develop a set of rules or do we just have to play it by ear? asked Sophia.

"Rule number one for most groups should be No means no. But I cannot imagine that there are insoluble border issues within this group," Amelia noted.

"In some groups, there might be jealousy because a couple only kiss and their spouses are kissing each other, and their spouses are going at it over the top full-gender. That wouldn't apply to us either," said Sophia.

"You know, these deck chairs are not meant for two. Shouldn't the ladies go into the comfort of their own bed and let the men change the house, or is that too bold at the moment? asked Angus.

"I would feel very safe in this situation with my spouse next door. And Sophia, if my husband tries to enter the wrong hole and doesn't take no for an answer, you have my permission to cut his balls off with a plastic spoon. exclaimed Amelia.

"Just kidding, Bruno, I know you'll treat Sophia with the same kindness and respect I get." She went on.

The swimming lesson went on as before, only this time Bruno and Amelia bombed the water and shouted: Rubba Dubba Doo!

The coffee on the terrace was drunk very quickly. Angus and Amelia went next door, Bruno and Sophia went upstairs.

Bruno and Sophia hopped into bed.

Sophia called her husband: "I'm about to pick up another man's cock, the first time since I met you. I love you," said Sophia.

He replied, "We're off to a slow start, but tonight my cock goes in Amelia's mouth and pussy, the first time since we met, it's somewhere else than with you. I love you, sweet dreams."

He hung up the phone and reached for the pussy.

"Oral sex in both directions, me on top, then lots of cuddling and a good night's sleep," Sophia asked.

"Sounds perfect," he replied, "Let me know if you're not feeling well or if you want me to do something special, can't wait to find the most sensitive parts of your pussy lips.

Next door, Angus and Amelia collapsed in armchairs, each with a glass of iced water, to get some rest before the main event. They recovered quickly,

Amelia approached him on her knees with a mouth full of ice. She took his cock in her mouth and used her tongue and swirled the ice and her tongue with great effect.

When enough ice had melted so that she could speak, she said, "I think if this was done properly, it would be alternately hot and cold.

How was that?"

"Incredibly good", and with that he moved her back to her chair and slowly fed ice cubes into her vagina with his tongue.

"How was that?"

"More than amazing."

So, they went upstairs and had Angus-on-top missionary sex and snuggled up until morning

The next day was a holiday. They all sat around the morning coffee cups and looked, as they say, like cats that had been in the cream.

They agreed to schedule an extra night once a month for their birthdays, holidays, National Windbag Day, St. Patrick's Day, King Solomon's birthday and any other special events that might arise.

THE NEW FRIENDS

My wife Mary and I met some new friends last Friday evening in a café in the city central when things took an interesting turn.

To describe Mary first, she has 5'6 long, taut legs, big 40D breasts that have just begun to yield to gravity, a round, firm ass and only a hint of a belly. She has long dark brown hair and beautiful deep brown eyes that give a hint of Indian descent. I am 1.90 m tall, have a shaved head to hide the quick baldness, broad shoulders, a somewhat thick belly, but overall a stature that is above average for a man.

We had been talking online with Ken and Kathy for a few weeks, we had met in a swinger's group and talked about movies and general nerdy stuff. This was to be our first meeting face to face, and a café seemed ideal. It is a neutral territory. Nobody feels pressured when they are near a private room, nobody is forced by alcohol to make decisions they might regret later.

When Ken and Kathy came in, I was devastated. We had of course exchanged pictures, even some naughty ones, but the camera didn't do them justice. Ken looked like a male model, like the hero on action figure packages. He was bald, full lips, dark eyes and a natural smile. His shirt bulged and rippled when he moved his arms, his muscles contracted and threatened to burst at any moment. Kathy looked like an Amazon. She was six feet tall, slim, dark night-black, with cheeky breasts, wide hips and long legs, accentuated by a miniskirt that constantly revealed her amazing ass.

I stood up and shook Ken's hand as they approached and gave Kathy a light one-armed hug. We talked for a moment, and then Ken and I went to the counter to order while the wives got to know each other a little. What attracted us to each other at first were movies, and it wasn't long before Ken and I talked at length about the new movies that were coming out, and what movies we thought were hot garbage, and which ones looked so bad they were good. While we waited for our drinks, I took a look back at the table and looked up Kathy's skirt for a moment, not sure if it was on purpose or not. I told Ken that Kathy looked amazing and he replied that Mary was an absolute knockout, an opinion I agreed with, but it was nice to hear others say that.

After a few hours of sitting and talking and three cups of coffee later, we decided to move this conversation to my and Kathy's house to play some board games and get to know each other over drinks.

As we both had a drink at the dining table, we started handing out cards for a few rounds of Cards against Humanity. It was a great icebreaker game full of inappropriate laughter. I kept staring at Kathy and noticed that Ken and Mary were also appreciating each other. After a few drinks and a few rounds we started to play a strip version. Whose card was chosen as the winner was allowed to choose one of the other players to remove an item of clothing. It didn't take long before we had Mary and Kathy stripped down to their bras and panties. Mary was wearing a matching black lace bra with lace-trimmed boys' panties, and Kathie was wearing a red bra and matching thong. Ken and I had both been stripped down to our boxers.

Mary won the round, and as she looked around the table, she finally said: "I just have to see what Kathy's nice tits look like to make the top girl burst! That made us all laugh as Kathy pulled up her bra and let her breasts out. They were smaller than Mary's and perkier, with dark nipple areas on her midnight skin and big nipples. Ken's victory made Mary lose her bra next, Kathy reached behind Mary and unzipped the bra that Mary threw over her head onto the pile of discarded clothes behind her. Her breasts sagged a little, but her fullness and voluptuous nipples still held her full attention.

Kathy won the next round and Mary lost her panties. My wife got up from her seat and stepped onto the table, taking care not to disturb the cards or the drinks, and slowly rolled her panties down her legs, spinning in a slow circle as she bent down and pushed it up to her ankles, she bent down lower and exposed both Ken and Kathy's ass and pussy, she turned her head over her shoulder to Kathy, "is this what you wanted to see?

"Is this what you wanted to see?" "You're damn right it is! The pussy's wet enough to lick stamps!" Kathy replied. Mary stood up and stepped out of her panties and left it in the middle of the table before stepping back. Kathy helped her down and ran her hand up Mary's inner thigh as she stepped back.

"Well, I guess I'm out of the game now, so I get to watch," Mary said as she sat down on the chair with her legs slightly spread.

This time I won, and I looked between the two new friends we'd made: "I can't wait to see Kathy's delicious pussy, but I think if Ken stays in these boxers any longer, his boner will come out of them and tear them apart, so let Ken see what you've got! This surprised everyone a little bit, but only for a moment before Ken started giggling and stood up and peeled off his boxer shorts and revealed a massive cock that was as coconut brown as the rest of him. It hung long and the stuff between his legs was a light ten inches and a good three inches in diameter. It was the second largest tail I had ever seen, and the largest was a soccer player we all hated to shower with in high school because there was simply no comparison. Ken pushed back his chair and occasionally stroked his cock to get it to full erection while Kathy and I finished the last round.

We decided that the only fair way to do this was to give Mary the opportunity to choose the winning card. This time it was Kathy who climbed onto the table and unfastened the strings on the side of her thong that was holding her, as

she climbed back down, Mary stood up and grabbed it. Kathy sat down on the table and Mary kissed her. I could see their tongues flirting into and out of each other's mouths.

Mary broke the kiss and lightly pressed on Kathy's shoulder to signal that she should sit back, which she did. Mary then began to kiss her breasts and licked the left nipple first, then the right. She moved her kisses onto Kathy's flat stomach and onto her hips. Mary kissed and then bit slightly on the skin of Kathy's inner thigh. Kathy arched her hips slightly upwards and Mary moved her mouth closer to Kathy's pussy lips. She teasingly licked her clitoris with the tip of her tongue. As I watched my wife lick Kathy's cunt, I pushed my boxers down and freed my hardened cock.

My cock is thicker than average, but only slightly, depending on my horniness and the weather it is between 6 and 8 centimeter's, it is quite thick, but the best part of my cock is the head. It has the circumference of a tennis ball, most of the women I have been with have no problem taking my full length, but my full circumference is another story. Mary herself had trouble with it until after our second child. Now I watched her sucking and licking this other woman's sweet-smelling pussy and I started to caress myself lightly.

Kathy moaned and pulled Mary's face deeper into her spread legs and lifted her hips as she orgasmed, only to finally calm down again. Mary sat up and then climbed over Kathy's body onto the table, curled up and kissed a new way up her body until she reached her face, kissing her deeply and passionately before turning around and lowering her own soaking wet cunt onto Kathy's eager mouth before diving back hungrily for more of Kathy's sperm. Kathy pushed her tongue inside my wife, licked the outer folds of her lips and then sucked on her clitoris.

As I rubbed my hard cock, I felt a hand gently caress my balls. I looked down and saw Ken massaging my balls, he looked at me and smiled, now I have never been with another man, I have never found any man sexually attractive. I've seen guys that look good, but they didn't do anything for me, but that was sending a little bit of electricity through my loins that became a full power plant when Ken bent down and started sucking just the head of my cock. He licked and sucked the head and let it jump out of his mouth with an audible pop every now and then. I leaned back the head and closed my eyes as he teased my cock. I had never kissed another man before, let alone had a duck on my cock, it was a strange feeling. I felt the stubble of his bread rubbing against my balls and thighs and tickling as he maneuvered my cock around in his mouth. He was talented at it, he kept bringing me to the brink of orgasm and then pulling me back again.

Kathy and Mary both orgasm together on the table, and Ken kept bringing me to the brink of orgasm before pulling back and letting me calm down. As the women came towards us, Ken stood up and kissed Mary on the mouth while Kathy fell on my lap and wrapped her arms and legs around me.

My cock found her dripping wet appearance easy and she started rocking her hips and pushing me deeper inside. Her pussy snuggled around my cock and stroked my length from the inside. I bent down and licked her nipple, took one in my mouth and bit her slightly. "Mmmmm", she moaned "harder!" I bit harder on her nipple and rolled it between my teeth. She bucked and pressed hard on my lap and I felt her sperm roll past my balls.

Over Kathy's shoulder I could see Mary bending over the table and Ken ramming his cock into her. She gasped for breath and moaned violently as he hammered into her, her hands gripping the sides of the table. She opened her eyes and watched as Kathy twitched in my lap before another orgasm. I grabbed Kathy's shoulders and began to push her body down while I pushed my hips up and penetrated deeper into her until I finally cramped my cock in her pussy and filled her with my sperm. Kathy moaned as I shot my load into her, then she leaned in and gasped for air, kissed me on the lips and then on the neck. She rose from me, small drops of our cum dripping freely and she made her way back to the table and climbed to the top in front of Mary. She spread her legs and pulled Mary's face into her neatly trimmed pussy. "Fuck you clean!" She moaned, "Lick your husband's sperm off my pussy."

That was all Mary needed when she drove her face in and wrapped an arm around Kathy's leg to hold her down. Ken grabbed Mary's hips and punched harder, obviously turned on by the show that was going on in front of him, until finally I saw his leg start to twitch and he cried out a deep throaty moan, and I knew he had just reached orgasm and was emptying his balls into my wife. Mary collapsed on top of Kathy, and Ken staggered back into the chair next to me.

This was the first time the four of us played together, but I hoped it wouldn't be the last.

THE SUMMER DAY

There is nothing more beautiful than a wonderful summer day in the cities. It was a Friday afternoon, and I was having a few beers with some friends in a bar by a lake. We are all teachers at a local high school and take full advantage of an afternoon without work. Joni is teaching social studies right next to me. Matt, who is also Joni's husband, is an English teacher at the other end of the building. Joni and Matt are a few years younger than my 31 years, and they are good friends with my wife, Kate and me. Kate is not a teacher, so she gets a bit jealous of our seasonal freedom.

We had a few pitchers of beer when Matt asked if Kate would join us later.

"I think so. She gets off work at 4:00 today, so she'll be down in about half an hour. Can we have dinner later?"

"I think we probably should," Joni replied, "This is the first chance we've had to hang out with you guys this summer. With all the time we spent in the cabin, we weren't sociable enough, and we'd love to spend more time with you guys.

She winked at me when she said that, which I found a little weird, but Joni has always been a little weird. Both she and Matt started working at the same school as me two years ago. We were friends, but it wasn't until this year that we became close friends. Joni was the teacher the kids loved. She was a hip young role model for the girls and a physical role model for the hormone-driven boys. I certainly didn't mind that a petite, strapping blonde worked 25 meters away from me. It kept my mind from wandering to the tits the teenage girls at school were so proud of and showing off with.

Matt doesn't mind that Joni is the object of so many teenage fantasies, and in fact, some girls (and a few boys) have a big crush on him. His fit physique, brown hair and eyes and short beard look strong, but he has a cool, literature-loving attitude.

After further conversations about how our summer had gone and about the students we keep coming back to, Kate showed up smiling. She was wearing a blue sundress that showed off her long athletic legs. Joni stood up to hug her and the contrast in her heights was dramatic. Katie had to bend her 1.5-foot frame down to meet Joni's 1.5-foot frame. It was a beautiful sight for Matt and me when Joni's short white skirt blew in the wind and standing on her toes strained her slender legs and tight butt. My wife leaned over and showed a bit more cleavage than she probably knew, and Joni gave her a quick hickey on the lips. When my wife was surprised, she didn't show it.

We sat together for an hour or two and talked, went to dinner and had a really great afternoon with great friends. "What are you gonna do now?" Matt asked. "I'd like to go home and let the dog out, but I don't want the evening to end. Would you like to join us for wine and let the evening continue?"

"That sounds great, but we live in the opposite direction and if I have more wine I might have to attack Dave here," my wife replied smiling and stroked my thigh.

"Joni gets the same when she's drinking. I'm surprised she hasn't fucked someone on the toilet today."

"How do you know I haven't?" she replied with a big grin. "Plus, we have this extra bedroom for both of your problems. If it's too late to go home, just stay the night with us."

Her conversation about Joni screwing someone else was a surprise, even if it was just a joke, but it turned her on a bit. We agreed to have a drink with them and we all got in a taxi. I sat in the front to accommodate my 6 foot 2-inch-wide shouldered frame, and the other three piled in the back. I could see Joni leaning into my wife more than she needed to. She sat in the middle as the smallest of the group and whispered something to Kate while Matt stroked his wife's leg.

We came to their place, and Matt immediately took out a few bottles of cabernet. Joni put on some music. While they did this, I used the privacy to tell my wife how sexy she looked today.

"Thank you very much. You look pretty sexy yourself, and it seems that Joni would agree with that. On the way here, she told me how she said she could attack you here too and that she was jealous that I would get fucked by it.

"She said this while sitting right next to Matt!?" I asked incredulously.

"I think he heard it and seemed turned on by it. She should also be a bit jealous, you're hot. Not that I'm not a bit jealous of her, Matt is a sexy man."

At that point, Joni came back and danced her jazzy beats Matt was right behind her while wine stared at Joni's swaying ass moving in front of him. Matt sat down in the armchair and Joni quickly took the middle of the sofa, leaving the ends free for me and Kate. As we sat and joked and listened to the music, the conversation continued to carry its sexual theme.

"I thought you were going to attack Dave?" Joni reminded Kate that.

"I have to admit I was thinking about that big piece of meat all night. Maybe I'll just drag him to your guest room and fuck him twice!"

"Big piece of meat, huh?" and Joni bent over and grabbed my crotch! I was definitely half-eased with all the sexual innuendo, not to mention the two sexy women sharing a couch with me. I tensed up, but Matt and Kate just laughed. "This feels really impressive! I'd love to see it. Kate, do you mind if I pull it out and take a look?"

I don't know if I was more shocked by Joni's audacity, Matt and Kate's laughter or simply the fact that my opinion didn't seem to matter. When Joni started unbuttoning my pants, I looked over at Kate and saw just a sexy smile, so I let it go.

"I'd love to see what kind of 'meat' you're packing," Joni said as she pulled my tail out of my pants. She started stroking it a bit so it could grow. "You're right, that's a nice dick!"

Joni stroked me until I was seven inches tall and tried to put her fingers around my thick shaft. While she was doing this I could see Matt's cock moving in his pants and my wife biting her lip with lust in her eyes and both of them watched as Joni slowly moved my cock to a full erection.

Joni broke the silence. "I know you're looking for some yourself," Kate stared, continuing to stroke my full length. "Since I enjoy your husband's, you could probably find something you can enjoy on your other side.

I looked across the room and Matt had pulled his own stand out of his pants and slowly stroked it while he watched his wife fiddle with mine. His cock was impressive, being over six inches tall and almost as thick as mine. He had a head that looked bigger and the veins bulged thickly. He looked at Kate and gestured to her. She went over to him and knelt down where she could inspect Matt's cock and take it in her hand. Since the boundaries had already been crossed, Kate bent down and took it in her mouth. I felt a touch of jealousy when I saw my wife sucking another man but I quickly got over it when Joni fell down and kissed the head of my cock. Her blue eyes looked up at me as she dropped her mouth and swallowed a good four inches. I put my hand through her curly blonde hair and pushed her further down. She gagged a little while she drooled all over my cock and it felt incredible. She tugged at my balls and stuck them further down her throat than Kate ever could. She bounced up and down while she stroked my shaft hard. Joni enthusiastically sucked a cock and it felt incredible.

As I looked over to my wife, I saw Matt looking at me smiling as I watched Kate do her best tricks that I knew so well. Kate sucked a mean cock and was really after Matt's thick stick. I had trouble pulling Joni off my cock but I didn't want to suck my cock too fast.

Joni has responded to this. "We have all night. It would probably be a good thing if you stuck one down my throat. Then you'd last longer if you start fucking me."

"There's nothing wrong with that logic," and I pushed Joni's head back on my dick. I still had no reason to rush, so I pulled her around. I put one leg over my ear and grabbed her smooth thighs. I always manage to delay orgasm when I'm busy eating pussy.

I don't know if she took her panties off when she wanted to turn on the music or if she was without them all evening, but under the flowing white skirt she was completely open. No underwear. No hair. Just a straight, sleek, shiny, wet pussy. While Joni put the head of my cock back in her mouth, I stuck out my tongue to taste her juicy pussy. I licked her slit up and down a few times, but her small frame made it difficult to reach her. I stuck my tongue into her pussy a few times and tried to suck on her clitoris, but our different heights made it uncomfortable. So, I tried what I could reach. I started rubbing her asshole. She took a quick shot and cramped up, but relaxed quickly. Joni seemed to take my licking on her back hole quite enthusiastically as she pushed her ass back towards my face. I licked around and stuck my tongue into her tight ring while she moaned around my cock. Kate is not as into ass play as I am, so I took advantage of the fact that someone is having so much fun. Then I knew my goal for the evening. To stick my dick in this fantastically tight ass.

"MMmmmmmmmmm!!" I was so engrossed in the blow job I was getting and the ass I was eating that I forgot about my wife until I heard her moan. I looked over, and she was sitting on Matt, who dropped on his dick. I felt a hint of jealousy. We had fooled around a bit, but now there was another man fucking my wife.

Joni might have felt it when she turned around and stroked my dick. "God, they look so sexy. See how much pleasure they feel? I can't wait to feel your dick deep inside of me." Joni moved one leg over my lap and looked me in the eyes. She lowered her pussy down to meet the head of my dick. The crown of my rock-hard shaft slowly worked its way in. Her pussy was wet from her juices and my saliva, but it was just smaller than what my cock is used to. We had to pull it out a few times and put it back in again to stretch her tight pussy. Eventually we worked it in so far that Joni closed her eyes and she just sank into my shaft.

Slowly Joni rocked her body back and forth. I grabbed her hips and pushed her body up and down. Her graceful stature made the difference to Kate's tall, slim body. We fucked slowly until I accepted that it was okay for me to fuck my girlfriend. And that her husband was fucking my wife. I think Joni sensed my lightness when she started to really go for it by fucking on my stiff dick. As my confidence in the situation improved, I started to take more control. I turned her around and put Joni on her hands and knees. As I pushed my cock back into her hot pussy, she sank down to her elbows and moaned.

"Fuck me! Fuck me! Fuck me! Fuck! Fuck! Shit! Fuck me with that big dick!"

I pounded her pussy fast and hard. Something about her still wearing a skirt and a top made her even sexier, but I had to get rid of the restriction of the pants around my knees. I withdrew to take off my inhibiting clothes and Joni took the opportunity to do the same. Her petite frame had perfect hand tits and a beautifully curved ass. I groped her tits and licked her nipples, but had to quickly get back into her hot cunt. I turned her back in doggy style and when I plowed a steel cock back into her cunt, she let out a soft moan. "I'll be right there. I "ll be right there. Keep doing that." I felt obligated and I grabbed her hips and slammed them hard. I was on this beautiful level of alcohol, where I was rock hard but got fucked forever. After a few more minutes of hard pounding in Joni's smooth pussy and fingers on her clit she started shaking and screaming.

"Fuuuuuckkkk!! I'm coming! I'm purring!"

I took advantage of her orgasm to distract her, to further my goal of getting up her ass. I took my pussy-juiced finger and pushed it in her back door when she came. I stuck it in up to the second knuckle when her asshole was squeezed around it. When she came down from her orgasm, she slowly kept bouncing back and forth on my dick. She also let her asshole relax a bit and allowed me to finger her tight ass while I continued to fuck slowly.

I looked over at Kate and Matt and saw my wife coming down from her own orgasm. I know her sex, and that was a big one for her. I expected her to turn over asleep at that moment, but other people had other plans. Matt lifted her off his cock but led her back on her knees and grabbed her head. He tried to get her to suck his cock right after he fucked her! Kate had denied me this pleasure in the past, so I started to feel sorry for

Matt because he didn't get his nut, but she opened her mouth and went down! My anger that Kate would do this for him and not for me was short-lived because I had two realizations. One is that Kate opens up and I will be able to cross more boundaries. Two, I'm goanna stick my dick up John's ass.

I watched Kate eagerly swallow as much of Matt's cock as she could bob up and down quickly and hard with her head. Matt grabbed her gently by the hair and helped her to speed up her blow job after fucking. He was in heaven when Kate swallowed his cock up and down. I could see he was about to blow, but I had more pressing and selfish concerns. I was still slowly rocking back and forth in Joni's tight pussy. I was still fingering her asshole. I watched as Joni turned her eyes towards her husband's cock as it disappeared and disappeared again in my wife's eager mouth. It definitely turned her on watching them while she was still bouncing back and forth on my stiff cock. As Matt began to buck his hips more enthusiastically into Kate's mouth, Joni started shaking again. Matt let out a deep "Fuuucckckkkk..." as he blew into my wife's waiting mouth and Joni came back on my cock while she watched with intense eyes. When Matt was done and my wife let his cock fall out of her mouth, Joni spoke up.

"Matt, honey. Why don't you run and get the bottle from the nightstand? Everyone came but Dave. I think that big cock deserves a real reward after all the work he's done." Matt started swinging his cock, and Kate grabbed a sheet to keep warm and curled up on the edge of the sofa. I knew what was coming towards me, so I pulled back to turn Joni around and kiss her deep.

"Here you go, buddy! Don't use it all!" said Matt as he came back and handed me the bottle of lubricant. I wondered how he felt so natural as he walked up to another naked guy and was so casual. I thanked him a little too enthusiastically and opened the lid.

I pushed a big teaspoon and started rubbing it up her asshole. I used my finger to push it a little bit into her asshole while she moaned. I squirted a little and rubbed it on my cock while moving my other greased finger further in and out of her asshole. Joni sat on her knees and moaned softly while Kate stared with big eyes. She seemed in awe and fear of Joni as I prepared us both.

"I can't believe you let him fuck you in the ass! I let him try, but I can't relax. Are you sure he "II fit? You've got such a small bottom, and it's..."

"Sooo... big?" Joni jumped in while Kate thought about how to describe the situation correctly. "And hard? And ready to fill my little bottom?" Joni really knew how to build up the anticipation. "I'm sure it will fit. Matt's dick hits my G-spot from this side when we do this. Not often, but a real treat when we do this. I think Dave hits it without too much trouble and hits it hard. I can't wait to get there while he fucks my ass. He just needs to take it slow to get started. You hear that, Dave? I've got a small ass and my tight little asshole needs you to let go of the fat cock real slow."

"Of course." I said as I started pressing my dick head against that sexy little hole. "I wouldn't dream of just sticking it in." I said, even though I wanted to do exactly that. "I'm just goanna loosen the tip a little bit."

My wife slowly lowered herself to her knees so that she could take a closer look. I still don't think she had blinked since she realized what was about to happen. Meanwhile, Matt sat back down on his chair and started rubbing his re-growing cock again. Joni had her eyes closed and took a deep breath. She made some sounds that were half grunting as if she was working on it and half moaning as if she was jumping on it. I played my part in this show by working my shaft into it piece by piece. I dropped some more lubricant where my cock and her ass were connected. Then I grabbed her left hip with one hand while using the right to guide my central appendage. I pulled back a little bit, more lubricant, then I let go a little bit. Kate still sat there like hypnotized and started to move more and more. Obviously she began to feel the excitement in her own loins. After a more torturous slow repetition of this cycle, I was finally about two inches inside Joni's bottom, and Joni's grunting had turned into a moan. So I began to make deeper strokes. I pulled it out almost all the way and then pumped it back in. Still slow but almost full strokes with my cock. I definitely hit the G-spot from behind every time I went deep.

Joni got off clearly and it spread. Usually too tender for a second round, Kate had started rubbing her recently fucked pussy while watching her husband tap her best friend's ass. Matt was fully erect again and had fallen to the floor behind Kate. She had kneeled down to get a good show and her legs were a little spread. Matt grabbed under her ass and started to help her work on her pussy and clitoris. She was almost hypnotized by the show as she let Matt readjust her position like a puppet while she could still watch closely. He pulled her down on her knees and spread her legs and put her in a similar position to Joni where she was right now. Once he had her in that position, he went down and replaced his fingers with his tongue. The room now filled with two groups of moans, the ever louder and softer moaning of Joni and the almost whispering moan of Kate.

"God, who feels so good... keep fucking. You feel so good in my ass! Keep fucking me, and I'm coming."

I didn't need the encouragement, but I took the direction anyway.

"Your ass is so tight! I fucking love it. I'll be there soon."

"Not until I do! It won't be long!"

"I can hold out for a few minutes, but soon I'll explode! Where will I come?"

"I'd like you to come on my face, but after all the hard work you put into my ass, it wouldn't be fair to force you to retreat, so you should just shoot me in the ass.

"Fuck, yeah. I'm goanna fill your ass with so much semen!"

As I kept fucking Joni at this now frantic pace, I could barely hear Matt asking Kate if she wanted him to fuck her again. She nodded slowly and let out her loudest moan yet as Matt came up behind her again.

"Could you... maybe... touch my bottom?"

I heard in a whisper. Because of my confusion, I almost pulled away when I heard Kate. She asked to be allowed to touch her butt? Ioni's thrill definitely made Kate question her earlier beliefs.

"Sure thing, babe," Matt replied. "I'll just use some oil to make it a nice massage."

Matt grabbed the oil and smeared it on Kate's ass. I could see him slowly rubbing the ball of his thumb around Kate's asshole. Suddenly I was torn back and forth what I was supposed to see, my cock spearing the sexy ass right in front of me, or my wife being fucked from behind while her asshole was being massaged by a very attractive man.

"How's that? Does that feel good?" Matt was very considerate and didn't want to scare Kate off.

"That's good. Really good. Please. Please keep doing that."

"Oh, God!! Shit! Keep it up. Fuck me!"

I wasn't sure who said that. Joni and Kate both seemed to be coming at the same time. I was numb myself, feeling so good with my dick deep up a tight, beautiful arse. Suddenly Joni's asshole started cramping on my dick. Her buzzing made her body shake. The pulse was in perfect timing with my thrusts. The grip of her asshole pulled the sperm right out of me and I sent several ropes deep into her ass.

At the same time I looked over to see Katie shaking as Matt pulled himself out. He sent his sperm all over her ass. He slowly and sensitively stroked his cock against her asshole as she came down from orgasm. My jealousy was washed away when I saw my wife, who looked so sexy, happy and wonton. Our sex life would change, so much is unknown, but I'm looking forward to it.

"Mmmm... I'm soooo tired..." Joni said as she collapsed on the couch. "I had originally planned to suck Matt's cock to sleep so I could get a taste of Kate, but he may have to wait until morning."

Kate twitched again, but I noticed that she didn't seem afraid of such a comment, as I had expected before that night.

"You have a shower in the guest bathroom next to the bedroom. I'm sure you want to clean up after our escapades. I know I'll want to take a hot bath. There are clean towels, and the sheets on the bed are fresh. Good night, you two. We had a wonderful evening."

"Thank you for your excellent hospitality. I'm exhausted, and I'm sure Kate feels the same way."

"Mmm hmmm..." murmured a naked Kate with heavy eyes.

"All right, off to the shower with you. Matt's sperm is still all over your ass." I said, as I helped her up on her feet and into the guest room. We entered the main hallway to the guest shower. Kate turned and held me as the warm water ran down our naked bodies.

"So... the night was... interesting."

"I gotta say. We're swingers now, my cock was in my colleague's ass, and you show up as a lewd bitch!"

Kate laughed at my generalization when she started soaping us both up. "What do you think about that? We've gone somewhere we've never been and we can't go back."

"I had a really hard time seeing you with Matt at first, but then I realized how sexy you looked, getting fucked like that in pure bliss. Since I'm usually the one fucking you, I hadn't seen you from that perspective. I was surprised when I realized how turned on I was. I mean, I was jealous when I saw some things, like you taking Matt in your mouth after he was inside you and making him play with your ass..."

While I was saying that, I casually dropped my hand on her ass and casually rubbed her crack up and down.

"How come I can't do these things?"

"Well, I was kind of caught up in that moment. A lot of things happened that I never thought I would do or agree with, but here we are. When I put Matt in my mouth, I didn't even think about how he'd been in my pussy, I just knew I wanted him to cum. Then I felt so sexy. It felt dirty, but empowering at the same time. And then when I saw how sexy you and Joni looked with your cock up her arse, I was jealous. Not that my husband was fucking another woman, but that she could enjoy anal sex so much. Made me wish I could do the same. I wanted to see if I could feel some of what Joni was feeling. Again, she felt dirty, but instead of feeling ashamed or disgusted as before, she felt dirty sexy. Somehow, I liked being that, what did you call me? A "wanton bitch"? Maybe we can try again sometime," Kate explained as she slowly soaped my cock. We had long since cleaned each other, but were still soaping each other up. I was hard again and wanted to make love to my wife. I slowly penetrated her with my finger and kissed her deeply. "Be gentle. I'm pretty tender from the pounding Matt gave me."

"We don't have to. We've both had a long night together and we don't have to overdo it."

"No! Please, don't... I need to feel you inside me. I need you to get inside my pussy! I just want you to be gentle. Please make love to me," Kate said as she started to pull my cock towards her opening. I put her back against the wall of the shower. I lifted her left leg so it was around her waist and slowly walked into her. We continued to kiss deeply while I gently stroked her in and out. As this position became a bit too much for Kate's back and leg muscles, I pulled her out and turned her around. She put her hands against the wall and spread her legs for me. As I entered her from behind, I turned her face backwards for another duel of our tongues. When I reached down and started stroking her clitoris, she immediately started to hum. Her pussy started to contract, which triggered my own orgasm. I pushed my cock as far as I could into her and got deep into her womb. It felt different than my previous orgasm tonight. It was amazingly sexy and pleasurable, but this one came from deep love.

We had been in the shower for over 30 minutes. I turned off the water and reached for the towels. I wrapped Kate in the fluffy white towel and kissed her again.

"I love you, honey."

"I love you, too, babe."

We slipped into the sheets and looked at each other. And we were both just laughing.

THE REUNION

Karyn rang the doorbell when she and Joe arrived at Walt and Jean's. It had actually been a year since the couples were together. From the inside, there was a muffled "Come in!" So the couple opened the door and went inside. Jean and Walt waited naked.

"It's so good to see you," Jean said excitedly. "I've been horny all week, just waiting for you to come!" She greeted Joe with a passionate kiss and began unbuttoning his shirt with one hand even before he closed the door. With the other, she felt his cock, which was growing fast in his pants, while Joe returned her greeting by bending down to suck her breasts. Walt did the same with Karyn, who was already walking up with her hands under her shirt and opening her bra.

Within a short time, Karyn and Joe were as naked as their hosts, their clothes scattered in random piles outside the front door, the four of them together with the spouses of the other side, who threw themselves directly into the activities of the weekend.

Jean and Joe lay on the floor. Walt let Karyn sit on the couch while he knelt between her legs. Jean and Joe eagerly explored each other's bodies, their hands clasped each other and familiarized themselves with the joys of their long-time sexual partners, who had been their first barter couple.

Jean happily felt Joe's cock as he sucked her breasts and rolled her nipples with his tongue. Their legs were intertwined, their bodies pressed together and rolled merrily on the floor.

"I missed your big cock so much!" Jean breathed hoarsely.

"He missed you too!" Joe replied, his cock was hard as a rock and throbbing as it felt its way between Jean's thighs. She felt it, reached out hungrily for him and began to caress him. Joe reached between Jean's legs and ran his fingers through her beautiful reddish-brown pubic hair. He found her swollen pussy lips and probed her inside with one finger, finding that she was wet and slippery.

On the couch Walt bent over and drilled with his tongue between Karyn's legs, which were spread wide to greet her. Jean and Joe looked over, just as Walt nibbled and Cudd on Karyn's labia, causing a purring excitement. He covered her pussy with his mouth, licked and sucked on her clitoris while she moaned with lust. She started rubbing her hips against Walt's face and then she clasped her hands behind his head and pulled him inside. She lifted her legs up on his shoulders and pulled him tight. Soon she rolled her head to the back of the couch and jerked her pussy hard against Walt's face, pressing his head between her strong thighs.

"Oh yeah, Walt," she called out. "I'm coming! Don't stop!"

Walt continued to whip over Karyn's clitoris until she spun and shook with her first orgasm of the weekend. When Karyn came down, Walt just kept going and pulled another climax, and then a third one until she finally straightened up and pushed Walt's face away from her pussy.

"Walt, that was fantastic!" she gasped. "Now it's your turn." She got up and they switched places. Walt's long dick pointed straight up at the ceiling, shaking with anticipation. Karyn bent over and kissed and sucked his cock head slightly and stroked his shaft with one hand while the other stroked his balls. She made happy humming noises in her throat and Walt just laid his head back and let the sensations of Karyn's mouth soak into his cock.

In the meantime, Jean and Joe had moved into a very nice, relaxed 69 position. Joe lay on the floor with Jean's pussy crunching on his face. She was lying on top sucking Joe's throbbing cock. Joe enjoyed the rich aroma of her vagina while she spread the thick juice of her arousal all over his face. Joe found it very sensual and arousing. The couple set a slow, leisurely pace for their intense oral explorations.

After a while, Joe and Jean noticed that things were starting to happen on the couch. While they paused to watch, Walt bucked his hips up off the couch, pressed his erection into Karyn's mouth, grunting and panting as she continued to suck on it.

"I will come," he told her, and she just nodded and hummed in agreement. "Oh yes", Walt moaned, and then, with a growl, he emptied his balls onto Karyn's face. Karyn eagerly extracted Walt's thick, milky-white sperm, applied every drop and then went back to collect the few drops that had escaped.

Jean and Joe enjoyed witnessing the mutual bliss of their spouses. It was incredibly hot to see Karyn carrying Walt's sperm on her face and tits and dripping it down. While she had blown Joe many times, it was somehow hotter to see her doing Walt.

Jean got up and moved to the other end of the couch, bending over her arm. "Come on, Joe," she urged, "take me from behind." Joe stood up, moved behind her and rubbed his cock against her wet pussy, annoyingly delaying her entry.

"Come on, Joe!" she shouted. "Fuck me! "Stick your big fat cock inside me and fuck me."

Not wanting to disappoint his friend, Joe pushed his hips forward and rammed the pulsating pole into her. Jean made a small gurgling sound in her throat as he pulled her almost completely out of her and rammed it back into her.

"Oh yes!" she shouted. "That's what I'm talking about!"

The couple settled into a steady rhythm. Joe bent over to fondle Jean's beautiful tits while they fucked. Joe enjoyed feeling the smooth, sweaty, damp skin of Jean's back against his chest. He loved to feel the beat of his balls against her clitoris at the end of each stroke. Soon, Jean gasped with the beginnings of her orgasm. As she reached her climax, she emitted a swaying moan, her cunt pressing Joe's rod as he slid further in and out of her. Eventually she shivered and trembled until the orgasm was complete. When he was sure she was done, Joe gave her one last forward push, palpated her to the core, then held on to her, his balls burst and sent a river of hot sperm into her before collapsing on the couch Karyn and Walt were watching.

Walt grinned as he listened to his wife struggling for breath. "This is how the weekend can begin," he giggled.

Everyone got dressed. Karyn and Joe took their bags to the guest room while Jean prepared a quick dinner. Then the friends went upstairs and piled into Walt and Jean's king-size bed.

After starting the weekend by mating across marriage lines, this time they mated with their own spouses. It was incredibly hot for Karyn and Joe to watch Walt and Jean make love, demonstrating their intimate knowledge of each other's bodies. While mating, Karyn and Joe made mental notes and even pointed out things to each other that Walt and Jean were doing and would try to do in the future.

Slowly and deliberately, Walt stroked Jean with his long tail while she purred and cooed with extreme pleasure as her husband's penis drilled into her deep. She wrapped her legs around his waist, then pushed them down his back, over his ass, and finally crossed her legs with his, fusing their bodies as she continued the waves of her horizontal mating dance.

Jean began to lift her hips from the bed and pressed against Walt's pushes, just as she had done with Joe before. He knew she would soon reach her climax. Her breathing was shredded and her hips snapped into her husband with increasing urgency. She began to moan to the rhythm of his thrusts, and soon Walt urged her: "Come with me, I want us to come together.

Walt began to roll his hips, aiming his spear at her core and grunting with every thrust, while Jean reached higher and higher plateaus of erotic pleasure. Finally, Walt growled, "Here it comes, babe!" and the two of them were lost in ecstasy as he sent his semen to his wife to mingle with Joe's earlier deposit.

Karyn and Joe watched as the mixture of Walt and Joe's sperm oozed out of her, around the shaft of Walt's cock, and slowly seeped into her ass. As they turned into position to watch, Karyn and Joe felt inspired by her example.

Karyn rolled Joe onto his back and began to slowly suck his cock, which pulsated with anticipation. She started with the balls and deliberately moistened every inch of his manhood sensually with her tongue, stopping at the tip to swirl her tongue around him a few times. This was all he could do to prevent him from getting right there and then.

With silky smooth movements Karyn glided along Joe's body, stopping to wrap her tits around his cock and give him a sultry titty fuck before continuing to glide seductively upwards until her breasts hung over Joe's mouth. Karyn moved from side to side, offering one breast first and then the other to suck while sliding her pussy back and forth along his upper body. As soon as her tits were satisfied, she slid back down and kissed Joe deeply. She slid further down until he could feel the tip of his cock pressing against her freshly shaved opening.

Karyn pushed further down until Joe's cock split her cunt lips, he could feel her warmth burning inside her. Slowly, Karyn continued until every inch of her favorite shaft was enveloped in the wet, sultry grip of her vagina until the base pressed against her pubic mound. Joe grabbed her ass cheeks and pulled them down, pressing the throbbing erection into her core.

As they had watched Walt and Jean, Karyn and Joe slowly fused their bodies until it seemed they were no longer two people but one. Joe's cock seemed to dissolve into the walls of his wife's pussy and every movement made every cell in their bodies tingle with erotic pleasure.

They mated slowly and sensually, for a long time, before the appreciative glances of their friends. Karyn and Joe put themselves on display for their friends and returned the former gift.

Joe held Karyn's body and enjoyed the feeling of feeling her naked skin against his own. Her breasts glided sensuously against Joe's chest, her nipples like little dots of erotic electricity that sent bumps through him. His hands caressed her thighs and ass cheeks and felt her muscles tense and relax with every thrust of her body. Finally, Karyn sat up and supported herself with her hands against Joe's chest. Her breathing became irregular and with each swing of her hips she became more determined and determined. She squeezed his cock with her muscles in her cunt, in time with her thrusts. In response, Joe began lifting his hips from the bed and urgently drove into her depths. Her fingers dug into his chest, and he gasped in pain after the little sting.

Then, with a soft howl, the dam broke from Karyn's climax. She twisted and writhed, trembling with the waves of orgasmic bliss that were crashing down on her. Her legs squeezed tightly around Joe's hips, and deep inside her a sob of lust surged forth. The sensations of Karyn's orgasm were as intense as anything Joe had ever experienced, so intense that he released into his own orgasm and joined her on a cosmic level of erotic bliss. Joe's body was riddled with orgasmic spasms and he felt as if the biggest charge of his life was shooting into her from his cock. He had virtually no control over his body. All he could do was let the orgasm run its course until it was complete.

When Karyn finally collapsed and struggled for breath, Jean spoke. "That was the most beautiful thing I have ever seen," she said.

"That's because you couldn't take care of yourself," Joe replied.

Then the four of them fell asleep happy and content.

In the morning, when the early sunrays were filtered through the blinds, Joe woke up dizzy and looked around. He and Jean were in the "middle" parts of the bed. Karyn lay on the edge next to Joe while Walt lay on the other side of Jean. During the night, Joe finally spooned with Jean, one hand cupping her breast. Joe thought it was a very pleasant way to wake up. He began to caress Jean's chest, squeezing it gently, stroking it, feeling its fullness and force. Joe's "morning glory" became even more pronounced and began to press into her ass crack.

Jean felt Joe's cock pressing against her ass and soon after, he came to Joe's attention. She turned her head to look over her shoulder. "Good morning, lover," she pulled reeling.

"Mmmmm. Good morning. Do you fancy a bit of morning fucking?" said Joe as he raised his hips to her ass and looked for a warm place to put his cock.

"Mmmmm. I'm always ready for a little morning fuck." She rolled her hips back to give the eager cock behind her better access to her pussy. She lifted her upper leg for a second and then reached between her legs to find the throbbing erection.

"Nice," she said to no one in particular. She led her friend's cock to her opening and pushed it into her. Then with the other hand, she pressed Joe's hand firmly against her chest while she slowly spooned. It was very relaxed, very gentle and unobtrusive.

After Jean and Joe had fucked for a while, Karyn turned around and got out of bed. She waded down the hall to the bathroom. When she came back, she went back to bed on Walt's side and started stroking his cock while she watched Jean and her husband fuck. When Walt woke up, Karyn rolled him on her back and started sucking his cock. She climbed on top of him, in the 69 position, Walt licked and played with her pussy while she sucked his cock.

Jean pushed Joe away briefly so that she could roll onto her back. She pulled him onto her, into a missionary position to resume the slow fuck. Slowly Joe pushed into her tight pussy, then pulled back until he had almost completely pulled out of her, then pushed back into her. She moaned as the thick cock spread her open and plunged in and out of her. When she began to hunch her hips, Joe reacted with even more violent blows until she whimpered with joy at her upcoming orgasm. A few more punches and Joe began pumping sperm into her again as she writhed through another orgasm.

Jean and Joe turned around and watched as Karyn and Walt reached their destination. She was now seriously sucking his cock, stroking it with her hand and bouncing her head up and down along its length. She whirled her tongue furiously around the tip of Walt's tail, the pleasure was clearly written on

Walt's face. He made a small gurgling sound in his throat and put his hand on Karyn's back and tried to speak.

"Kar-," was all he could get before a sound came out of his throat somewhere between a grunt and moan, and he sent his semen back to Karyn's face and tits. Karyn made a happy purr when Walt came and continued to suck his cock until she had cleaned it thoroughly and his now soft cock slipped out between her lips.

Then she slipped backwards and presented her pussy to Walt's face. Walt gasped for breath for a few minutes, but this only had the effect of making him drink the rich, musky aroma of Karyn's cunt even deeper. When Walt had taken enough air, he drew back on Karyn's hips and put them on his face.

Karyn was happy to crunch her pussy on Walt's face and Walt in turn dipped into it with relish and made big slurping noises while licking and sucking his friend's wife. She moaned and groaned with relish as she rode on Walt's tongue and felt it enter her canal before finally settling on her clitoris. This caused Karyn to roll her hips at breakneck speed until she came with a trembling moan.

Walt might have thought his morning duties were over, but Karyn was not finished with him yet. As she lifted herself off his face, she turned around him and positioned herself on his tail. At first, she just spread him out by rubbing the crevices of her slit along the length of Walt's shaft to make it hard again. Jean and Joe smiled as they watched his cock expand. When she felt his hardness, Karyn lifted herself up for a moment and Walt's tail jumped up in readiness.

"I think he's ready," said Karyn and winked and smiled at her audience. "I can't believe it's Saturday morning and I haven't had that gorgeous long cock inside me yet. And with that she sat down again and slowly and deliberately impaled herself on Walt's stake.

Inch by inch, Walt's tail disappeared until she had swallowed it whole. She turned sensually on his shaft and purred with erotic pleasure to feel him penetrate deep into her as only he could. For several minutes she just sat still, pressing his shaft with her shells and enjoying the feeling of having penetrated to the furthest corners of her vagina.

Slowly she started rocking back and forth, rubbing herself sensually against Walt's long stick, moving it from one corner of her pussy to the other, moaning with erotic pleasure.

Walt adapted to her slow rhythm, pushed his cock into her depths and then relaxed. Her spouses watched with fascination as they enjoyed her erotic dance.

Karyn moaned undaunted about the feelings that Walt's cock evoked in her. She steadily increased her speed until her ass was practically blurred as she pumped against his cock. Finally she came with a trembling moan that made Walt moan again when he shot his second load of the morning into her.

In the evening someone had the idea to put on some music and dance. Jean found a CD with dance music and we joined forces - Karyn danced with Walt and Jean danced with Joe. Of course all four of them were naked, it didn't take long before things started to move in an erotic direction.

When Joe danced with Jean, he felt increasingly aroused by the feeling of her naked body against his. He let one hand slide down from her waist to feel her bottom, stroking her cheeks, feeling her firm muscles as she moved and danced across the room. Jean snuggled up close to him, her left breast stomping against Joe's. He bent over and took her nipple in his mouth, rolled it on his tongue and enjoyed its taste and texture.

As Joe's cock hardened, Jean had a mischievous look on her face. She subtly tried to turn around to rub against Joe's throbbing erection. They stood face to face, bodies pressed tightly together, their breasts crushed Joe's chest, their hard nipples practically bored inwards. Joe grabbed her butt, one cheek in each hand, and she did the same. They kissed passionately, tongues intertwined, probing the corners of each other's mouths. Jean spread her legs slightly so that Joe's throbbing cock could rub against her pussy lips. Then they looked into each other's eyes, pulled each other tight and Joe's cock slid into them.

As soon as it was inside her, she pulled her legs together again, making her pussy feel even tighter. Of course, we really stopped dancing. But the standing fuck was even better. Normally her pussy was quite tight, but by pressing her legs together, it felt amazingly tight. Joe was pumping in and out of her. She was quite wet, but the friction from the increased tightness alone raised the sensations to an even higher level. Joe knew he wouldn't last much longer and as his climax approached, Joe sat down on the couch and Jean rode him. Soon it was grinding towards its own climax. When Joe knew she was coming, he raised his hips and sent another load of white-hot sperm into her.

While Jean and Joe recovered, he bent down to suck on her wonderful tits a little more while they watched their spouses. Walt left Karyn standing on a chair. She wrapped her arms around his neck while he hooked his elbows behind her knees to hold her up off the floor. He lowered her slowly until her opening met his cock. Then he slowly dropped her onto his cock, her whole weight pressing her down on him. Between Karyn's hands around Walt's neck and his arms that supported her knees, they could control her movements quite well. Joe watched in awe as they limped together vertically. It was obviously quite an athletic movement - Walt had to be strong enough to carry both their weight and still help Karyn to cope with the pressure of her own weight pressing on Walt's cock. And Karyn had to be strong enough to hold herself up with her arms.

They fucked like this for several minutes. When they got tired, Walt put Karyn on the couch and crawled between her legs to finish missionary style. Walt's long cock pumped in and out of Karyn's sweet pussy until she breathed, "Come with me," and he sent his thick white cum back inside her.

Sunday was their last day together. They had formed a loose tradition that their last day together was the "day of three". They began by alternating the men with both women. Walt lay on his back while one of the women rode on his cock and the other one on his face. After each of the women had an orgasm in this position, they switched places until each came back. This time Walt Jean pumped the pussy full of semen when they were done.

At Joe's place both women sat next to each other on the couch while Joe licked their pussies. He loved to lean close to enjoy the smells and tastes of his two favorite vaginas. Jean was freshly filled with her husband's sperm, which contributed to the experience. As Karyn shivered through her second oral orgasm, Joe moved up and pushed his cock back into her, stomping furiously into her until she received another deposit of his hot sperm in her box.

Next it was Jean's turn to take on both men, she was dizzy with anticipation. Jean just loves it when two men take care of her pleasure at the same time. This time the boys "roasted her on a spit". Jean went in the "doggy position" on hands and knees, while Walt went on his knees in front of her and Joe went on his knees behind her. Jean sucked Walt's dick while Joe fucked her

from behind. At some point she practically threw Walt deep into her throat, with the thrusts from behind pushing her onto Walt's cock. The men managed to time it so that they let go almost simultaneously, with Joe's sperm squirting into her pussy and Walt's into her mouth.

When Walt and Joe had recovered enough from Jean to get a hard-on again, Walt sat down on the couch. Karyn reached for the bottle of lubricant and coated Walt's cock with plenty of lubricant. Then she sat down carefully and pressed her pussy against the tip of his cock. Slowly and gently she curled up on Walt's erection, stopping several times to adjust to Walt's length. As he sat well and safely with his cock in her cunt, she leaned back and invited Joe to lick her clitoris. Karyn moaned at the sensation of both types of stimulation. Walt started to slip and slide in and out a little faster while Joe tried to match Walt's movements with his tongue. Karyn writhed and writhed in front of the two sensations. She quickly reached her climax and she began to twitch, writhe and moan uncontrollably as the waves of lust rolled over her.

Walt and Joe just kept going, pulling orgasm after orgasm out of her one by one until she splashed on Walt's cock and Joe desperately tried to suck it all up until Karyn waved it off, spent. The boys stood over her and jerked off until they let their last load of this visit fly over Karyn's tits.

THE DIRTY WORK

It was the last class of the week, and so far my time had passed quite well. As a young and quite pretty substitute teacher I was used to badly disciplined school children with constant barbs about my shapely stupid blonde appearance. Dealing with the hooligan dynasty of alpha males and spiteful females trying to maintain their dominance was also a further prerequisite for survival. If nothing, then it considered me mean and harsh on the outside, even if I flinched on the inside. The jealous looks of the girls I taught, knowing that their friends wanted me more than they did, were also a constant in every class that I tried to control as much as I could. I was quite small and slightly overweight compared to the more marriageable cheerleaders in the class. Since I was only twenty-three years old, it seemed more like curvature than anything else. Unfortunately, despite my rather large bottom, I was quite flat-chested, and on those days when I was only filling in for other teachers, I didn't see any downside in filling out my bra to make me look stronger and more intimidating. I could handle teasing about my bottom, but since I was a teenager, I was very sensitive about my lack of cleavage. I must say that I cut an impressive figure with an accentuated bust, my light cream power suit and my red 4-inch heels. Even though I didn't always like some of the ruder comments that were often put in my way, if I'm honest, I knew I could have discouraged them with more.

Anyway, that Friday I found myself in a fairly upper middle-class high school in a mid-sized town in my home state of California. I had gone to high school there and was only a twenty-minute drive from my new apartment. It was my dream to find a permanent job here, and with my college debts growing exponentially, it was almost a necessity. Some of the staff remembered me from my time here as a rather uncouth favorite student, and certainly

Principal Harding appreciated me very much, although he might have preferred to remember me in my cheerleading outfit rather than my more elegant business suit. During the lunch break, I caught one of the older girls in my current class shitting the pants of a classmate and informed the principal. As a former victim of such pranks, I had no mercy for the perpetrator. I hoped that she would get into trouble and assumed that she would be given an immediate suspension so that I would not have to deal with her again as she had a rather scary appearance. So I was quite surprised to see her strolling into my last class and approaching me calmly, almost reluctantly.

"I am so sorry for the former Miss Gatting. It will never happen again. Please take this cup of coffee as a token of truce and no hard feelings. I know what I did was wrong and I hope that you can forgive me. Papa called me a terrible name..."

Papa? What did she mean by that? I was looking at my class list of names. I looked at my class list. The girl's name was Sylvia, Sylvia Harding, and she must be Principal Harding's daughter. Oh, God, how could I be so stupid as to think that that wouldn't have improved my chances of getting a permanent job or even a reference. So, in an effort to reconcile, I graciously accepted the cup of coffee, even though I neither drank coffee nor even liked it.

"Well, that's really a lovely gesture, Sylvia. I must say I was a little tired, so a cup of coffee should really cheer me up. Thank you, my dear, I hope you didn't go to too much trouble," I replied and tried to ingratiate myself with her.

When I took a sip of the coffee, I thought it tasted strange, but when she looked up at me excitedly, I looked down at her and nodded my appreciation. Within five minutes, thank God, I had drunk the whole cup and was able to get through my last lesson of the day comfortably. Everyone seemed to have behaved remarkably well so far, and I even began to relax a little and enjoy the lesson.

Then, about ten minutes after the class started, I felt a strange fullness in my stomach. As I stood at the blackboard trying to explain the relevance of the Canterbury tales to a disinterested bunch of teenagers, I suddenly felt a big pile up in my stomach. I stumbled briefly and could feel that the class noticed my discomfort. I tried to ignore it, but thirty seconds later the fullness gave way to a stronger cramping pain in my stomach. I felt the increase in pressure in my stomach and struggled to my stool to get a temporary respite.

But it was no use. The pressure pushed down through my intestine and the cramps became almost unbearable. The urge to empty my bowels was insatiable. I knew immediately that something terrible would happen if I didn't get out of this classroom soon. I tried to stay as calm as possible, turned to the door and told the class that I would be back in a minute. I could feel their giggle and reuse as I stumbled, sweat building up on my forehead towards the door. I knew I didn't have much time as I turned the door handle before I was planning to flee madly down the hallway to the bathroom.

It no longer bothered me that over twenty-five pairs of eyes from eighteen-year-old students, all senior high school students, witnessed my embarrassing escape. But when I let the door come back towards me to open it, I realized that it would not move. For five desperate seconds I pushed and pulled desperately and without success, while the class became more and livelier as they watched my curious escapades. My need to defecate was overwhelming and as I looked back at the class, I could see that Sylvia was almost unimpressed by the madness of her classmates and the panic that emanated from me unabatedly. She was the only one who didn't seem

surprised by my irrational behavior. Another convulsive tremor flowed through my body, and only with intense physical will could I prevent the fatal faucal accident from happening. Finally, and with a devastating feeling of fear, I knew that I could not hold out much longer. I realized that someone had locked the door and asked for a key, but while the words were still leaving my mouth, another wave was seeping through my system.

"PLEASE, SOME HELP..." I cried out in horror as the reality of what was happening quickly dawned on me in class, when a horrible, elongated, flatulent event echoed from my rear end, drowning out even the loudest laughter in the class.

A vibrating fart bursting into decibels echoed wildly from my big ass. Only with my greatest willpower could I stop the fart before it changed from gaseous to semi-solid form. Nonetheless, this anal eruption made the class laugh, and it was clear that I would not get any sympathy from these teenage hyenas. Although it was only a fart, I knew I could not hold back the insidious forces that were holding my body hostage for much longer. Whatever was inside me was determined to leave, and with great reluctance I knew that the class would probably get a show they would never forget. Bizarrely, in the half seconds before the ultimate anal explosion, I resignedly debated in immense existential despair whether or not I would perform the nasty deed in my pants and make a massive mess of my clothes, or squat on the floor and empty myself on the floor. Neither, of course, was appealing. When I realized that I would have to leave the building later in some kind of clothes, I made the humiliating decision to quickly slip my suit trousers and panties over my ankles and squat in an inelegant manner in front of the class. This humiliating act brought the boys a primal spasm and the girls a hideous grin. Unfortunately, I didn't really hold my own down there. My blond bush was quite wild, and even in spite of the enormous situation I found myself in, there was still a clever Alec boy commenting on something ridiculous, which caused even more derisive laughter. So I squatted in my 4-inch heels, naked pussy and ass, which were displayed to over twenty children, and waited in disgust while a last, all-encompassing, throbbing and viscous wave of pain went through me until finally I could not stand it any longer. When I looked up, I noticed that by now all the kids had left their seats, and they followed my dirty demonstration in deepest excitement from all imaginable angles. They knew that they were witnessing something truly monumental.

When the resistance of my sphincter finally eased, I could feel an almost volcanic eruption shooting out of me. Some children from behind could actually see the poop lifting off my butt and starting its long fall to the floor, while others in front watched my trembling, sweaty face with tears falling down as I contorted mercilessly while aware of the exhibition I was offering. Only then did I see the multitude of telephone cameras, even a video camera, all of which caught me at an unflattering angle, and although I knew it was a terrible view, I did not want my naked image to be broadcast while I was performing this most evil of acts. So in a moment of madness I reached for my panties, and when the first elongated turd fell off my butt without further ado, I tore up my white cotton panties, caught the excrement in mid-flight and pulled them back up towards my still gushing butt. When it came in contact with my butt, it rubbed and squeezed itself around my now freshly covered butt. The smell was foul and the scene was relentless.

Unfortunately for me, the shit just kept coming back. Within seconds the panties filled up and almost unnaturally I felt that my now destroyed panties were full to the brim and the feces like riverbanks at high water flooded my panties in all directions. I was amazed at the sheer volume and speed of the action, for I am sure it was the bound schoolchildren.

The sinister look of disgust and ridicule continued when, after a short pause for breath, another massive surge of electricity came out of my anus. This time the discharge of excrement was so violent and explosive that even as I squatted there in my four-inch high heels, with my hands on either side of my cramped stomach, the sheer volume of faeces made my panties slide down my legs, leaving a brown, dirty trail. When they landed on my ankles, I knew immediately that they had destroyed my cream-colored pants, but that was the least of my worries at the moment.

The scene was unbearable. All these people stared in macabre fascination at their teacher, who humiliated herself in such a horrible way. Again, I saw the cameras pointed at my crotch and my bottom, which was now, of course, covered with an unbearable chocolate mess. The sheer volume was staggering, and finally it seemed as if the river, which had long been beyond my control, had come to a halt. My face begged for mercy, my mouth was incapable of speaking, while the bodies and cameras of my students around me pressed around their positions. The sound of flashes and giggles from the class continued until one boy held his camera almost directly under my crotch. I immediately clasped my hands to my stained pussy, hoping to fruitlessly fend off these photographic intruders. No sooner had I done that than I realized my mistake. The poop was frozen to my once blonde pubic hair, and when I touched it with my hands now, a big sticky mass ran onto my fingers. I looked down in horror, as if the events that were taking place were a nightmare, but as this was accompanied by further shockulence, I saw a camera in my face capturing my broken emotional state. Again, almost unconsciously I tried to shield my face as if the images had not already said a thousand words of humiliation. I put my hands in front of my face and as soon as I did so, my grave mistake became clear to me. The smell was obscene, but when I blocked my face with my hands, a volume of poop splashed over my once beautiful complexion. The make-up I had been wearing, already discolored by tears, was now drowning in the soft, sticky excrement from my intestines. Instead of protecting my face, I smothered it in my foul-smelling brew. More photos were taken and even more atavistic laughter was captured from the audience who, if they had once felt pity, were now completely immersed in my horrible ordeal. Still squatting, I tried to stand up, thinking my bowels could certainly not produce more, but when I bent my stomach to hear another original rumble from behind, it squeaked out. This time the contents were looser and gushed out painfully in one quick burst that lasted no longer than three seconds. But the effect was undeniable. A scatological spray formed like a puddle under my writhing body.

From the crowd of teenagers further collective cries of disgust were heard. The pain in my stomach began to subside and I looked down at my dirty panties, my legs and ankles, and the feelings of humiliation were overwhelming. I wanted to be somehow clean so that I could hide from the relentless looks. I rubbed my dirty hands off my sky-blue blouse to somehow free them from their impotence. Unfortunately, all I did was unknowingly leave another brown trace on my blouse. Everything I did was recorded, and every move I made was accompanied by the sound of "UGH!" and "GROSS!" or a variation of them.

In the midst of all this chaos, I once again encountered the bright light of Sylvia Harding, who seemed calmer than all the others, much like a peaceful lioness watching other lions tearing up scraps of meat. But in her eyes, I saw a serenity that I needed, and in my humiliating paralysis I felt that maybe she could offer me a break from this situation.

Almost instantly she jumped out of her chair and in an instant, she divided the crowd in front of me and looked down on me with something I felt was between pity and disgust.

"My goodness, what a mess you've made. Don't just stand there and admire your dirty work, why don't you at least try to cover your dirty vagina with the suit jacket?"

I still felt paralyzed, but amazingly the girl stepped behind me and almost involuntarily she slid the shoulders of my suit jacket over my flaccid arms and back. In one quick movement she wrapped the suit jacket around the front of my upper body. She was right; at least my front was covered, even though my bottom was still completely exposed. Maybe she was trying to help.

"Now do exactly as I say and this nightmare will soon be over," she whispered to me.

I obeyed as in hypnosis. Suddenly the laughter of the crowd in my head stopped and for a while I only heard the voice of Sylvia who helped me out of my crisis. I nodded submissively and when she ordered me to take off my blouse, since I had destroyed it with my dirty hands, I couldn't help but obey her. Slowly I opened the blouse and wiped even more shit from my hands while pressing the buttons. Finally I had taken off the blouse and looked at Sylvia for further instructions. She told me to throw it in the corner of the room and as I did so I heard another collective "OOH!

Now only dressed in a bra and with a jacket wrapped around her crotch, I looked at Sylvia for further instructions.

"Oh my God! Is your bra padded or what? I'm sure I can see that there's paper hidden in your bra," she asked almost rhetorically.

I was too stunned to answer, I just looked down and could only slightly see the paper loop hanging loosely from my ruffled oversized bra, but I couldn't believe that in the midst of all the other hustle and bustle she would have noticed it so quickly. My stunned expression and my guilty behavior were answer enough for Sylvia.

"You're lucky you have something to wipe your dirty ass with MsSCATing," Sylvia announced as she dug her hands into my bra and like a magician pulled paper out of one sleeve and unfolded the huge rolls of paper until my bra hung listlessly and loosely from my body.

I wondered if she was calling me Miss Scating for a moment as I complied with her request.

When she handed me the bundled toilet paper that gave me confidence, she ordered me to clean myself.

I knew that what I was doing was ridiculous, but I was still trapped in the room, and since I had no other options, I just stuck to the one person who seemed to have authority. Still on my heels, the lower half of my body covered with poop, my face grazed too much, as if I had just had a poop facial, but my upper body only with traces. My white bra and my white body offered a strong contrast to all this. I crouched down to wipe my bottom and as I did so, the suit jacket slipped off and revealed my smudged front again. Once again exposed I tried to follow Sylvia's orders when she told me to ignore my nakedness. Unfortunately, despite the toilet paper I didn't make much progress in the mess I had made. I tipped the dirty cloth on the floor in the stinking puddle of excrement where I was standing.

As a variety of thoughts flashed through my mind, including how I might ever get home or even get clean or get over this incident, I felt Sylvia unhook my bra in the back... "You're still dirty...need something else to clean yourself...hmmm, how about this thing, it doesn't seem to work anymore.

Crazy, despite all I had been through, I still felt humiliated because of my not very luscious breasts. On another day it would have been a shattering experience if I had been discovered that I had falsified my appearance as I had been. It shouldn't have mattered in connection with the last fifteen minutes, but when I submissively started to remove my bra from my body, I wished the bottom could have opened up and swallowed me right there. Instead, more people than ever before got an unencumbered view of my naked breasts as in the midst of a fresh round of quick-tempered and angry laughter and the dots, glances and flashing cameras I tried to use my bra to wipe my dirty bare bottom clean.

In each cup I scooped a large amount of the sticky, smelly substance. My hands were now completely brown, as the excess was matting on my skin. I couldn't believe that I had wiped my butt completely naked in a classroom full of students after I had performed the most private of all actions right in front of their eyes.

"OH MY GOD, THIS IS THE MOST REVOLVING THING I EVER SEE", exclaimed just one of the many voices that penetrated the crowd.

"AND OH MY GOD, LOOK AT HER TINY TITS. I CAN'T BELIEVE I THOUGHT I THAT THAT BITCH WHAT HOT!', cried another voice.

How humiliating and for some reason the barbs on my tiny breasts still hurt deeply. Maybe I should cover them, I thought to myself, and almost in post-traumatic shock I tried to adapt the dirty bra back to my body. Immediately I felt the poop being squeezed against my breasts and dripping into my stomach. Sylvia looked at me with dismay.

"This is just disgusting, if you want to leave this classroom, I suggest you take this oversized bra made of poop off your body. I mean really, just look at the mess you've made of your clean and perverted little bosom. It seems to me that you must have a scat fetish or something," said Sylvia, leaving me little choice but to take the bra off again and let it fall to the floor so that now a boob covered with steaming poop appears.

"Luckily, my dad gave me the key to school, so why don't I escort you to the locker room and you can borrow this... "and you can wash that dirt off the body. I mean, oh my God, look at you, you're fucking disgusting now, right? Now take off your dirty panties and pants and we can take care of it!"

I couldn't help feeling the disgusting taste when I wiped them with my hands so dirty. She was right, I was disgusting, but when my mind gained temporary clarity, I thought why the door was locked, why, if she had a key, she didn't try to open the door earlier.

"Stop hesitating and take it off at once," she moved again and threw those thoughts out of her head again.

Anyway, the task wasn't so easy in four-inch heels and standing in a puddle of excrement. I knew I had to take off my heels to get the job done, but I didn't want to stand barefoot in my own mess, so I was hoping briefly to be able to take the dirty clothes off my feet while I was still wearing my heels. So, I stood my left foot on half the clothes and quickly raised my right foot to do the job. This turned out to be even harder than I imagined, and as I jumped from foot to foot trying to take off the dirty clothes, I saw my whole body vibrate wildly. If I had big breasts, I would know they would be swaying madly now, but when I suddenly released the left side of my panties and pants from my left heel, a new swing made me lose balance with my right and slipped, as if on ice, first face the pelvis below. The consistency of this looser, more liquid pile was quickly washed all over my body when I hit the ground, practically swimming. The front of my body was now completely covered with various shades of brown, including the face, and while I was soaking in the search for air, I tossed my body on my back to open my mouth to the air. Lying there in what was now a complete humiliation, I looked up at Sylvia, who was rising above me. She was now laughing mercilessly at me and I saw evil in her eyes. And then he hit me almost like a stone between my eyes, as bright as day. Coffee, keys...

6 stories: Taboo Stories of Forced Sex

Amira Red

Table of Contents

CLUB CITADEL

Renee's heart hit her chest so hard that she thought it would explode, right then and there in front of everyone. But nerves are funny things. It was part of the thrill, part of the anxiety about what was to happen. Especially the imminent fate of her long, shiny hay-brown curtain.

The world had no limits, as long as it was safe, healthy and compatible. And hair fetish was a big part of it for some people.

As a long-standing subjection and wife, Renee was very aware of her Master and husband, David's fetish for hair and hairstyles. David was also an enigmatic owner of the Club Citadel, where they played mostly on the weekends.

"Hey, you okay?" Lana asked Renee in the locker room, who almost jumped on her voice.

"I'm... okay, I guess," Renee said, unsure.

Lana smiled to her heartily and let Renee be with those friendly bear hugs without another question. Yeah, Renee needed it the most now.

"Thank you," Renee said. "I'm really nervous as hell."

"Well, it takes courage to agree to this demo," Lana agreed.

It was a ritual at Club Citadel that every third Saturday of the month, a seasoned demo master demonstrates a scene with different things involved. Sometimes it was Shibari, an electric game, any kind of edge game or fetish. Today's demo was: a hair fetish. Master David took it upon himself to demonstrate to the crowd how to do sub climax while giving it the extreme hairstyle that House preferred for Sub.

When David asked Renee to agree to this demo, she couldn't refuse her Master. It wasn't a forceful or blind surrender, but a deep longing to find her own pleasure in serving her Master. This thrill intoxicated her.

"I'm excited and terrified; it's hard to explain," admitted Renee Lana.

"I know that feeling. I felt the same when Xan first picked up the cane," remembered Lana. "But you'd do so well in this demo, Renee. I'm really excited to see it. I'm actually supposed to sit quietly and kneel at Xan's feet all the time," she said with a giggle.

Renee closed her eyes and bit her lower lips. "God! Everyone would be there," she remembered.

It wouldn't be the first time she'd been to the demo, but it was really important.

"I think you should be in the hallway by now," Lana remembered Renee. "Master David hates being late."

Renee quickly fixed the silk robe around her. "Oh, yes. I can't afford the punishment now. Bye!"

She hurried into the room as fast as her wobbly legs could lift her up and relaxed a little, knowing she wasn't late. But a giant leather chrome-plated barber chair with the right plinth in the middle of the room sucked the breath out of her lungs.

"I can do it," she said to herself, and slowly laid down to the chair.

She knelt down by the chair while people were gathering around. Most of them were homes and submarines, masters and their slaves, and several trainees. Renee was expecting a large crowd because no one had given up watching the championship of a master as experienced as her husband, David.

The low murmur of the crowd suddenly melted when she felt a male hand gently caressing her head. She knew the touch too well and greedily leaned towards it.

David bent a little bit, whispering in her ears, "High course, Sub. Make me proud."

Renee nodded her head. She knew that "High protocol" meant she wouldn't talk unless she did. The safe word was a caveat, but with David, she almost never needed it.

As a neat owner and host, he welcomed the people around him and turned to his beautiful submarine. "Stop", he ordered to give her his hand.

She did it gracefully like a swan. Quickly, the robe was unfastened and removed from her body, leaving her gloriously naked. At the back, he tied her brown hair with a medium length back and helped her climb onto the chair.

Renee twisted a little when the cool skin came into contact with her naked derrière. The chair was extremely large. Quickly, her hands were tied to the armrests, and her thighs were unbuttoned because her legs were also limited.

"Hand tied is optional." Master David turned to the crowd. "But make sure her legs are wide open for your access." To show, he quickly redirected his fingers through her already wet slit several times.

The low noise of consent from the crowd intensified the exhibitor in Renee.

Then, at the snap of a finger, the intern pushed the instrument cart forward. In the corner of her eyes, Renee took a break on him. She had various pairs of shaving scissors, several hair scissors and at least a handful of appetisers, as well as combs and hair styling products.

He took a wide comb and started brushing her in the gentlest way. "My sub has beautiful hair, as long and beautiful as you all see," he said proudly, and then added, "Although it won't take long once I'm done with it.

His words were like adding fuel to the fire in her nerves. He divided her hair into two ponytails, pinned up with poor rubber bands at the bottom of her head.

With one hand he pulled her hair, and with the other he pulled a new shiny pair of scissors out of the cart. "If you plan to give your subordinate a hell of an experience, I'd advise you to skip the cape." "Let him feel every bit of hair on her delicate breasts. Or cool drops of water when you use the spray."

He brought one of the ponies between the sharp blades of his scissors and started cutting. The movements were slow and purposeful; Renee felt the cold steel at the back of her neck, while the constant "schnick, schnick" kept humming in her ears. When the sound finally stopped, she heard low breath from the crowd. Women, especially those from other domes, stared at her widely.

David kept his long hair cut like a trophy and then dropped it at her feet. He quietly taped her naked breasts in his big hands and whispered: "You're making a big submarine." Relax. I just started." David was deliciously intimidating. The duality of his actions always kept Renee on the edge of thrill.

He jerked her head off once again when he started cutting off her second ponytail. The ominous sound of scissors through her precious hair danced in waves around her and suddenly stopped again. This time the crowd cheered a little more when the ponytail joined the previous bunch.

"Doesn't she look beautiful without that long hair?" David happily talked to the crowd while running his fingers over her sensitive neck. Renee already had an idea that her 16-inch hair was gone.

Then he took an aerosol bottle and wetted her hair. The water was extremely cool; a few drops were flowing down the neck line and flowing down the valley of her naked womb. "Make sure your submarine's hair is nicely moist. She better feel like you're cutting her beloved hair," David showed.

"Let's give her some fringes now." He combed her face with a nice piece, and the curtain of hair caressed her chin. A strong grip held her crown, while the scissors began to cut the locks about half an inch above her forehead.

Fragments of damp hair slid down and settled between her chin-lined thighs, tickling. Renee started jumping on the seat to rub her thighs to satisfy the growing damp heat.

David quickly twisted her nipples, telling her. "Did I give you permission to move?"

"No, sir," she said quietly.

Then he picked up the cutters and notified the crowd: "Now the real haircut begins."

Renee swallowed the gas, wondering how far she was going to go. Perhaps if she had reached the climax earlier, all this torment would have ended. But he was ready to pull it off on his whim.

The killer dicks were connected and immediately roared to life. He attacked her back with a vice on the top of her head and pushed her chin into her chest. The cut hair fell all around her and the vibrations on her scalp fell on her toes. An involuntary moaning escaped from her mouth when a sensation started to attack her nerves.

The hair in the back of her head had already been cut to half an inch. Suddenly, she felt her head lean to the side as the menacing scissors were heading towards her left. Behind her shoulders a huge piece of hair accumulated, but some of it slipped back onto her knees again. The slight panic she felt in her bones at the thought of losing a shiny brown mane, mixed with the excitement of the hair cutters on the virgin scalp, was exciting.

"I love how her sweet ears are exposed," David chuckled as he folded her ears and ran the clippers around him. The crowd murmured in excitement as well.

Renee was beating down in a heightened pleasure when suddenly the clippers were off. To add to her mortification, he skillfully ran his fingers through her crack, which was now wet.

"So wet and beautiful," he whispered in her ear and then licked around the rim of her ears to increase the heat.

"Never tell your ward what hairstyle to pick up", he instructed the crowd and started to cut the other side of her head. A strong hug from her Master with a humming machine on her temple drove her mad. Renee couldn't see how short he was cutting her, except that every second she grew a pile of cut hair on her knees.

Among the crowd, Lana sat at her Master's feet. Her Master, Master Xan, leaned slightly and asked her: "How do you want me to do it with your hair, baby? Should I fuck your hair or shave you bald?"

Lana didn't know what to say. Some of them wanted to get the climax while her master banged her head while the other part was scared of shit. What would she look like if she was cut off from the crew?

"Whatever you like, master," she managed to escape.

Xan squeezed himself lightly into her hair and kissed her on the head. "Wonderful, my little one," he complimented her.

In the center of the stage, Master David managed to cut Renee's back and sides off half an inch. At the moment, he was working on her head. He skillfully grabbed a piece of hair between his long, male fingers and cut it off an inch from the scalp. The moistened pieces of hair clung to her cheeks and the whole naked skin, giving her a furious pile of sensations.

"Shall I take my fringe off?" asked the crowd cheerfully. The answer was yes, because everyone liked how she was cut like a sacrificial lamb.

"Yes," David agreed with them. "I don't like fringes either. I'd prefer much shorter hair, like a short, neat look."

Instead of using scissors, he used a clipper over a steel comb technique to quickly cut off the blunt fringes he had previously cut. But he didn't stop there. The comb brushed his hair back, held it between his fingers, and Clippers did the job.

When the top of his head was a little less than an inch, nicely tapering half an inch back and sides, he started piercing short hair with his fingers to move the tiny pieces. Renee finally understood how drastically short her hair was.

"Doms and Masters, if you're not proficient in haircutting or narrowing your gaze, I suggest you have a butcher's cut." All you need is a good hairdresser. But always cut your hair in stages, the fun is all about waiting," he added with a satisfying smile.

"Will you take it shorter?" asked him from the crowd.

"Absolutely, yes," he replied, playing and kneading her breasts. "My beautiful sub had long hair all her life. With this haircut, she won't need a comb or brush for a long time." Electricity poured through her veins on his words when she almost reached the climax.

He stopped the cutters and asked the crowd, "What about number two?"

Renee had no idea what "number two" meant, and neither did the women in the room. But somehow everyone agreed with the cry of joy.

"Very well then."

Another clipper came to life with a growling roar. David stood behind her with a hand hook below the chin to keep his head upright. "My sweet lamb," he whispered. "I'll give you a little clue what I'm going to do. In a moment, you'll get the shortest haircut from your barber."

He unceremoniously drove the cutters over her head - from crown to forehead - like a lot of hair added to the pile. "How could the pile get bigger?" Renee was wondering before the scissors' noise got worse.

David deliberately slowed down his movements, allowing the vibrations on her scalp to give her the chills. Renee was moaning uncontrollably and begging to be released.

To add to this thrill, the Master pushed her down her head in the dominant Western way and drove the clippers over her head to buzz down to 1/4 inch. Renee's excitement had already reached its climax, breathing down the limits.

David, sensing her reactions, leaned in a whisper: "Say goodbye to your fancy combs, conditioners and styling tools, sub".

She reached a climax, then and there. The threads of the tightening nerves melted away, revealing a new wave of pleasure. All the sounds around her were lost, except for her Master's relentless, gnarly tone and terrible haircutters.

And when her brain finally came back to normal, she realized how invigorating the experience was. The crowd noticed how to make subklimax with a simple haircut. It was about control and submission to the master's will. Fear and excitement was a deadly combo, Renee realized.

"I hope my menagerie liked it because I'm not done with it yet," he announced with pleasure. David's excitement was tightening in his pants for what he was going to do next.

"As much as I love keeping scissors on her, I hate being attached to her." With a smile, he took off his guard and clenched his hand on her head again. "Let's take her to another notch," he said.

This time the machine attacked the remaining soft strand of brown hair on her back, mowing it to zero. "Oh, my God." Renee whispered to herself, realizing he was scalping her.

"No, no, no, no, no," she kept whispering to herself as the next swollen wave of unbridled pleasure began to rise.

The Clippers only approached the occipital bone, leaving white skin behind. Tiny hairs tickled her everywhere, provoking the approaching climax. Then, the balding dicks climbed over her ears to an inch.

"Should I take the side a little higher?" he asked the crowd ridiculously, even though he planned to take it higher and harder. As expected, the crowd agreed.

"I thought so much."

The machine buzzed loudest in her ears when she felt it move up, almost at eye level. Renee tried so hard to imagine what she looked like with her short hair, but she failed. There was no mirror, and she was at the mercy of her demanding Master.

Before David finished scalping her sides and back, Renee was covered in a delicate shine of sweat. Her muscles were tightly rolled, and warm liquid was accumulating between her legs. She discreetly bullied her hips to allow a little friction against her swollen clitoris.

"Let's turn it nicely and clean up now." David chose a different kind of clipper and still mixed the soft beard on the top of his head.

Renee couldn't stand it anymore. A second wave of pleasure went through the roof with vibrating clippers on the scalp that mixed soft beard with bald skin on the perimeter.

"Doesn't it look beautiful when it's clipped like this?" David smiled proudly. His control of the submarine was astonishing.

Renee lost her breath and had a beautiful time. The fear of being cut naked has already turned into a delicious experience she hasn't forgotten before.

"At the last minute," said David. Before Renee could figure it out, she felt the warm foam massaged with hard fingers in the back of her head. Soon it was spread out on her sides, moving upwards. She looked a little weird with the white foam covering her head, except for a small part at the top.

The crowd watched the final stage of the hair fetish demo with great interest. Not only was Renee wet. Lana, whose breasts shaved up and down in shame, was equally wet. The thought of sitting tied up and naked and getting an extremely inductive hairstyle shook her inside. This and her master's hand kneaded and massaged her breasts.

"Don't you dare sleep," Master Xan whispered in Lana's ear even though he knew how dangerously close she was. And then he added another delicious threat: "If you do that, you'll be in that chair, buckled up and naked." And I'd love to shave you bald in front of everyone."

"Oh, God," Lana closed her eyes, wondering how great it would feel. But deep down, was she ready to be bald at the price of an overwhelming orgasm?

Master David, on the other hand, brought a sharp razor, but Renee had no idea. "If you don't know how to use it properly, never use it on a submarine," he warned the crowd with a serious tone, and then he turned to his boat. "I want you to stay put."

He started scraping the foam with small, careful strokes. Any tiny hair was left in the back of his head, the sides were carefully shaved with a blade. The remaining skin was smooth as ever, and there was no hairline around the neck. Instead, only a small strand of hair covered the top and front of the head.

A warm, damp cloth wiped the remaining foam and then shaved afterwards. There was nothing left of her hair that could change a comb or hairbrush. So David took a doll of styling gel and vigorously massaged her head.

The thorough treatment of the rough massage felt like an after-shave treatment.

"Thank you all for your participation," David turned to the crowd. "I'd like to take care of my submarine in private."

He unbuttoned her stripes, freeing her completely. Knowing that her hands were tight, Master David would punch her in the shoulders as she wrapped them around him, and walked out of the room into one of the private rooms.

"May I see my haircut, Master?" She was purring cutely, and he just couldn't refuse her.

"All right," he said and led her to the mirror. "Here's your new look, little submarine."

Renee froze when she looked in the mirror. She couldn't recognize herself. She instinctively ran her fingers through the back of her head and was surprised she was smooth. It was really a very short haircut, as he promised.

As if he was reading in her mind, he said: "It's called Tall and Tight." It's a popular military haircut."

"Oh." That was all she could do. "This is really... really short, Master."

"Do you like it?"

"I'm still working on this whole look," she said honestly. "It will grow back," she said, comforting herself.

"It will grow back, yes." David agreed with the smile. "But I'm not gonna let it grow. I like that tall, tight little submarine on you. Get ready, you'll be scalping again in two weeks."

He kissed her hard, erasing every rational thought from her mind and consuming her body in the most pleasant way she knows.

THE PARADISE TANNERS

Millicent Jamison scanned the job offers page on her laptop. This has been a regular habit since she was fired from the Peerless Upholstery Company. She loved her job as general manager of the office, taking phone enquiries, booking deadlines and a hundred other tasks that made her days interesting and varied. Now that her husband, Stephen, has been on short notice, she was desperate to find a new position. So far, she has not been able to find anything to suit her experience. At 49, Millicent did not want to completely change her career path.

Come on, bingo! That must be it, she thought that since her eyes were focused on the vacancy, which looked like it was made for her:

"A small family business with old-fashioned values is looking for a general manager of the office who will take care of bookings, appointments, welcome customers and a lot of other duties. Salaries to be negotiated, according to experience. Please submit your application together with your CV and two references to Paradise Tanners under heading number XX1".

Feeling excited and more positive than for centuries, Millicent wrote a cover letter and attached its impressive CV. The references were joined by Mr Brockleban, CEO of Peerless Upholstery, and Mrs Wandless, President of the local Mother's Association branch.

Ten days later a letter came from Paradise Tanners informing Millicent that she had been selected for the post and invited her to an interview. My luck is changing, Millicent told herself.

On the day of the interview she wore an elegant suit in a style that she thought would match the "old-fashioned values" advertised by Paradise Tanners. Millicent was a little surprised when she arrived at the address given in the job interview letter. It was quite a large, Victorian semi-detached house, nothing seemed to indicate that it was a business address. With its exuberant net curtains and a potted plant in the bay window, it was very similar to all other houses on the street. How strange. Millicent was expecting a small factory or unit in a business park, like her old company.

Millicent rang the doorbell and after a few moments you answered her about 40 years later. "Oh, you must be Mrs. Jamison. Welcome to Paradise Tanners. I'm Mrs. Paradise, this way, please." Millicent was brought into the cozy front room and invited to sit on the couch.

"I've read your resume, Mrs Jamison, and I must say I'm impressed. I also spoke on the phone with Mr. Brocklebank, and he spoke most about you. You seem to have all the qualities we're looking for. Before we move on, maybe I should ask you what you know about our business, Paradise Tanners."

Millicent was blushing. She really didn't know anything about the company. She assumed it had to be about leather goods. Mrs. Paradise smiled at the inconvenience of Millicent. "I think I should explain. When we announced this position, we were rather discreet and did not reveal the true nature of what we were doing." Millicent's face fell, wondering what she could afford.

"Oh, don't worry Mrs. Jamison, it's not illegal. We don't grow weeds or anything. But this is something we have to be careful about. The thing is, Paradise Tanners make movies with spanking. We spank ladies' asses and film them. We sell them as DVDs or publish them on the Internet. It's perfectly legal, but of course we have to be very discreet."

"Oh, I see," said Millicent Jamison, surprised. "What would I have to do, Mrs. Paradise."

"Well, just what we put in the ad; answering phones, making bookings, keeping files and generally making sure the office is running smoothly. You wouldn't have to get involved in spanking." "You wouldn't have to get involved in spanking. And then I add, "unless you're obviously interested in this website."

God, that's not what Millicent expected when she applied for this job. But what a pity, she justified it. She'd be happy to fill in by updating her calendar, answering her phone and making coffee. If the ladies got spanked in another room, what did it matter?

"Well, Mrs. Jamison, now you know a little more about us, would you still want this job?"

"Yes, ma'am, Mrs. Raj. When do you want me to start?"

"Will Monday suit you? We're expecting quite a busy week."

Millicent was a little vague when her husband asked about her new job. "Oh, general office work, just like my previous job," she answered his question.

On Monday, with a mixture of nervousness and excitement, Millicent arrived at Paradise Tanners ten minutes earlier. She was received by Mrs. Paradise. "Call me Sylvia," she said. "We are like family here at Paradise Tanners. Come with me and I'll show you around."

Sylvia took Millicent to the living room where she was interrogated. "This is the room we use for home scenes, such as the daughter coming home at midnight, two hours after curfew. She has to go through Daddy's knee. You can imagine the scene, I'm sure of it."

Millicent, wanting to show interest in her new job, she said: "Oh yes, Sylvia, I remember one evening I came home a little late and went over Daddy's knee." Sylvia, she looked at her new employee with new interest.

"Oh, you have some experience with being flogged, so?"

Millicent started regretting her impulsive attention. "Just a few times," she assured her new boss.

Sylvia moved to another room. "This is the school room." The room had a whiteboard, a teacher's desk, a few student benches, a wooden stool with a headgear and other school accessories, including a range of sticks. The third room was quite a conventional bedroom. Finally, Sylvia showed Millicent the study where she was to live and the waiting room, which was rather similar to the one in the doctor's study.

"This is where you should ask the ladies who come in for spanking to wait until we're ready for them. I'll tell you a little trade secret here, Millicent. We have a rule of thumb for the ladies to always wait a little, even if we're ready for their visit. "Waiting increases their anxiety and builds tension."

When the tour was over, Sylvia left Millicent in her office. "Your first task will be to welcome Joanne Thimble." Sylvia was looking at her watch. "She should be here in half an hour. She's a newcomer who answered one of our announcements. She's gonna have a spanking audition that I'm gonna run. If everything goes well, maybe she'll come back for a more intensive session. Make her coffee and show her in the waiting room. You can direct her to the waiting room when I'm ready. I'll call you on the intercom." The intercom was a model similar to the one Millicent used in her previous job.

Mrs. Thimble arrived fifteen minutes before her meeting. Millicent was surprised at what she looked like, just like a hundred other middle-class housewives. "Oh, I'm sorry, I know I'm quite early, but I wasn't sure about the address. I hope I'm not bothering you."

Millicent made good use of her people, assuring Mrs Thimble that everything was all right and took her to the waiting room.

"Do you want a cup of tea or coffee?"

"Oh, coffee would be lovely. Just a drop of milk and no sugar."

When Millicent brought the coffee a few minutes later, Mrs. Thimble was nervously playing with her purse. "Er, you'll, umm," she got stammed up. "Er, will you, umm, spank?"

"Me"? Oh, God, no. No, I think it'll be Mrs. Paradise. She'll call in a minute."

Just then, Millicent heard a noise at the back door. She went to the investigation, leaving Mrs. Thimble alone with her coffee. A middle-aged man, carrying a big bag, just walked into the building. "Hello, you must be the new office manager. I'm Cecil Paradise."

"Nice to meet you, Mr. Paradise. I'm Millicent Jamison. Mrs. Thimble is here for questioning."

"Oh, good. My better half does the honors. I'm an operator this morning. I'd better go and set up the equipment, or I'll get smacked." Cecil Paradise, grabbing his own joke, fell into the living room with his equipment.

Millicent returned to the waiting room. "Is the coffee all right, Mrs. Thimble?"

"Yes, fine, thank you. Please call me Joanne."

"So, Joanne, I'm sure they'll be ready for you soon. It'll be Mrs Paradise to spank you while Mr Paradise films it."

"Oh, I see." Joanne blushed. "This is my first time. I'm a little nervous."

I never would have guessed, Millicent thought. "I'm sure you'll be fine, Joanne."

"I really hope so. I was looking forward to a new experience, but now I'm here to do it. well, I have to admit I'm a little scared.

Millicent was about to offer further reassurance when a woman's voice came over the intercom. "please show joanne thimble to the rec room."

After guiding Joanne through the lounge to meet Mrs. Paradise in the lounge, Millicent returned to her office to inspect the equipment. There were all the usual office paraphernalia found in any small office: computers, staplers, paper clips, a paper cup with pens and pencils, a telephone, etc. Then their attention turned to a television screen. It was divided into quarters to transmit the video footage from a number of security cameras. One showed the front door, another the back door, and the other two quarters were just gray panels. Obviously, they were not in use.

As Millicent moved her office chair, a sudden movement on the screen caught her eye. A third quarter of the screen had suddenly become active. A camera panned around in the lounge, shifting the focus from a blur to a sharper image. Millicent noticed that Mr. Paradise had his camera on, and it was set to transmit the view to the monitor screen. Gradually, the view calmed down and showed Mrs. Paradise and Joanne sitting at the table.

Millicent knew she should turn away. She felt guilty as she watched the scene in the lounge. Something forced her to keep looking. There was no sound, just the black-and-white picture. The scene changed when the two women stood up. Millicent's heart raced when she saw Madame Paradise pulling up Joanne's dress. Mr. Paradise adjusted the camera lens to zoom in on Joanne's lace-clad black panties.

Mrs. Paradise's hand raised and lowered itself, striking Joanne's lace-covered black buttocks, a tattoo. Millicent swallowed hard and felt Mrs Paradise's humiliation out of pity for Mrs Foxglove. Then Mrs. Paradise pulled Joanne's panties down and revealed the pale flesh that had just begun to take on a pinkish red colour. Millicent blushed when she thought about how grateful she was that it was Joanne who got spanked and not her. What was the German word that summed up the feeling of enjoying someone's discomfort rather than being compassionate? Oh, yes, that's it; "Schadenfreude."

Joanne began to fidget and squirm. Obviously, Mrs. Paradise made an impression on the inexperienced woman Foxglove. Then, oh God! Millicent instinctively put a hand to her mouth in shock. Mrs. Thimble had chosen a leather device shaped like a ping-pong paddle and began to slap Mrs. Thimble on her bare bottom. Mr. Paradise had zoomed Mrs. Thimble's bottom very close. Her legs were spread and revealed the maroon fluff that adorned her matronly slit.

Millicent swallowed hard. She was shocked, but undeniably tickled by her voyeuristic gaze. She herself was surprised at how much she enjoyed Joanne's discomfort in the hands of the formidable woman Paradise.

Schadenfreude!

At last the ordeal was over. Frau Fingerhut rubbed her sore bottom before pulling up her panties and straightening her frock. Guiltily, Millicent turned off the monitor and, while trying to control her breathing, waited for Joanne to come out of the lounge. As she came out, she gave Millicent a faint smile.

"Was everything all right, Mrs Thimble?"

"Uh, very invigorating, my dear."

After Mrs Thimble left, Mrs Paradise came into the office.

"Millicent, I would like you to add Joanne Thimble to our database. Complete today's entry and find an opening for next week. Our Mrs. Thimble is a natural talent for spanking videos, she has a perfect backside that was made to be spanked. Next time her Mr. Paradise will introduce her favorite belt.

"Why, certainly, Mrs Paradise. No problem, mrs. Paradise. I'm completely familiar with Microsoft Office. I'm sure your database will present no problems."

"Good, and when you've done that, pull up the file on Kandy Kreme. (That's with two K's, by the way). She's going to be on camera this afternoon for a scene Kandy is a total bitch, but very much in demand by our clients. She is 29 years old, but can pass for a college student in a short skirt and white blouse".

Curiously, Millicent brought up the database entries and searched Kandy Kreme. From the number of entries, it was immediately clear that Ms. Kreme was a very productive artist. There were several images included that showed her in some of her roles. Millicent added Joanne Jamison to the database and closed the system. She noted that she should ask Mr. or Mrs. Paradise for a picture for Joanne's database entry.

Kandy arrived exactly on time. She was wearing a long coat, which she left in the waiting room. She was wearing a tiny tartan skirt that revealed her white cotton panties every time she moved.

"You must be new," she watched as she checked Millicent up and down.

"Yes, hello, I'm Millicent, delighted to meet you. I'm the new office manager."

"Oh, yes," Kandy said. "I was wondering if you were here to get your ass kicked." Then she demonstratively removed a pack of gum from her mouth that she had been chewing all along since she arrived.

"Sorry about the gum, but it's part of the script for my scene."

"Screenplay?" Millicent looked confused.

"Yeah. Not much of a script, really. The idea is that Mr Paradise catches me sticking it under my desk and decides to beat my naked butt with a rod.

"sounds like a pretty harsh punishment for something as trivial as sticking gum under your desk."

"Yeah, any excuse to get my drawers down. Besides, I have a reputation to uphold for my fans. I am the ultimate bad girl. I have to be naughty and get spanked to keep my fan base.

"Doesn't it hurt to get your naked butt spanked?"

"I'd say it does, but there's pride in a job well done. It fills me with satisfaction that I can do it without screaming. A lot of the girls scream and cry at the first spanking, but not Kandy Kreme. I think Mr. Paradise is frustrated that he can't get me to scream for mercy. Of course I squirm a little. The fans like it when I wiggle my butt after each stroke. And, oh, yeah, the money's good too. Better than working."

Then a stern voice came over the intercom. "Miss Kreme, get over here right away."

"It's happening again, and the marks of my last beating have not quite disappeared."

As soon as Kandy Kreme went to Mr Paradise, Millicent turned on the monitor, hoping the scene would play out. She thought she was very much looking forward to seeing Kandy's performance.

The camera zoomed in on Kandy's right hand while she pressed a pack of gum into the desk cover. Then she panned to an angry looking Mr. Paradise, who seemed to be protesting with a rebellious Kandy Kreme with standing

Armakimbo. Millicent wished she could hear what was being said.

Mr. Paradise grabbed Kandy and in a fake outburst of rage, tore her across his knee. Her short skirt was pulled up, revealing the tight-fitting white panties that were tucked over her round bottom. Millicent's heart raced as Mr. Paradise began to slap Kandy on the ass, first on one cheek, then the other. It was obvious the man was deadly serious. He seemed determined to force his favorite victim to surrender and beg for mercy.

Mr. Paradise grabbed the waistband of the cotton panties and peeled them down to his thighs, depriving Kandy of any protection. The slaps continued raining in a moderate rhythm. Even with the limitations of the black and white monitor, Millicent could see that the young woman's buttocks were turning color.

Then Mr. Paradise allowed Kandy to stand up. He pointed to something that was not on the screen, and Kandy moved out of the shot, returned a few moments later, carrying a stick, and handed it to Mr. Paradise.

Almost ashamed of the voyeuristic pleasure she was getting from watching, Millicent's eyes were riveted to the screen. She watched as Kandy bent down as Mr. Paradise pushed the cane through the air with a few practice strokes. Then, with careful aiming, the first blow landed on Kandy's expelled floor. The impact made the young woman's pale flesh tremble, and a clear line appeared clean above her buttocks.

Mr. Paradise paused and let the full effect work before lifting the stick for a second blow. Millicent pressed his thighs together in anticipation of the next stroke landing. She wondered why this dirty scene had such an effect on her. She was shocked at the sexual excitement Candy's suffering caused her.

As several more strokes landed with infallible accuracy, a series of clean parallel lines marked Candy's beautiful bottom. Millicent rubbed the area between her thighs, and when the camera zoomed in and the delicious butt filled the screen, she had an incredible orgasm.

The slapping finally came to an end and Kandy had to go to the "corner of shame" with her skirt up to show her tube-striped butt.

Millicent was very thoughtful as she started to walk home.

"How did the new job go today, Millie?" Millicent's husband, Stephen, looked over his glasses and put down the Racing Gazette for a moment.

"Oh, fine, thanks, Steve. I'm just getting into the swing of things." Stephen grunted without obligation. He was back studying the odds of the 3.30 Doncaster race.

"Were you ever tempted to spank me, Steve?"

"Why did you do that?"

"Oh, nothing dear. I just wondered."

For the rest of the week, women of all ages, shapes and sizes came to Paradise Tanner to get spanked. One rather buxom lady in her late 40s looked familiar, although her name - Betty Boobs - didn't mean anything. Millicent couldn't quite place her. When she was in the studio and Millicent was watching on the monitor, the buxom woman proudly and confidently showed her huge tits and big ass. The penny dropped - it was the woman who ran the underwear stand in the market hall. In addition to conventional underwear, she kept a number of exotic underpants, some of which she had just disposed of.

Mr. Paradise lost no time when he started working on his tits and bottom with a small leather paddle. Betty Boobs was obviously no stranger to being treated in this way by men. In fact, she seemed to enjoy the treatment that Mr Paradise gave her.

Mr. Paradise must be having the best time of his life, Millicent thought, especially when Betty fell to her knees to suck Mr. Paradise's penis. Meanwhile, Mrs. Paradise allowed the camera to continue filming. This was to be a special production.

Millicent was more and more fascinated by the activities at Paradise Tanner. To say that she was tempted to try it herself was perhaps overstating the case. That is, until she had updated the accounts on the spreadsheet. She noticed that Kandy Kreme had earned more in an hour than she would earn for a whole working day. Why not give it a try, just once? It couldn't hurt, could it?

Millicent plucked up the courage to approach Mrs. Paradise. "Sylvia, I was wondering if I could have an audition to get spanked."

Sylvia curiously glanced at her office manager. "Well, I don't see why not. Your predecessor has succumbed to temptation; we can try if you'd like. Just a word of warning: Mr Paradise and I do not treat our staff lightly. They get exactly the same treatment as the other ladies, a good thrashing on the bare bottom. Do you think you can handle that, Millicent?"

"I think so, Sylvia.

"Very well, Millicent, perhaps you should make an appointment.

Millicent could feel her heartbeat when she booked an appointment in an empty seat.

She had noticed that most of the ladies in her age group wore stockings with suspenders during spanking sessions. Millicent couldn't remember the last time she had worn them, but she found them in her underwear drawer. When the day arrived, Millicent felt a mixture of excitement and nervousness.

The morning dragged on as Millicent filled her time with trivial tasks and waited for her 2 pm appointment. It's like waiting for a dental checkup, only worse, she told herself. Eventually, the appointed time came.

"Mrs. Jamison, please come into the parlor." Millicent, swallowed hard and entered the lounge. Mrs. Paradise was behind the camera, which was mounted on a tripod. Mr Paradise rose from the sofa on which he had sat and greeted his employee in her new role as Spankee.

"Millicent, are you still glad to be able to continue? If you've changed your mind, that's perfectly all right."

"no, mr. Paradise, i haven't changed my mind. I'm happy to go on."

"very well. Did you sign the release form?" It was a rule that all ladies had to agree in writing to corporal punishment before each session. Millicent confirmed that her signed consent form was on file. She confirmed that she agreed to receive corporal punishment on her bare bottom by hand, strap and stick,

"In this case, I think we'll start with a standard above the knee warm-up. Please go above my knee, Millicent." Ms. Paradise began recording the session when Millicent was above her employer's knee.

"Ouch!" The first slap over her dress came as a shock. It hurt more than she expected. I must pull myself together, she said to herself. The beating hasn't really started yet. Millicent managed to take the next few slaps without shame, although a fire began to smoulder in her best panties made of creamy lace.

"Time to remove some of your protection." Mr. Paradise pulled Millicent's dress up to her waist, revealing her stocking-clad legs and pretty panties. He grunted his approval of the enticing target. The warm-up continued as slaps continued to rain down on the panty-covered buttocks. Mr. Paradise smiled to himself as the woman above his lap began to writhe in discomfort. After a few minutes, he decided it was time to strip Millicent of her last layer of protection.

Millicent was relieved after the temporary pause for breath when her tormentor interrupted the beating as he cautiously began to loosen her panties in his butt. He pulled her across her hips to a position midway between her buttocks and knees. He examined Millicent's buttocks carefully and noticed that the previously pale, alabaster-colored flesh took on a pretty pink color. His experience told him that the pink would soon turn into bruises. Ms. Jamison's inexperience made her particularly vulnerable. At this stage of a beating, Kandy Kreme or Betty Boobs would have barely visible marks. Millicent couldn't remember the last time anyone but her husband pulled her underwear down. Basically, she couldn't remember the last time her husband pulled her underwear down.

The beating continued with the sound of flesh on flesh as the beater's hand met the naked cheeks of the naked behind. Mrs. Jamison did her best to keep her thighs closed and tried to avoid exposing her furry female charms. She had noticed how the ladies almost always exposed themselves when they were spanked. So Millicent held her legs tightly together.

Unfortunately, as Millicent was to find out, a serious spanking comes at a time when it's no longer a matter of maintaining one's dignity. The struggle to avoid the burning pain is exhausting. When she felt the heat, she began to wriggle and squirm, trying in vain to escape the agony. Mrs. Paradise was able to take many revealing pictures between Millicent's thighs. She desperately tried to protect her bottom with her hands, but Mr. Paradise was too experienced a wrench for that. He controlled her arms slightly with one hand while he continued the blows with the other.

"Okay, that's enough. You can stand up now, Ms. Jamison, but hold your dress up. We all want to see your bottom." Millicent came to her feet wobbly and carefully felt her bottom, convinced that, judging by the terrible burning, it must be badly damaged. At

Mr. Paradise's request, she stood in the corner of the room facing the wall while holding up her dress in favor of the camera.

"Don't worry, there's no harm done, although your pretty ass will look pretty bruised tomorrow and may be a little tender. I think we should end our session here for now. If you want to experience the kiss of a leather strap or the sting of a stick, please sign up for another session. I am sure Mrs Paradise or myself would be happy to help you.

"did you have a good day at work, millie ?" Stephen Jamison looked up from the Racing Gazette.

"Oh, not bad love, not bad at all. You know how it is, all jobs have their ups and downs. Sometimes it's great, and some days it can be a real pain in the ass."

Stephen giggled. "To true love. You got that right." He turned back to his paper. "Shit! Charlie Boy at Newmarket let me down. "If I'd been romping around the square, I'd have been fifty pounds overweight. He's a real pain in the ass!"

THE HAPPY ENDING

God, it's been a long day.

Meeting after meeting with unsuspecting board members; shy, mouse-grey interns scurrying up and down office corridors; a stack of paperwork in his inbox, ten inches high.

The height of a man's inbox should never rise to the length of his dick, thinks Aiden crookedly to himself and enjoys his own confident humor.

But he assumes that everything came with the territory. Just as he had passed his third decade, the company he had inherited from his father had overtaken its fiercest competitor in the marketplace, and so Aiden's bank account had finally passed the nine-figure mark. His "birthday billionaire blowout," as he liked to call it, had been an alcohol-soaked stain of breasts and booze, so much so that Aiden soon could no longer distinguish between the strippers and the women on the guest list, so desperately everyone threw themselves at him in their unrestrained stupor.

Yes, so the whole thing had certainly been worthwhile. He is still not sure who was the one who finally got him released, or how it had come about in the first place, but this night of debauchery had purified him.

Today, however, he longed for a different kind of cleansing, and if the hands of the clock are right, he had better hurry and prepare himself.

Aiden strolls down a modern hallway sprinkled with expensive artwork specially selected by his senior art consultant. He makes his way to his bedroom, the huge king bed, perfectly made and furnished with decorative pillows.

With deft fingers, Aiden unties the Windsor knot that holds his tie and throws his suit jacket on the floor, where it falls into a puddle of charcoal grey. Melinda will pick it up again later. The same nimble fingers work their way down his shirt and undo the buttons with a deft ease, revealing a dyed belly above a deep V of the pelvis.

This too, together with his trousers, makes the belt buckle clang. And finally the boxer shorts, constricting elastic waistband that was finally torn from his hips.

His cock hangs down and he tugs at it longingly, but there is no time until Marie comes and he hates being interrupted so much. He wouldn't want to take out his frustration on the young woman.

When the doorbell rings, a loud ringing sounds through the air, and Aidan hurries to put on his navy blue and silk bathrobe - he puts the belt around his waist and ties it into a knot as he walks back down the hall to the foyer where, through the private glass windows that frame the oak door, he can see that Marie is floating on his doorstep.

His cock is still half hard from those few long blows and the thought of pushing him into something warm and moist, but he has already made her wait.

So he opens the door wide, a glow of lust warms him as he catches the flash of her eyes down to his pelvis and then up again.

"Marie?" he asks.

"Yes, sir," she replies in a low voice, and Aidan suppresses a grin. She has good instincts. Or maybe the agency had sent a memo. Or maybe Collette had passed along the knowledge of his preferences after he let her go. Delays can't be allowed.

But Marie had what it takes to be a good substitute.

The V-neck of her dress, issued by the agency, drops just deep enough to expose the soft curve of her décolleté, whose soft material embraces her at every turn. She looks at him anxiously, but eagerly, and he immediately knows that she must be a new hire. The newcomers were always anxious to please him.

"Let me show you the terrace," he tells her, turns around and gestures inside. She steps forward and Aidan drops a hand on her back, lets it slide down a little too far and leads her into the house, her little satchel clinking with the oils on her side.

"We'll be working on a terrace?" she asks, obviously not used to the concept of doing her service outdoors.

"Oh, yes," replies Aiden with a slight upward twitch of his lips - more a suggestion of mischief than a smile. "But don't worry. It's pretty remote. I'm sure you'll enjoy it."

"I'll take your word for it," Marie replies, and something in her tone makes Aidan think there might be more to her than just a shy girl. Another side, maybe.

He leads her through the French doors to the terrace and holds his hand in this too low place, satisfied as they walk all the way to the massage table without her squirming or asking him to move it. But for Aidan, this was a practiced game. A natural ease to find out how far he could go.

Marie turns away as he undresses, but Aidan knows the effect he has on women. I'm sure she's curious, if nothing else.

The area is lush and green, trees and shrubs transform the backyard into what many women he had brought here had called the "fairy garden".

He lies down on the table, and a moment later Marie puts a blanket over his lower back and buttocks and begins to exercise his muscles, working her tiny but strong fingers into his knots and kneading them until his body bulges upwards in her touch and she has to guide him down again.

Her hands work so quickly and so skilfully, bringing deep physical pleasure that spins his head. In him the longing rises that her hands should move under the blanket she had draped over him at the beginning, and so something else also rises.

It is as if the pleasure and longing that encapsulates his muscles have nowhere else to go, his body has no other way to deal with it but to let blood rush down, let his cock get stiff and hard and long for redemption.

It takes every bit of Aiden's willpower not to grind into the bed beneath him just to get a little of the satisfaction his cock is calling for.

He moans as Marie digs deep into the curve of his shoulder blade and runs her fingers down, down, down.

"Does it feel... feels good?" asks Marie cautiously, but Aiden swears he can detect a hint of intrigue there, a double meaning of the question he knows Marie is probing to see if the rumours are true. If he asks her.

"That's my line," he blames her as if she were a misbehaving schoolgirl.

"Oh, oh", she mumbles and then giggles.

If there was any doubt at all whether she wanted him to ask her, he'd leave now. But at the time, Aidan expected it. They always wanted him to ask. Dirty whores, all of them. All it takes is the promise of a bunch of hundreds and a look at his perfectly toned body, and they become putty in his hand. He'd even made some of them beg for it, the feeling of his cock in their hands, making them wet and desperate. But Daddy doesn't reward begging. Daddy rewards achievement. Because in reality, the bundle of cash, as tempting as it may be, is not the reward, not the tip for a job well done. No, he had a very different way of showing his gratitude.

"But we are nearing the end of our time," Marie informs him.

Hm, how quickly an hour goes by.

"Of course," replies Aiden and slides himself under the blanket, turns on his back and leans on his elbows.

Now that he has turned around, his aching tail is hard to miss, stretching the soft tissue and twitching with hope. Marie's eyes focus on it, the desire shimmers. She licks her lips as if she doesn't know she's doing it. For a long moment Aiden lets the uncertainty between them linger in the air, turning Marie's beautiful cheeks a deep pink, her soft, flaky lips slightly parted.

"So before we finish, I would like to ask for a full body massage," smiles Aiden.

"That's, uh, that's extra, sir," stammers Marie, clearly trying to make sure the two are on the same side before she makes a move.

"Oh, I know. It won't be a problem, I've arranged the payment. Now, shall I remove the sheet or will you be a good girl and remove it for me?

"I'll be a good girl, sir."

She steps around to stand by his side and Aidan looks up at her as she pinches the towel in each hand and slowly pulls it from his body, exposing his rock-hard cock, which rises hungrily six inches into the air. The towel falls to the ground with a soft blow, but Aiden doesn't hear it because he is too distracted by Marie.

"Oh", she gasps, her deep brown eyes widening at the sight of his cock. The sound she makes at the back of her throat is involuntary, random and oh so telling.

"You like what you see, don't you?"

Instead of answering, Marie makes another tiny moan.

"I bet the sight of my cock makes the pussy nice and wet, doesn't it? Better not let it distract you from your work."

"No, sir, of course not, sir. May I begin?"

"What a good girl, asking permission," purrs Aiden. "You may."

With that, Marie raises her hand and runs her sweet pink tongue across the palm of her hand, which is covered in saliva. Twice she does this with agonizing slowness until her palm is shiny and smooth.

"Let me relax you, sir," she pulls and wraps her long, slender fingers around his cock, lubricates the saliva, teases his head and makes sure his shaft is completely covered.

Aiden sighs briefly and marvels at how soft Marie's hands are as they move up and down his cock and tie him up with a twisting movement of the wrist as he lifts up.

She works slowly at first, strokes in a steady rhythm, making him sway in a comfortable suspension of lust, not so much that he has to fight not to come, but so much that he is desperate for her to continue.

A moment later, she adjusts her grip by holding his cock so that with each stroke her thumb hits the sensitive spot at the base of his cock head and with each touch triggers a slight jerk of his legs.

Marie's eyes are longing as she stares incessantly at his swollen cock, and Aidan snaps to attract her attention by temporarily shifting his focus from his own pleasure to hers.

"Come closer now."

She obeys and doesn't miss a beat as she strokes it.

"Use your other hand. Tuck up your skirt and pull your panties aside for Daddy. I want to see how wet you are."

After careful consideration, Marie lets one hand slide over her body, pauses to caress her tits and pulls up the hem of her dress to reveal a pointed black thong barely big enough to grab her bulging pussy lips.

"Pull her aside, Marie."

Marie follows his command, brushes her panties to the side and holds them there, giving Aiden full access to her pussy. As his hand gets closer, her hand wraps around his cock, making him shudder. He strokes along her slit with an index finger and enjoys the juices that collect there. He takes a moment to swirl the padding of his finger around her clitoris, already swollen with lust.

She emits a sharp moan.

"Quiet," Aidan demands and holds up his soaked index finger. "Cleanse him, whore."

Obediently, Marie tilts her head, bends down to wrap her tender, chubby lips around his finger, swirls her tongue around the tip as if it were the head of his cock, and Aidan's eyes close, a gasp escapes his lips.

He can imagine it so perfectly, her lips tight around his cock, gliding up and down, up and down. Her tongue, licking at the tip, sucking and whirling, teasing him and forcing him closer to the edge.

Marie moans around his finger.

"I thought so," he smiles contentedly and shares her lips with his fingers before plunging one into her, her tight hole swallowing him. He rubs against her G-spot, firm movements in time with the jerk of her hand around his cock. He revels in the way her hole nestles around his fingers, warm and smooth and soaked in her juice. What a good, wet little girl.

Aiden removes his finger and pushes it sideways to the top of her slit where her clitoris

is swollen and begging for his attention.

Her moans turn into almost lustful moans as he rubs himself in angry circles. He lets her enjoy it for a minute by letting her work ever closer to him before he moves on to a new technique.

Marie's clitoris is so dammed up in her desire for orgasm that Aiden can pinch it between his fingers, and he does. He rolls her between his thumb and forefinger, intensifying her screams and her pleasure. And just when she seems to be about to climax, he lets go of her completely.

"Unnf," she moans. "Please, please, sir... . . .oh, God. . . . . . .please give it to me. I need it. God, my clitoris is throbbing, please."

Your begging gives Aidan a wave of joy and a satisfied grin.

"You want me to keep going, bitch? You want to cum for me like the dirty whore that you are? I bet you're desperate for me to cum on you."

"Oh, ooh, I do, sir. Please, please, please finish me off, I need it so bad, I'm begging you. Finish me off."

Aidan just looks at her for a moment and judges the waves of lust that roll down his aching cock and bring him closer and closer to the edge. A moment later, he made a decision.

"Finish it," he orders, and he realizes that she was itching for it, that she longs for it because the hand that wasn't busy stretching his dick is flying to her clitoris. He takes cruel pleasure in forcing the girl to settle for second best, and he knows that nothing will ever satisfy her as he could have, that the thought of his deft fingers working her clitoris will stick in her memory. That the memory will always rise again. Whether she is alone or with another man, she will allow the memory to push her over the edge.

And Marie seems to know it. Her hands work faster and faster, she increases in speed, just as her two moans increase in volume. God, he can feel his climax coming, rising, powerful and overwhelming.

He uses his freshly freed hand to push the collar of Marie's V-neck to the side, and works his hand inside her bra to pinch her hard, pointy nipples between his fingers, just as he had done a minute earlier with her clitoris.

Maybe this is what finally sends Marie over the edge, but Aiden feels her climax before she reaches it and tells her

"That's right. Be a good girl. Lock up for me, my little whore."

And she does it, her body twitching and shaking as she moans in ecstasy, eyes rolling back into her head.

Her hand tightens around his cock as her orgasm unmasks her and puts her back together again, and the effect of all this, her hand, the pressure, her moaning, her supple tits and the way she begged for him and the resulting desire to deny her makes him go over the edge.

From the tip of his cock, thick, white sperm spurts out, dripping down the side in hot, rope-like strands.

"Cleanse him."

"Yes, sir," Marie says, bowing her head and nodding.

Her voice is soft and breathless, the girl is obviously still staggering before her orgasm, but she still obeys, bends over to run her tongue over his cock, licks up every trace of sperm, and leaves his cock sparkling clean. She swallows every trace of his cum with an innocent grin, has pieces of it smeared over her lips before licking them clean too.

"That's a good boy," Aiden says to her and runs her hand over the top and along the back of her head. A moment later he stands up, a satisfied tingling sensation buzzing up and down his legs.

He goes to a small shelf on the house wall and takes out a bundle of hundred dollar bills, counts them out for Marie and loves how greedily she stares at the cash - almost as hungry as she had stared at his cock.

He pushes the money into her hand and pulls her towards him to squeeze her ass one last time.

She giggles and Aiden looks at her for another moment. Yeah, he thinks she shows promise, sure. As long as she's on time, she'll do fine.

"I love stories with a happy ending, don't you?" asks Aiden and begins to pull at his silk robe, tugging at its silk robe, and laces the belt again to hide the rooster Marie had been so desperately drooling for.

"I do," confirms Marie, her voice still breathless. "Did I play to your satisfaction, sir?"

Aidan smiles again. "You can tell the agency to book another appointment next week for the same time. and make it twice as long."

"Of course, Sir," Marie says to him, giving her voice a tone of innocence with big eyes and makes her way back through the French door and through the front door, so that Aiden is more than satisfied.

THE BUS DRIVER

I work full-time. I have been a bus driver for many years. This year, I happen to be driving for your children. Every morning, you and your children stand at the bus stop Every morning, you smile at me and flirt a little. In the afternoon, I bring your children to your house. You are my last stop of the day. I spend my evenings thinking about your sexy smile and fantasizing about all the wonderful things you could do to my body. The last day of school, you finally have the courage to ask me out. I agree to meet you at your house later that night. The plan is to go out and have a few drinks.

I'll come over to your house in a long flowing dress with red floral print. It's got a slit that goes all the way up to my hip. Spaghetti straps and a low neckline that shows off my cleavage beautifully. I combined it with strappy red block heels. The straps wrap my leg. When you open the door, look at me from top to bottom and lick your lips. My smile grows knowing that you like what you see. You compliment me and we go for a drink.

We'll talk for hours and enjoy each other's company. You tell me you're a single father of three wonderful children. That you've been single for over a year, doing everything alone. You tell me that it is lonely and how much you miss the company of a good woman. You also tell me what you want from a woman, but I notice that you are holding something back. I'm telling you that I'm a single parent too.

I have two children, and I've been doing this all by myself for six years. I also mention that I haven't had sex in over a year. You ask me why, and tell me I'm a beautiful woman and should have no problem finding a man. I smile at your compliment and drop my eyes. I feel the heat on my cheeks as I debate telling you my secret. You reach out your hand and stroke my cheek with your right index finger. The night has gone so well, and I'm afraid to ruin it.

I take a deep breath and decide that the best way to do it is to just do it, like ripping off a Band-Aid. I look up and tell you that I haven't been with a man in over a year because I am a submissive person who needs a dominant man. A master man who dominates her sexually, but allows her control over her own life when she is in the midst of the norms. I tell you, I need a man who can use me as his personal, dirty little slut, but who is still a good master who treats me right. You almost smile, then your face becomes solemn when you ask me if I am ready to prove it.

I look down at my hands and think about it. After a moment I look up and ask you to kiss me so that I can make up my mind. You get up and lean over the table. You take my face in your hands and whisper to me that nothing would make you happier. You kiss me long and hard. You explore my mouth with your tongue and leave me breathless when you pull away. A moment later I can still feel you on my lips and feel a burst of energy reaching my innermost being. I look into your eyes and tell you: "Yes, I am ready to prove it. You only live once, right?

I look down at my hands to think about your challenge. After a moment I look up to ask you to kiss me, but you get up and wave me to silence. "A true submissive does not make demands unless he begs," you reply flatly. When you come around the table to my seat, lean down after you have collected the hairs on the back of my head. You hold me firmly but gently with your lips, which are only a few centimetres from mine, and shout, "Do you understand?

My eyes are wide open as our conversation turns to my darkest desires, and I manage to stammer "Yes, yes".

"Good girl." Her hand lets go of my hair as the other hand cupping my face:

"Nothing would make me happier than your surrender. You growl softly before you take my mouth and kiss me long and hard. Your tongue explores my mouth, gets entangled with mine and leaves me breathless. As you pull away, the hard glint shimmers in your eyes as I lift trembling fingers to my lips. A moment later I can still feel you on my lips and a surge of energy shocks through my core.

I meet your eyes with mine. "Yes. I will prove it to you." And risk it. "Master."

You instruct me to go back to my house, put on something slutty and take you home in thirty minutes on my bus. Thirty minutes later I arrive at your house on my bus as ordered, wearing the same red strappy heels and a naughty schoolgirl outfit. I think it's appropriate, since you asked me to drive the bus. The top is black and see-through. It has short sleeves and a deep V-neck. It's also a low-cut top. My stomach is almost completely naked. I have decided not to wear a bra, but a tie that goes with my skirt instead. My tie is a little longer than the shirt itself. The skirt is red plaid with black lace trimming and rests nicely on the middle of my ass cheeks. In the front it is a bit longer, just long enough that you can't see my panties when I stand up. Not that the panties I've chosen for tonight have much to hide. Tonight, I'm wearing a red thong with black trimming.

I feel slutty and exposed and I love every second of it. When I get to your house, I notice you standing outside with your own backpack. I smile and open the door. You drink in my appearance as you get on the bus. You sit in the first row of seats, but on the opposite side to me. You tell me that I have done a good job to be on time and I smile. You instruct me to drive to a dirt road a few miles away. I turn onto a heavily wooded road, and about two miles later you let me stop and park the bus.

You tell me to show you my submissive position. I get out of my seat and kneel beside it. I spread my legs wide, fold my arms behind my back and look down at the floor in front of me. You tell me: "Good girl, then ask me if I have hard boundaries and a chosen safe word.

"Sir, anal. Feces and water sports. Drifting. I can't stand people fiddling with my feet, sir. What happens between us must remain private. I am a trustworthy member of the community; I work with people's children, and it would not be good for me if anyone found out about me. Your head tends to bend speculatively when you ask if that's all there is to it.

I say, "Um, sir, there are two things. Sir, I don't do ass to mouth resuscitation, and I don't want to have bruises or welts like they would if you hit me with a stick. I don't have a problem with whipping and flogging and whatnot, except for the bruises. Sir."

You cross your arms while your eyes get hard and sarcastically ask me if there is something I actually agree with. My cheeks blossom with your displeasure as you ask me again, "Is that all?" I nod my head, "Yes.

Your anger increases and you grab my hair and pull my head back. With the other hand you roughly grab my jaw and tell me: "I can't hear your head rattling from there. From now on I expect you to answer me with your words.

If I answer quickly, I say, "Yes, sir. I'm sorry, master." You let go of me and tell me to take up my position again and answer your question. I say, "Yes, sir, that's all."

"Oh? No safe word?" My face turns crimson again. "Yellow," I murmured.

"Hmm. Appropriate."

You walk away from me towards the back of the bus. I can tell you're processing everything I told you. I'm taking the moment to examine you. I look at your ass and the way you walk. I love your build and the way you carry yourself. When you reach the back of the bus, turn around and look at me. You catch me looking at you like this.

"Tsk, tsk, tsk, tsk. You must be very rusty or a very bad submissive. A good submissive knows that making eye contact without being addressed is bad etiquette. Bad girl. Cost you two lashes."

I apologize and look at the floor.

As soon as you arrive at the front of the bus, open the doors and let me up. You leave the bus and stand outside. You grab every door and look up at me and instruct me to lie down over the driver's seat, facing the back of the bus, and tell me that you want to see my ass. You tell me to put my hands behind my back. I do what I'm told quickly.

Once I'm in position, you walk back up the stairs. I feel your eyes all over my ass, and it's making my pussy tingle. I know now that if you looked, you could see that my cunt is wet. My cheeks turn pink when I think of what I must look like in this position. I can hear you taking a deep breath. A short moment later I feel your hands graze my ass while you fold my skirt onto your back.

You caress it and my thighs. I moan softly. It's been so long since anyone has touched me. You sit on your knees and inspect me. You pull my ass cheeks apart and watch the string of my panties sink deeper into the crevice.

You kiss each butt cheek and hook your finger under the string of my panties and slowly slide it up and down under the string as you start talking. You tell me that anal intercourse is the only one of my boundaries that you don't want to break. It doesn't have to be tonight, but if we go any further, it will be a requirement at some point. This is the moment when I put your finger on mywrinkled hole. It ripples under your touch and I take a sharp breath while you say, "Relax. It's a nice, tight, little hole, and I can't wait to use it."

I am relaxing. You slide your finger down a little further and push that little piece of cloth aside. You get a full view of my wet pussy. Your mouth curves into a smile. "You must be a submissive little bitch. I've barely touched you and I can see the moisture coming out of your pink little pussy. I'm getting red again. I can hear you inhaling my scent, and my blush turns bright red. Your finger's running across my slit as you keep talking.

You're telling me you're not gonna push my limits tonight. Tonight you're gonna tie me up and use me, and if I prove to be a good bitch for you, then we can talk about our relationship between Dom and Sub.

I'm nodding eagerly. "Yes, sir."

You're going to stand up again and pat me on the right ass cheek. I jump a little bit because I wasn't expecting it. They rub it roughly and grab my ass cheek and squeeze it hard. It stings just enough to let me know that you left a red handprint. You pull your hand back and admire your work. "Very nice. You'll do well." Then you ask me if I'm ready for my punishment of two fisticuffs earlier.

Swallowing, I manage to stammer, "Y-yes, M-master." How quickly I am on the verge of tears.

"Good. Count out every sway out loud. If I don't hear you count out loud and clear, we start again. Do you understand?"

"Yes, sir."

The first blow hits me hard on the left cheek. I won't jump this time, but I'll say "shit" as soon as you connect. I take a deep breath and say "one". You shake your head and tell me, "I'm disappointed in your little submarine. A real submarine should know how to count right." You tell me to say the number, and sir, and then a thank you for punishing you as you deserve. I apologize to you and I'm mentally preparing for my next assignment.

You gently rub my ass cheek and ask me, "Are you ready to be a good bitch and try again? I answer, "Yes, sir." The next blow feels harder than the last as it lands on my right cheek and brings tears to my eyes. I take a short breath and say, "One, sir. Thank you for teaching me, sir. May I have another, please, sir?" You like that very much. You fondle both my ass cheeks and give the right one a tender kiss. I give a sigh while you comfort me.

They tell me that the next blow will be the hardest yet and ask me if I understand. I say softly, "Yes, sir." Your hand immediately touches my pussy. I scream in pain and tears come down on my face. It takes me a few moments to get my composure back. Softly I say, "Two, sir. Thank you for teaching me, sir. May I have another, please?" You kneel beside me, rubbing my aching pussy and telling me that I did well and that you're proud of me. You say that two lashes was the punishment I deserved and that I won't get another now.

You turn me over and you kiss me hard. You tell me to turn on the interior lights in the back of the bus and go to the sixth seat on the bus. I push myself up from the seat, turn on the lights, then get up and go where you directed me. You sit on your seat and rummage around in your bag. You find what you are looking for and approach me with a ball gag, leg irons and handcuffs. You tell me to stand with my feet together and turn towards you. You put the handcuffs on my ankles, but don't hook them together.

You bring your hands up against my body from my ankles and make me tremble. You tell me to open wide and you push the ball in my mouth and turn me around so that you can fasten it on the back. You tell me to turn around and face you. I do as I am told, another delicious tremor runs through me. You tell me to strip and keep my tie and panties on. I slowly take my shirt off over my head and feel my tits burst open. My nipples harden immediately. I lower my skirt down to my ankles and step out of it.

I begin to reach for my heels and you stop me and tell me to keep them on. You put my hands behind my back and caress my chest at the same time. Then you lick each nipple, one by one, and then you suck hard on them so that they make a popping sound when they slip out of your mouth. They stand up and tell me to turn around and look to the back of the bus. Then you pull my hands behind me and put the other handcuffs on my wrists. This makes my chest stick out. They tell me to stay facing the back of the bus and put one knee on each seat.

My legs are openly spread across the aisle of the bus. They reach down and tie each of my ankles with the small ring on the ankle cuffs and a tie from your pocket to the bars that are under the seat. You stand behind me and press your body against my bound back arms. You grip your hands around me and start squeezing my tits. You pull on my nipples while you bite and kiss my neck and collarbone.

You keep pulling and rolling on my nipples until they hurt from your abuse. You pull them out as far as you can stretch them, and then you do the same by pulling them up and down. You seem happy with my tolerance for it and the distance you can stretch them. I have drool running down my chin and dripping on my chest. You are smearing it on my chest while you are telling me: "You might be a good little slut I could use after all.

You stick around, keep playing with my tits with one hand and slide your other hand down my stomach to my panties. I can feel you sticking a finger in my waistband and pushing it right and left, back and forth. You growl in my ear that you fuck this sperm-loving pussy and that I'm going to love being your dirty sperm slut tonight.

Your finger slides further down until you reach my clitoris. You snap your finger and slide it further down my slit. In the opposite direction you take your hand out of my panties and rub my juices under my nose and on my upper lip. You tell me to pick it up and smell it. Then you suck on your fine one and tell me, "You taste wonderful... ...for a little sperm bitch." Without warning, you get down on your knees and slide my panties aside.

You look at my pussy and tell me I'm a dripping mess. My pussy lips are a bit swollen from my previous punishment, but you like the way it looks and smells. You tell me you can't wait to use my little pink pussy any way you want. Then you pull your tongue with a slow lick from front to back over my swollen pussy. I moan and let my head fall to my chest. I stick my ass out a little more.

You tell me that I have a very good pussy for a dirty sperm bitch, and you wonder how tight it is. You're talking more to yourself at this point than to me. I'm whimpering with anticipation. You take both hands, you pull up my pussy lips and tell me it's such a nice pink pussy. I try to thank you, but with the gag in my mouth it comes out all distorted and in the end I let a stream of drool run down my chest.

You slap my ass and say, "Shut up, bitch." I bow down in devotion. You rub my ass for a second and say, "That's more like it." You spread my pussy lips again and stick your tongue in it, fuck me with it for a few moments with your tongue. I roll around on your face. You stick a finger in and tell me to shut up, or you can untie me right now and we'll be done in a second.

I'll stand still like a statue and try to say "yes, sir" one more time. I got drool in my panties. You keep on fucking me with one finger, then with two fingers. If I take the third finger with ease, you ask me how much I think I can take. I try to answer, but it's all just a mumble You ask me what that was while you're driving your fingers faster and harder and faster into my pussy

I am panting violently through wildly flared nostrils at this point. You're telling me I don't have permission to cum. You're not done with me. That I'd better not jerk off when I know what's best for me. Then you insert your fourth finger. I feel the warm feeling deep in my stomach. It tells me that I'm going to cum hard and it's going to be a gush.

I start to shake my head, no, and scream "I'm coming!" into the ball gag. They do a few more hits, then quickly pull the hand away. You wipe my juices on my thigh, and I cry about your fingers not being in my pussy anymore. You giggle and call me a needy little bitch. I'm whimpering again because I didn't come to jerk off. I'm also very proud of myself for not coming and doing what I was told. They tell me I'm a good little whore and that I'm being rewarded for it.

They loosen my ball gag and remove it. You slide under me and come towards me. When I look at myself from top to bottom, I see in your expression that I am a wreck and I know it. I blush violently as your eyes wander over my body. My make-up has run over my face in streaks. I have red lines from the ball gag straps on my cheeks. I drool down to my panties. My nipples are so hard and painful after your touch. Between the drool and my juices my panties are soaked to see how wet they are. I know that when I look down, I see a puddle under me.

They lift up my chin to look into my eyes. A pinch on my nipple confirms that you tell me I look like a beautiful sperm slut. You order me to tell you if I have come. You're sure I didn't, but you want to hear it from me. Your fingers squeeze my nipple a little harder, pulling hard on it. If I tell you, "No, sir, that whore didn't come. This one was a good bitch and did what was asked of her," you let go of my nipple and pat me on the tit.

I scream and you tell me, "Yes or no, come on, bitch!"

"Yes, sir! I'm sorry, sir! Fresh tears streaming down my cheeks.

You tell me you're gonna fuck my pussy, then you fuck my mouth. And only after I clean your cock will I get your permission to cum.

I nod my head and immediately try to correct myself by saying "Yes, sir". But I'm not fast enough. You frown, but tell me it's okay that I fucked up. That I tried to correct my mistake, but I'm still being punished for it. I sigh and look down and say, "Yes, sir. I'm sorry, sir." They tell me that this time I'm going to get four punches, and I'd better count them right, or it's going to get a lot worse for me. This time I say, "Yes, sir."

I keep watching your face as you rub your hands together, which creates friction and warms your hands. Then you slap me on both titties, hard and at the same time. I yell, "One, sir! Thank you for teaching me, sir! May I have another, please?" between sobs. They smile quite cruelly and say, "Yes, you may, bitch. You've earned it."

You rub your hands together again, and this time the punches are going to my areolas. The sting makes my nipples stand upright and burn in pain. I sob harder. After a moment I pull myself together and repeat my mantra "Thank you". They smile again and tell me that maybe I will have another one. I pull myself together as you rub your hands together again and this time one hand comes down hard on my left tit and grabs my nipple. I scream, "Fuck! Ooooohhh, fuck!" and take a deep breath and repeat, "T-thank you, s-sir. M-may I have another one, please?" My voice raises in a crescendo of pain. You smile and quickly come down on the other tit. You catch my other nipple, like you did with the last punch.

There are tears in my eyes all the time now, and I take a few deep breaths before thanking you one last time. I open my mouth to ask for one more, and you shut me up. I slide back under my legs, get up and stand behind me. I hear your zipper open and your pants fall to the floor. You kick off your shoes and step out of your pants and then kick them behind you.

I feel you aligning your cock with my pussy and rubbing your head against it a couple of times. You remind me not to cum. You spread my pussy lips open and push your cock in a jerk all the way into my soaked but narrow channel. My breath stops. Your cock is big and thick and I feel it being stretched mercilessly by him. You pull it all the way out, slap my ass and tell me to be quiet.

My pussy's dripping wet and your cock's missing. You bend down and lick my pussy. You untie my ankles and tell me, "On your knees, look at my face, bitch." I do as I'm told. I turn around and I kneel down in front of you. You stroke your dick with your hand, then you tell me to open it wide and suck it like a good bitch. I open my mouth and take about a third of your cock between my lips and over my tongue. I pull it back, stick out my tongue and start licking it all over. You put your hand on the back of my head and tell me to suck it while you press my head on your cock.

You keep your hand on the back of my head but give me back control as I lead you deeper and deeper with every stroke. Tell me what a good cocksucker mouth I have and how well I do my job. You tell me that you want to hear me gagging on your cock and that you want me to look you in the eyes while you do it. I mumble "Y-ll-esss, Sthirr" with your dick in my mouth. I look you right in the eyes and I swallow your cock until I gag. I see your eyes roll back into your head while I choke on your shaft.

I do it again. This time you grab my head with both hands and hold my head still while you fuck my mouth. You're fucking him harder and faster with every stroke. I choke so often that my throat burns. Fresh tears are streaming down my face. You tell me you're gonna cum and I'm supposed to show you before I swallow. You squeeze my mouth one last time, hold me on your cock while I wave my hands behind me with my cuffed hands. The bulbous head blocking my throat swells up, rippling pulses run down my flattened tongue while your sperm squirts out in many hot bubbles.

One of them hits the back of my throat. One hits my chin when I pulled back too far trying to breathe. The last one lands right on my tongue. You put your hands on the seats near you to calm yourself down while you look down at me. I tilt my head back, on my knees, tongue out, mouth wide open, and show you your sperm. You tell me what a dirty sperm slut I am and that you enjoyed using me tonight and that I can swallow. I swallow your sperm and thank you for doing it and for using me.

You tell me that I have been a good girl and that it is time for me to get my reward. You let me sit back in the seat and stretch my feet in the air. I put them on the seats on either side of me. I'll spread them out for you. You get down on your knees and press your face into my needy pussy. Your lips go straight to my lust bud and suck it hard while your tongue swirls it and licks it mercilessly. Your fingers find my soaking wet opening, rush in to fuck me to the point where I go crazy with my desperate desire. You get up and pause.

Beg me to come, my pretty, dirty sperm slut," you demand.

"Please, sir," I say, "C-can I come?

"No," your terse answer comes. "Not before I hear you begging. Really begging."

"Please, sir, may your sperm slut come? I-I-I'm so close it hurts. I want to cum. I need to jerk off! P-please, sir? Please, sir? Master?"

"No, not yet, bitch." Your last denial is a cruel grin.

"Please, please, please, please, please, please, please, please, please, sir," I sing desperately. "PLEASE!! Uunnghh..." my summoned plea ends in a grunt as you press four fingers into me until your thumb stops your thrust. I pant violently: "P-please. C-can. I. Sperm?"

"You may cum, bitch. All over my face." When your mouth comes back to my pussy, I'm gushing all over your face. You swallow it greedily as you continue to finger me. You also suck on my clit and delay my orgasm as long as possible. I scream and cry and laugh and finally writhe in lustful pain while the sensations overwhelm me. My thighs cling to your head while I try to stop your onslaught.

"N-no...n-nothing more. I can't go on. I can't go on... Lord. Please..." I beg weakly, this time I beg for a break.

You raise your head and look at me, and there's... recognition in your eyes. Your smile illuminates them, and my own gratitude skyrockets when I hear your last two words.

"Good girl."

THE SUMMER EDUCATION

I had been travelling around Europe for almost four weeks with my college roommate Helen. We had started in Greece, worked our way through Italy to France and finally to Switzerland and on to southern Germany. Helen had to leave from Frankfurt to begin her first semester at the graduate school. That left me three days to get to Vienna's Schwechat Airport via Austria and catch my flight back home to the States.

Vienna is a beautiful city. I would guess that it is even nicer if you have more than a few euros left in your backpack upon arrival. Sadly, one August day, at the beginning of August, I showed up by train.

I think I should introduce myself first before continuing with my story. I am Melissa. I was almost 22 years old when I made my trip with Helen. I'm not pretty; well, maybe on a good day I'm average. I have light, clear skin, dark hair, and a slight weight problem; however, I had lost a few pounds during that trip: more on that later. I am almost 1.52 meters tall and I don't remember the scales ever telling me that I weigh less than 150 pounds... at least not since high school.

Helen and I had a great time in Southern Europe. We drank too much, visited all the great museums, and each of us even had a brief affair. She was seduced by an Italian boy with a Vespa, and I had an interesting night with a Scottish boy I had met in a Parisian enemy country. I adored his accent, and he loved that I swallowed to come.

Anyway, Europe seemed to become more expensive the further north we traveled. When I dropped Helen off at Frankfurt Airport, I ran out of money. Helen gave me the rest of her money, but even with that money I knew I would run out before I made it to Vienna. I knew that in an emergency I could ask my parents to transfer some extra money to me, but I was determined not to get involved with my parents bailing me out. If I had to starve, so be it. In fact, I had already lost ten pounds during the holiday. That was partly due to thriftiness... and partly because I had to walk everywhere.

When I arrived in Vienna, I was given a loaf of bread and a small tin of coffee in a café. Then I bought myself a seat in a tour bus and went on a long tourist tour through the charming Mozart city. My flight was to leave in two days. I decided that I had enough money for a cheap hotel stay, so I stayed the first night in a dingy place and the next day I visited some museums and Habsburg monuments. My plan for this last night was to arrive at the airport and sleep in a lounge. My flight left the next day at ten in the morning.

The idea to sleep at the airport Schwechat became even less attractive when I realized that I had no clean clothes left. When the public bus dropped me off in Schwechat, I was desperate to have a beer, although I am usually more of a wine drinker. I found my way to an airport bar and sat my tired ass on a bar stool. The bar was quite full of travelling tourists and some businessmen in suits: two of them were having a friendly conversation in German while sitting on the stools next to me. I was rummaging around in my wallet for coins to buy a beer when the bartender came by. He looked coldly annoyed when I asked him how much a beer cost. I thought he was joking when he told me the price of a draught beer. If I bought a beer, I couldn't eat for 15 hours before takeoff. I was discussing my purchase when the man in the suit sitting next to me bent over and spoke to the bartender in English.

"Hey, Frank. Put your beer on my tab, and a big one." Then he returned to his conversation with his partner in German.

I was a little upset that he had interfered without even asking me or talking to me, but I wanted a beer. So I decided that I had to say thank you, even though I hadn't wanted any help. When his employee went to the toilet, I said, "That wasn't necessary, but thanks anyway.

He smiled at me. "I'd say that was damned necessary. I saw how much money was in your purse. Besides, I'll put it on my expense account anyway." His friend returned and they continued in German. While I was enjoying my beer, I made an assessment of my fellow American. He was at least 40 and maybe as old as my father, who was 47. He was wearing a well-cut suit and a crisp white shirt with a nice complementary tie. His clean appearance made me more aware of my shabby condition. He was of medium height, and he was not heavy. He was not handsome either. Conversely, there was nothing unattractive about him. He was the definition of average.

Finally his partner stood up, the two men shook hands warmly, and I was left sitting next to the American. My beer was almost ready, and I got ready to leave.

"I'll have another beer. Would you like one?"

"I could not impose."

"Oh yes, you could. Have you ever had a schnitzel here in Vienna?"

"No, not yet." The idea of the veal cutlet sounded delicious and made my stomach gurgle loudly.

"Sounds as if your stomach wants one."

I started to say that I wasn't hungry, but he had already given up on the bartender. The two men talked briefly, this time in German. I understood enough to know that he had ordered two more beers and two meals. My stomach demanded that I stop arguing against the idea.

While I enjoyed my meal, I told my generous host the stories of my European vacation (minus the few sexual exploits Helen and I had experienced). His name was Keith. It turned out that Keith was an American from the West Coast who came to Vienna on business several times a year. In return, he had learned German, although he explained that almost all German speakers were fluent in English.

When I had finished telling my holiday story, Keith asked, "So, is this the story you're going to tell your parents?

"Hm?"

"It's a nice synopsis, and it completely omits any romantic stories."

"What makes you think there was a romance?"

Keith had a big smile. "Well, Melissa, a young lady can't go to museums forever."

I laughed out loud. "I don't think my parents would be interested in the other part. Not that there was much."

"But there was a lot. That's good. So, what time's your flight?"

"Just before ten."

Keith looked at his watch. "Shouldn't you check in soon?"

"Oh, he leaves tomorrow morning at ten o'clock."

"Will you stay at the airport hotel tonight?"

I felt flushed. I didn't wanna admit I was planning on sleeping in a chair in the Concourse Lounge, but I didn't wanna lie either. I clearly hesitated too long.

"You don't have a place to sleep, do you, Melissa?"

"It's all right. I've spelled it out at an airport before."

"Don't take this the wrong way, but I have a suite. She has a couch. If you want it, you're welcome to it. In fact, you can have the bed, and I'll take the couch. I have a meeting at 8:00 in the morning. I'll wake you up in time for your flight."

I guess I looked a little scared because he went on. "Melissa, I'm offering you a place to sleep. "That's all. You can use the laundry service if you want, and they'll even bring up breakfast."

"Laundry service? Are you saying I smell?"

"Boy, are you defensive. You said you've been skimping for weeks. I guess the laundry wasn't a priority."

I didn't like the idea of sleeping in a plastic chair and then getting on a transatlantic flight. The thought of a bed, a shower and clean clothes was like a vision from heaven. The idea that my parents knew I wanted to spend a night in a strange man's hotel room was like a vision of hell. But my parents were five thousand miles away and I was drinking my third big beer. "If you really don't mind?"

"Then it's a deal." Keith asked for the bill and he paid it.

The suite was magnificent. It was big and clean, and the sofa looked nicer than most of the beds I'd slept in the last month.

Keith told me to do a load of laundry, and he picked up the phone to call the valet. "There are bathrobes in the closet. Just leave out the one you want to sleep in, and I'll let you wash the rest. It'll be on the doorstep before you wake up."

"I really can't..."

"Expense account. Now go get changed."

I took my rucksack into the bathroom and put on my last clean pair of underpants, a pair of running shorts and a T-shirt. I quickly made a bundle of dirty clothes and wrapped it in my sweatshirt. I left the bathroom and put the laundry by the door.

"Take a shower, Melissa. I have some e-mails to send." He opened his laptop and put on his reading glasses.

I'm not sure how long I showered, but I enjoyed every second of the hot water and privacy. When I finally came out, wearing a bathrobe over my underpants and T-shirt, I saw that the laundry was gone. "My clothes will be back in time, won't they? I can't really travel in running shorts and T-shirt."

Keith carefully closed the laptop. He'll be back at daybreak. These Austrians are anal retentive. I think I'll have a show too when you're done in there?"

"I'm done."

"Are you sure you don't want the bed?"

"Yes."

"I know better than to argue with a woman. There are blankets and extra pillows in the closet." He went into the bathroom with it.

I sat down on my couch and I thought.

Keith left the bathroom in boxers and a T-shirt. "I half expected to find you in my bed."

And that confused me. Did he expect me to accept his offer to sleep in bed while he took the couch, or did he expect me to wait in bed to sleep with him? "Would he have expected me to wait in bed to sleep with him?"

"I said I only half expected it. A man can dream, can't he?" And with that, he climbed into bed. "Turn out the light when you go to sleep. Sleep tight."

I turned off the light quickly so he couldn't see my embarrassed and confused face. As I lay there in the dark, my mind was whirling around. In 12 hours I was to board a plane. I would never see Keith again. He was not gorgeous, but he was not unattractive, and he was clearly a nice man. Besides, I've never been with a man who was age-inappropriate for me. I had friends who did, and their general criticism was that older men were much more adept and patient than the "boys" we were all usually with.

I fell asleep on the spot. When I woke up, I turned around to see the clock. My first instinct was to think I had overslept, but the clock showed 23:54: just as a European Cinderella would turn back into a kitchen maid. I got up to go to the bathroom: The beers had taken their toll. As I washed my hands, I decided to be brave. I left the toilet in the dark. As I approached the bed, I said, "Are you awake?"

"Yes. Yes, I'm awake."

"I don't wanna run off to bed." I stepped forward carefully until I found the bed. The covers had already been pulled back.

"Come in, Melissa. I'd like to let you sleep here."

I crawled into bed with this.

"I'm so glad you came. You don't have to do anything you don't want to do, but I think you're pretty." He bent over and kissed me. At first it was a gentle kiss. As it progressed, he became more and more passionate, and he slowly rolled over on me. Now I felt an apparently enormous penis on my legs. I stretched more as a means of examination than as a foreplay movement downwards. Oh my God, Keith was hung like no other man I had ever been with, let alone seen.

At that point, I wished I had stayed in my couch, away from that monstrous weapon of love. Keith's hands were under my shirt, rubbing my breasts as he kept kissing me. Finally he broke off the kiss and asked me if he could take off my panties. Before I could answer, they slid across my wide hips and Keith slid his face between my legs. I hadn't been eaten in ages: It seemed all the men I knew thought the road to sex was a one-way street called Blowjob Boulevard, never Cunnilingus Court.

Keith was an expert pussy eater. He tried different things, and he listened to my verbal cues. What I didn't respond to with enthusiasm stopped, and what I could approve of continued. My friends were right about older men. I felt as if I was soaking the bed in my own luscious juices when Keith lifted his face out of his crotch and came towards me to kiss me.

"I have condoms in my bag in the bathroom. I'll be right back." That was it. He was gone. The bathroom light came on and he came back. The room was no longer pitch-black, and I could see his cock for the first time. When he knelt on the bed, I noticed that he had trouble putting the condom on. I assumed that this was due to physics and not inexperience.

"Don't you want me to suck your cock?" I asked.

"Maybe later. Right now you're very wet. We should try it now."

It almost seemed like a warning. As if to say that if I wasn't wet enough, his dick would never penetrate me. He was right, I was wet, and yet it seemed like a great effort was required when his dick wanted to penetrate me. This situation was made worse by the fact that I had only had sex once in the last few months. He was patient and eventually pressed most of his cock into me. His penis was not excessively hard, but the sheer size could not be denied. I could see that he did not try to fuck me with the full length of his tool.

The feeling was unique and delightful. I have always had the bad habit of making more noise when I approach a good orgasm than when I actually come. So several of my partners misunderstood my approach to orgasm as the real thing, and I was all too often left hanging on the edge of the abyss when another gentle (or not so gentle) nudge was enough. It turned out that this was not a problem with Keith. He read me perfectly and continued to fuck me even after I got calm and came. I was able to jump in rapid succession from my first to my third orgasm.

I think at that point he knew that I was satisfied and he could enjoy me for his own purposes. He began to hammer me harder and deeper. I felt like my whole being was fucked... not just my pussy. On some of his deeper thrusts I swear he hit my cervix; it was disturbing but not entirely unpleasant. He was not a loud lover, and since he wore a condom, I have no idea how much he shot into me.

He kissed me tenderly, went to the bathroom, then returned to me, held me tight and stroked my shoulders.

I smiled in the dark. "Your wife must hate you?"

"No. She's quite fond of me, actually. Why do you say that?"

"Having to serve your beast can't always be fun. How does she manage it?"

"Tequila," he laughed.

We both fell asleep quickly.

I heard an alarm go off. I was in a state of mind where, for a moment, I had no idea where I was: A month away in strange hotels and enemies does that to you. I could feel Keith hugging me, and then he just rolled over my back.

"I have time for a quickie, Melissa. Are you in?" he said as he opened up a pack of condoms.

"you seem pretty sure i am." I pulled back the blanket. "why not? we'll both go right now."

"That's the right attitude." He came between my legs and started fingering me.

"Ouch," I said sharply.

"Are you okay?"

"Damn, my pussy's sore." I touched myself and felt that I was raw and red. Keith got off me.

"I'm sorry, sweetheart. I was too rough on you last night."

"Not too rough, just too damn big."

Keith started getting up.

"You lie back down, mister. Just because I'm angry doesn't mean I'm useless."

"No?" he smiled as he lay back down.

I slid down his body. Now that there was some daylight in the room, I would finally get to see the gun that had attacked me. It was an impressive sight, I admit. My usual plan of attack was to suck a guy as deep and as fast as possible until he came. Today, with this strategy, I would notice how I puked on the fresh white sheets. I think he noticed that I was hesitating.

"Can I give you some advice?"

Normally I didn't want or need advice from a guy who sucks dick, but today I realized that I was overwhelmed (forgive the bad pun.) "OK".

"Just suck the head and lick the shaft. Use your hands to jerk me off. I'll try to come quickly." He hesitated: "Do you swallow?"

"Fuck yes, I'm swallowing." And with that I put my mouth over the huge tip of his dick. I'm sure it made me look like a landed perch. I also started pumping his shaft with my hand. I noticed that my fingers didn't even come close to meeting when they slid down his fleshy penis. I let a lot of saliva run down the shaft to lubricate my efforts in the manual labor. I also took breaks to rest my jaws, and I continued nibbling and kissing his penis. I even teased his hairy balls with my tongue. I realized that my hand was bringing him close to the point of no return, so I pulled back. I figured that at 21, I might see the biggest dick I'd ever see. I wanted to savour the moment.

"Don't tease me, darling," he encouraged me.

I noticed that if I rotated my hand while pumping up and down, Keith quickly started moaning louder. I decided to stop playing with him and let him come. After all, he could have split me in half the night before, but he didn't.

"Oh God, yes. Go on. I'm coming."

With that brief warning, he grabbed my head. In the past, I'd gotten very angry when boys tried to grab my head when I performed oral sex, but Keith seemed gentler. He did hold me down, but he didn't try to force his cock down my throat. Maybe he knew that I was having a hard enough time getting the head of his dick stuck in my mouth. I felt his tool twitching and I prepared myself for the eruption. I've always appreciated men who gave some kind of warning before they came in my mouth. It's an unpleasant situation to suddenly find your mouth full when something looks like a pint of sticky, hot sperm.

A rich, creamy liquid seeped into my mouth. It was not a large amount, nor had it exploded by force, and after the first dose, the second and third shots were even smaller... the last one was almost nonexistent. I found it ironic that although a double-barrelled gun was put in my mouth, the explosion was gentle and not fatal. Keith tasted good and had a thicker consistency than most guys I'd sucked off. One quick sip and it was all over.

I went back to bed. Keith rubbed my stomach and commented on his pleasure at my services. He kissed me and then got up to take a shower. I fell asleep. When Keith poked me, he was wearing a suit.

"I left your package of clean clothes next to your backpack. I also ordered room service, which brings you a hearty breakfast. You should get dressed; they'll be here any second. Here's a little tip for him," Keith gave me a few euros, "and please leave this money for the maids. Then he took a break. "And take this money for tips on the plane and in the airports when you go home."

"I don't want your money, Keith. I'm not just some whore."

"No, you're not a whore. You're just a slut. A whore wants money. A bitch just wants sex." He smiled, kissed me on the forehead, and I wasn't mad at him anymore. He grabbed his suitcase and his briefcase and left the suite. The sumptuous breakfast arrived a few minutes later.

A few hours later, I took my seat in the narrow carriage seat of a transatlantic airliner. My pussy and my intestines in general felt very sore. I tried to make myself comfortable, but I couldn't.

It took days before I no longer felt sore. It was a fun experience to be with Keith, but I was glad that it was his wife who had to deal with that huge cock every day.

In the years since that night, I have never again found a man who was Keith's equal. Unfortunately.

THE ASSESSMENT

Since matriarchy took over the country six months ago, every man has been given a penis control chip that makes it impossible to get an erection without permission. We have to apply for a license to have any kind of sexual pleasure - even just jerking off without a license is illegal. My appointment is today and I am looking forward to finally getting a feeling of liberation.

I arrive at the Male Ejaculation Assessment Center, fill out the paperwork and am assigned my Waiting Allocation Number Kollar, or jerking off number. I have the wank number linda.

I sit in the waiting room, which is filled with other men, and assume that we are all here for the same reason and all avoid eye contact with each other. It is an uncomfortable room to be in, but hopefully the result will be a good one.

"Wanker linda, come to my office," I hear from across the room. I get up and go in. I am greeted by a woman in a doctor's coat who tells me to stand in a square painted on the floor and strip naked. Then I am to put my clothes in a basket to the side of me. "Is it possible for the door to be closed? I have a clear view of the waiting room."

"No," she says, "it is very important to have transparency during the process. If this is a problem, you can always leave and not get your allocation papers. Now be a good fucker and take your clothes off."

I take my clothes off and put my clothes in the basket and I'm totally ashamed.

Your assistant comes in and takes the basket away. "Don't worry," she says, "you'll get it back in the end. Let me look at you now. Stand with your legs spread and your hands on your head."

I do as I'm told.

She walks around me and looks at me from top to bottom before returning to her desk and writing something in my file. "I will temporarily disable your penis control chip for the next part of the process. Do not touch your penis until you are instructed to do so."

I feel a sudden jolt in my shaft as it's turned off.

"Now lower your arms while I show you some images on the screen."

The first picture is of a woman lying naked on a bed. It's the first naked woman I've seen in the six months since porn was banned. I can feel my dick growing when I look at her.

"Standard response to visual stimuli, which is good. Not the biggest I've ever seen, but I guess not all men can be well-hung," she says, updating my file. "Now for the next picture."

It shows a naked standing man with an erection. I don't like this picture, but it's the first erection I've had in ages, so I try to remember the first picture so I can stay hard.

"Hanging tough for homosexual visual stimulation... interesting. Now I want you to hold your penis. Start stroking it. I'll play you a video that you can watch." The video starts and it's a man sucking on another man's cock.

I ask for a heterosexual video instead, but she says, "Once I make the selection, it's final. If you don't stick to it, you won't pass this evaluation and you'll never be able to get an erection again. Now", as she lets out a giggle at my expense, "go ahead.

I have no choice but to continue stroking and watching. I feel so humiliated that I have to masturbate to gay porn in front of the other men waiting outside the door. But to be able to masturbate at all after six months is a gift. After a few minutes my penis suddenly becomes soft before I can cum.

"That's right, cum linda. That concludes this part of the evaluation process. Jerking off is not part of this evaluation. Oh, you look confused, I have full control of your penis thanks to your chip. I can make you hard or soft at the touch of a button.

Then I feel several blows running over my shaft while she makes me hard a few times and then soft again to prove her point. In the process she lets out a dirty chuckle. "I know you wanted to cum, but you haven't gotten your papers yet, and if I'm honest, one of the benefits of this job is seeing you so frustrated and confused. That concludes your evaluation. You will be informed of the results in a few days. You can pick up your clothes at reception on your way out.

I hesitate when a feeling of fear overcomes me - I realize that I have to walk naked through the waiting room.

"Now go on, I have other men to see. But not before they see you." She laughs. "Go on, get out of here."

I start walking out the door and feel the jolt of the chip as she makes me hard again. I keep walking and feel my penis go soft several times and then hard again. The other men in the waiting room look at me as I turn around to look at them. She laughs at my embarrassment.

I collect my clothes and leave hoping that I have passed the assessment.

The letter informs me that I have passed my assessment - I will be allowed to ejaculate twice a week - and that I must return to the assessment centre to discuss how the process will proceed. I immediately set off for the centre.

As I go into the waiting room, a man pushes me. He is completely naked and looks nervous. He must have just finished his evaluation, like I did yesterday. He pushes past me, goes to the desk to get his clothes and runs out the door before he gets dressed. I sit down and wait for my call.

"Motherfucker linda, come to my office."

I get up and go in. It's the same woman from yesterday. "Congratulations on passing your evaluation. I hope you enjoyed the process as much as I did. Now take off your clothes and we'll begin."

I'll undress, put my clothes in the basket and watch them being taken away.

"Well, you seem to be getting used to our process. You didn't even ask for privacy this time."

I nod and look out into the waiting room. After I walked through there naked yesterday, standing here doesn't seem so bad.

"You have been selected for stages one and two of our ejaculation extraction program. Stage One will be the first, and we will use a machine to make you ejaculate. This is so we can keep the sample. I planned for you to do that after this meeting. Stage Two is scheduled for tomorrow, and that will be manual extraction, also known as "you will twitch and purr".

I smile at the thought of the extraction and feel a jerk in my shaft as she pushes the button to make me hard.

"Now you look like you're ready to begin stage one. Follow me through the door and we'll begin."

Through the door is a line of men, standing close together between metal railings, all waiting. "Well, stand in line," she says. "Space is limited, so you'll have to stand as close as possible to the man in front of you."

I go and stand about a foot behind the man in front of me.

"No! Closer." She grabs my dick and pulls me forward until my dick touches the ass cheeks of this random man. "There you go, as close as you can get. Keep pushing against him, it helps the line move in an orderly fashion. I hope you have no problem touching another man with your penis, not that it matters when you do it. She laughs.

I feel so uncomfortable, but the chance to cum is so close that I have no choice but to stand here. Another man comes along and I feel his cock pressed against my ass. I turn around and look without thinking. As I turn around, I feel my dick sliding down the ass of the man in front of me before I hit the dick of the man behind with mine. We make eye contact for a moment and I feel so ashamed and embarrassed.

"Jerk off linda, foaming is not allowed in line! Tails must always point forward! We didn't know you liked that. I'll update your file."

I'll look ahead and put my dick back on the butt cheeks of the guy in front of me.

The line begins to move forward and curves around a corner. As I stand there, I can see the machine being used. There is no privacy, so I can see a man who is strapped in, his arms and legs tied to metal posts and a VR headset in his face. A woman slides a thick black tube over his dick. A tube comes out of it.

It looks like we're all being made to do it in front of the other men. Every few minutes a new man is strapped on and made to cum.

Now it's my turn, and I'm embarrassed to have to climax in front of so many people. "Jerk-off number 16734, step forward and I will strap you in." I do as I'm told and have leather cuffs put around my wrists and ankles before I'm strapped to the bars. I feel so vulnerable and unprotected.

"Since this is your first time, I will explain how the process works. I will put a VR headset on you that plays a video that is connected to the extraction device so that it simulates sex for you. I have selected the video based on the data we gathered during your evaluation - it will be of a man sucking you until you cum. The device will automatically turn off if you close your eyes for too long".

I am trying to explain that I would like to have a heterosexual video.

"Well, I've already set it up, others are waiting, and since you're already strapped in, your objection is pretty pointless, isn't it? She laughs as she puts the VR headset on me. "It may feel a little damp, but what wouldn't it be if fifty men were to jerk off in it?

I flinch when I feel the sperm soaked extraction device on my dick.

The video starts playing. I see a man kneeling before me on his knees. As he leans forward, I feel my cock sliding into his mouth. I try to look away, but it is useless - I am stuck, watching and feeling him sucking me.

Every time he moves his head back and forth, every time he licks my shaft, I feel everything. I try to think of something else, someone else, but I can't. The simulation is so real, it's all I can focus on. I'm forced to watch him. I try to fight the urge to cum, I don't want to get to it, but the feeling builds up and I can't control it.

My balls cramp up and I start to orgasm. It is so intense that I let out a long moan.

"Oh, that was a big deposit - are you sure you're straight?" She giggles as she takes the headset off. "Let me just take the extractor off. I should warn you, you're gonna be pretty sensitive after the extraction, so when I take this off, it's gonna feel very intense."

When she starts pulling the device off me, I moaned again.

"Oh... ...it seems to be stuck. Let me try and get it off."

My cock is so sensitive after the buzz that I can't stand the intense feeling when the device shakes it up and down my cock. I let out a moan, then I beg her to stop.

"Oh, behave yourself, I've nearly shaken it off." She keeps on shaking. It feels like I'm about to come off. She pulls it off just as I climax and drops me on the floor while I'm suffering a ruined orgasm. "Oh, I didn't push the button to soften you up after the extraction. Hopefully that'll teach you not to question what I'm making you do next time. It must be embarrassing to have such sperm in front of all those other waiting men."

She was right. I've never been so humiliated. I feel the jolt in my shaft when she pushes that button to soften me up, giggling like she does. "Now I'm going to untie you. Normally you would walk out the door behind you after work, but this time I want you to get back in line, past all the other men. She untie me, and I'll get a handkerchief to wipe the other men's sperm off my cock. "These are for my use only. You'll have to wait until you get home to clean yourself up." She grabs the box from me.

I walk towards the snake, and she orders all the other men to turn left to make room for me. There's not much room and I have to slip past them. Each of them has an erection, which means that I have to rub my now soft cock, which is still covered with sperm, against each one of them while looking directly at them. Finally I come to the end of the line - I must have just rubbed myself on forty tails. When I reach the reception and ask for my clothes, I'm told to be back tomorrow for level 2.

I hope it's better than today. I have never been so humiliated.

I arrive at the centre and am asked to go down the corridor to a different waiting room than yesterday. I go in and sit down. In the middle of the room there is a short post with two loops in the middle and nine more men waiting. I'm looking forward to this session - being able to masturbate normally and come will be great.

After a few minutes a woman comes in, the same one who operated the machine yesterday. "Good, now that you are all here, we can begin. Push the chairs aside and gather in a circle around the post." We do as we're told and form a circle in the middle of the room.

"Most of you have done this before, but since Wank linda is new, I'll explain how it works. This is a manual ejaculation extraction. You will be asked to manually stimulate the penis until orgasm. You will undress and place your clothes in the basket provided. You may wonder why you are standing around a post - anyone who cannot follow orders will be tied to it and for, well, let's just call it target practice. "Take your clothes off now."

I'll take off my clothes and quickly put them in the basket. I don't want to give her any reason to see me standing in the middle, and after the last two days it's become easier to stand naked in front of other men.

"Good. Now I'm going to activate your penis chips and we can begin."

I feel this familiar jerk running down my shaft, and I feel my cock growing and getting hard. It's weird to see the cocks of the nine other guys all getting hard in unison.

"Now all of you take a step forward so that you stand shoulder to shoulder and extend your right hand with the palm of your hand upwards. She walks around in a circle with a bottle of lubricant and gives us two squirts, one on the hand and one on the head of our cocks. "Now that you are ready, you may begin. Reach for your right hand and hold the man's penis next to you."

I feel the man next to me grabbing my cock with a firm grip. I hesitate, but I have no choice but to hold the hard cock next to me. "Oh linda, you look confused I said that you would stimulate a penis until orgasm - I never said it would be yours. Go ahead, go ahead, I'm sure he wants to come as much as you do." She laughs as I start to move my hand up and down the length of his dick

It feels so wrong for a man to rub his hand across my shaft while I feel another man's throb in my hand. It makes me feel so hurt. I try to look at the woman who makes us do this. If I have to come off like that, at least I can be looking at her.

She walks behind me. "Look ahead. I'm not here for you. Do you like holding a real dick in your hand? You must enjoy it - you look like you're about to burst."

I shake my head. When I open my mouth to speak, she straps a ring gag over my mouth and forces my mouth to stay open. "No talking allowed in here." She goes back to her desk, looks at her computer screen. "Take your seat, I have other groups today," she shouts before looking at the screen again.

We all do what we're told. With the increase in speed, I feel my balls start to cramp up as I reach orgasm. Just as I stand on the edge, I feel a jerk and my penis becomes soft.

"All stop!" She walks towards me. "I've just looked at your chart, and you're only allowed to come twice a week. And, well, with the extra I gave you yesterday, that's your limit. What a pity for you," she laughs. "Since your instructions for today were to jerk off and come, but you can't finish now, I'll have to have you strapped to the post.

The two men next to me grab my arms and pull me into the middle, force me down on my knees while she ties my hands to the loops behind my back. I am now at eye level with every cock in the room.

She goes away and sits down at her desk again. "Reform the circle and return to what you were doing."

I turn away from the rooster right in front of me, but every time I turn around, it's another one, all hard and about to come off. I will be covered by them. I hear the man behind me moaning and feel a hot, wet jet of cum hitting the back of my head and running down my back. As soon as the first man came, the others all start buzzing within seconds and I feel one shot after another hitting me and running down my naked body.

The man in front of me is the last one to arrive - he shoots me directly in the face, in my mouth, which is kept open by the ring gag. It is salty and makes me gag. Kneeling here, unable to move, feeling him running down my body before he drips to the floor, is the dirtiest and most humiliating feeling I have ever experienced.

"Good. Now go get your clothes." The other men all go and get out. "Now linda, don't look dirty; I hope this has taught you a lesson about following orders and why you're here. You came to this trial because you thought it was for your own pleasure. But it is not. You are here for our pleasure. You will be here again if from now on you do not "follow every order without question".

She unties me and orders me to stand up before she removes the ring gag from my mouth. "After two more weeks of coming to the centre, you will be given a review. Depending on your behavior, we may enroll you in further levels or our program. Nod if you understand."

I'm nodding my head.

"I am nodding my head. I'm sure you would like to get cleaned up, but unfortunately we don't have the facilities for that, so you'll have to wait until you get home. Pick up your clothes on your way out, and I'll see you next week."

I turn around and start walking away.

"linda, you forgot to say thank you."

"Thank you," I say and start walking away.

"Thanks for what?" she says with a giggle.

"Thanks for covering me with semen," I say.

"Oh, my pleasure," she laughs and looks up and down at me. "Now go, I'm done with you for now."

I go and get my clothes and pull them over my wet skin. When I start to go home, I'm afraid to go back next week - but I'll do anything they say not to be used like that again.

11 stories: 10+1 Roleplay Sex Stories

Amira Red

Table of Contents

SHOWER GIRL

As in other parts of the country, I am on self-quarantine, everything that is of interest is closed until who knows when. I experienced the interruption of normal life first hand when I finally had to go shopping.

When I arrived at the grocery store, a small snake was waiting for me. Yes, they limited the number of customers in order to maintain social distance. The line moved pretty well, one out, one in. Luckily, people just got what they needed and went out again.

Once inside, I noticed a young woman from the gym, who usually works out on the elliptical machine in front of me. She usually comes in with her husband, a military man. I can't say that we really know each other; we may have spoken a few times over the year.

A week before the gym closed, I noticed that her husband was not with her. I asked about it, and she said that they had put him on for a while, so she would come alone for a while. About the only other thing I knew about her was that her name was Janene and that she was an elementary school teacher and not from this area. Not that I didn't want more information, but she didn't open up much.

Janene waved to me from the production department, I waved back as usual and continued shopping. She checked out in front of me and so surprised me by waiting for her outside. It is uncomfortable to maintain a safe social distance when you try to have a conversation, but she started talking.

"Bob, can you help me since you know my husband has been deployed and I'm here all alone?

"Sure, Janene," she thought she needed help with the shopping bags.

"Bob, I really need a place to shower, my apartment complex is having water problems. The manager can't seem to get a plumber to fix it. First the hot water went, then all the water stopped, it can work for a few minutes and then stop. I almost got a cold shower, but the water stopped while I was soaped up, and when it was running again, it was brown water".

"I don't know any plumbers, I don't know how to help."

"Could I come to your house and take a shower?"

Janene is a young, attractive, thin woman with a nice, firm butt, at least from my point of view at the gym. I'd like to help her, but immediately I hear my wife's voice in my head saying, "No way.

After a long pause: "Okay, I'm sure my wife won't mind.

As soon as these words came out, I knew that I had committed myself to something that my wife would object to.

"Janene, give me your phone number, I'll text you our address."

Chapter Two

Later that day she called: "Bob, the situation is even worse now, I have to leave my apartment because several tenants tested positive for the virus. I'm scared... what am I gonna do?"

"What do you mean you have to leave, are you infected?"

"No, but several of my neighbours have tested positive and are now in quarantine. My husband suggested I go away for a while to be safe."

"Did he suggest a place where I might go?"

"No, I can't go back home because my parents' place was quarantined and I can't go where my husband was stationed. Please help me, I don't know anyone else in this area I could ask."

"Okay, we have a guest room, you can come over."

"Thank you very much, I bring my own shopping and I have my own toilet paper."

My wife almost blew up when I told her that she needs more than a shower, she has to stay for a short time until her apartment complex is repaired. I hesitated to mention that several of her neighbours had tested positive for the virus, but for our own health I had to mention it. I played down the health risks, but my wife said she would call her friend who was a nurse to get advice.

Her diabolical Angelia is a dental hygienist, not a nurse, but I would not stir the pot.

"Angelia said we can contact a doctor, she knows it, and he can do a telemedicine video check to examine your friend.

"Carol, I called the doctor to figure out how to do this safely. He told me your guest should take off all his clothes and leave them outside in a plastic garbage bag. She should go straight into the shower, shower with bacterial soap if you have it, and then contact me for a telemedical examination. If she passes the health check, she'll be safe with you. You should wash her clothes with a small amount of bleach to kill any germs before she can use them.

That one arrived at the front door, I told her to use the garage entrance. I printed out the doctor's instructions and taped them to the inside garage door.

She knocked on the inner garage door, "Bob, you can't be serious about these instructions, I can't do this

"Janene, this is Bob's wife, Carol. These instructions are from a doctor, we don't want to get infected with the virus. If you don't follow these instructions, you cannot stay here. I'm sorry."

A few minutes later, she knocks on the door: "Okay, I'm undressed, can I come in?"

"Can I come in?" "Anything? Including your underwear and shoes?"

"Yes, I'm standing here completely naked."

"Okay, I open the door, go straight down the hall to the bathroom on the right. It's all there, special antibacterial soap and towel. When you're done, come into the living room and we'll contact the doctor."

"Carol, Bob's not gonna see me naked, is he?"

"Janene, I sent Bob to his office in the back room, he won't see you."

Carol opened the door and got out of the way so Janene could go right into the shower. Then she sprayed Lysol on the door handle and took the garbage bag with Janene's clothes and put them in the washing machine. She wanted to separate everything, but she remembered that it was about disinfecting.

Janene was done and went back to the living room with a towel wrapped around her as ordered. The towel was not big enough to cover her top and bottom at the same time. She decided to cover her breasts.

Carol reached out her hand, but then remembered the new greeting: "Hi, I'm Carol. Sorry for the extreme precautions, but doctor's orders."

"Thanks Carol, I know this is an imposition but I have no choice and I'm scared to death. Especially since my husband is on God knows where."

"Janene, we'll call the doctor and do your telemedical examination so we can both calm down."

Carol tried to get the telemedicine doctor on her iPad, but couldn't get the connection. In her desperation she had to call me to help: "Bob, I can't get this damn iPad to work, can you help?

I entered the living room and noticed that both Janene and Carol were tapping the iPad everywhere, a total violation of the virus protocols. "Hey, ladies, step back, I'll do it after I wipe the screen with an alcohol swab."

I typed in the number, and the doctor was on-screen live in seconds. Dressed in a white lab coat and a face mask, he certainly looked like he was following proper protocol.

"Hello, I'm Doctor John Hopkins. I assume the woman with the towel is the patient. Please let her get closer to the iPad so I can get a better look." I'm speaking in an Indian accent.

Janene moved closer to the iPad to please the doctor.

"Thanks, I need to take your vitals, Carol, do you have that thermometer I requested?"

"Yes, doctor and I have the pulse ox and BP you requested."

We have a number of medical devices left over from years of taking care of Carol's father.

"First, Carol puts on examination gloves, then she takes her blood pressure and puts the pulse oxymeter on her index finger.

"BP 120/65 and pulse ox 98."

"Good, good... Take her anal temp now."

"Janene, bend over so I can take your temperature."

"Whoa, wait a minute, you're not sticking that up my ass!"

"Janene, this is the best way to get an accurate temperature. One of the first symptoms of the virus is an elevated temperature." Said the doctor.

Janene gave way and bent over the living room chair, her pale white butt exposed.

Just as Carol was about to insert the thermometer, the doctor's voice told me to hold the iPad so he could see her butt. Then she told Janene to spread her ass cheeks with her hands to make it easier for Carol to insert the thermometer.

That asshole croaked in anticipation of the foreign body being inserted. Not only was her ass visible, but her labia were also visible.

After an initial gasp, Jenes ass accepted the thermometer. The doctor warned Carol to leave it in for a full two minutes.

"98.4, Doctor," shouted Carol as she tried to take the temperature.

"Okay, that's good. Janene, we're gonna have to start at the top and examine you further. Carol, can you take a tongue depressor and look down her throat? Bob, can you move the iPad so I can see, can you put a flashlight in it so I can see better?

"Okay, well... I don't see any inflammation. Janene, I need you to remove the towel now so we can do a breast exam."

"Breast exam? What do my breasts have to do with a virus?"

"The virus can have many symptoms and can lie dormant in several places. If fluid is leaking from your breasts, it can be an early indicator. If fluid leaks, we can take a sample and have it analysed.

Janene looked confused. "I think that's fine, but does Bob have to see my breasts?

"I understand Janene, but Bob has to hold the iPad while Carol examines your nipples. Bob will keep his eyes closed if that helps."

After Janene has removed the towel from her breasts, "Carol, you need to palpate her areolas. If you feel anything unusual, stop so I can see."

Carol palpated them carefully and found nothing to report.

"Next, you pull on her nipples as if you were trying to milk them and look for signs of fluid leakage. If there's a stop and you take a sample, we can have the lab analyze it. Bob, I need you to move the iPad closer so I can get a close-up of her nipples.

I thanked the doctor and moved closer to Janene's nipples. I watched them harden as Carol pulled and twisted them; I think she became aroused. She didn't notice that I hadn't closed my eyes.

This went on for several minutes, I think Carol enjoyed playing with her nipples and could have gone on like this for longer, but the doctor said that was enough as there was no fluid.

"Last step Janene, I have to do a pelvic exam. There could be signs in your vagina. Sit in the chair, then I want you to move your labia apart and Carol will use a tongue pusher to hold your labia majora open so I can see your cervix. Bob, shine a flashlight in here so I can get a clear view."

As she removed the towel, her blonde pubic hair was cut off in a small, clean triangle that ended just above her pussy. I expected her to object to this further penetration of her body, but she agreed to it for fear of contamination.

Imagine this: My wife has a tongue depressor in a strange woman's pussy while I'm holding an iPad and a flashlight shines in her. Never in a million years did I think something like that would happen.

"Carol, move the handle to the right... "now to the left... Now I want you to pull back the clitoral hood, the little flap of skin where the inner lips meet."

Janene gasped as Carol uncovered the clitoris, and when she touched it with the tongue depressor, she pushed her hips forward and moaned.

Carol immediately stopped thinking she had hurt her, "Sorry, I didn't mean to hurt you."

The doctor threw in: "Yes, hmm ... the clitoris is swelling up ... that's a good sign. Okay, um... all done. I see no signs of a virus."

We all sighed with relief before the doctor continued: "Anyway, you should take your temperature in the next two days, just a precaution. If her temperature gets above 99, call me back."

Together we thanked the doctor and ended the iPad session.

Janene looks at Carol: "Now you know me inside and out."

"I'm sorry we had to put you through this examination, but the doctor said it was for all our safety."

Janene said, "I guess there's no hurry to put my clothes on now, I have no secrets now.

"Janene, when you're sitting on the furniture, please sit on the towel." Carol said casually, as if it were normal to say something like that.

A naked Janene went to the panoramic window of the living room and shocked Carol as she stood naked in plain view, watching the neighbor.

"Janene, would you like a tour of the house?"

She accepted, and Carol led her through each room, including the guest room, until she reached the rear covered patio. Janene, was admiring Carol's flower garden as the flowers appeared. Absent-mindedly, Carol suggested that Janene go outside and take a closer look, forgetting that she was naked.

"Wow, the sun feels so good" as she stood in the backyard.

"Carol, you should try this, being naked outside feels so free and natural.

Carol didn't answer. Carol just stared at Janene's young, slender, naked body as she walked around her backyard.

When they finally got back to Carol, Carol yelled, "Bob, can you put Janene's laundry in the dryer, I forgot all about it.

I expected Janene to ask if her suitcase was still in the garage so she could have clothes, but she seemed content to stay naked. Later, Carol suggested that I spray her suitcase with Lysol and take it to the guest room.

Carol surprised me with her reaction to Janene running around naked. I thought she had a problem with me looking at a strange naked young woman, but I think she enjoyed seeing her in that way herself.

"Carol, I hope you don't mind, but I think I'll go to the guest room and lie down for a while.

Carol took the opportunity to have a private conversation with me in the kitchen: "Bob, did this doctor look familiar to you?

"Familiar as who? ... we don't know anybody with an Indian accent, let alone a doctor."

"I thought it strange that he called you by name. You didn't tell him your name."

"My Skype ID is bob32, maybe that's why."

"I also thought it was weird when he went for a pelvic exam and the nipple exam was a bit suspicious. Not that I didn't mind, but it seemed weird." Said Carol with a raised eyebrow.

"Well, you had to admit he was thorough, and I'm now very confident about her health, and it was for our safety.

Later that night at the diner, Janene appeared in a light-colored gown that barely covered her nakedness.

"Carol, I'm sorry to cause you all this trouble and thank you for getting a doctor to examine me. I didn't want to bring germs."

"You're welcome. It's the least we can do for you."

Janene's bathrobe kept opening up, giving me a look at her tits. Carol chose this time to ask about her apparent lack of embarrassment with nudity.

"Carol, I love being naked, when I'm at home I don't wear clothes, I like the freedom of being naked. If I could, I would go to the gym naked. I'm not ashamed of my body, but I could stand to lose a few pounds.

"Well, we don't have a problem with you being naked, do we, Bob?"

I could only nod affirmatively for fear of choking on my mouth full of food.

When they cleared the table, I went to the garage to make a phone call.

"Carl, or should I say Dr John? What were you doing? I just wanted you to take her temperature and give her an okay."

"Bob, I couldn't resist when I saw the body. I wanted to explore it in every detail. You can't tell me you didn't want to see those tits. I just wish I could have made a house call."

"Carol would have made you in a heartbeat. She was still suspicious, but she left thinking you were a real doctor. She'll kill you if she ever finds out."

In his Indian accent, "What do you doubt about Dr. John?"

"Best April Fool's joke ever, pal, but Angelia's gonna castrate you if she finds out you took advantage of a young girl at her best friend's house."

"Good point, I won't tell anyone about this, neither can you, or Carol will castrate you too."

When I got back, Carol said, "Bob, who did you call?"

"Just a friend from the bowling league."

"You know, Bob, I've been thinking about the telemedicine doctor and Jane's checkup. I think I should let him examine me, just to be sure."

"Do you have any symptoms?"

"No, but he's had such a thorough examination, but I want to be sure. He should examine you, too, after you've done so much shopping."

THE POLICE HARRASSMENT

I'd gone to the library to return some books to my mother. When I walk home, I can go through a small, clean alley, which cuts my walking distance in half. So here I was trotting down the alley when three men came into the alley from the other end. When I talk about men, I suppose they were about my age, eighteen. I knew they were, if I remembered that we all had birthdays in the same month.

Now I was white and a girl and they were black and men, but was I worried? Certainly not. The three of them were very nice, and I had been in class with them at different times. I assumed it would be just a case of just saying "hullo" and passing each other and continuing on our way. It was not to be.

Even before we reached each other, this policeman stepped into the alley behind the men. He slammed his nightstick hard against a fence and yelled at the boys.

"All right, you scumbags," he yelled. "Stand by the fence and take up your positions and don't even think about running. I'm armed and perfectly willing to shoot."

I saw the consternation in the men's faces and the irritation when they saw that if they tried to run they would have to knock me down. They used highly inappropriate language as they turned and leaned against the fence, their weight on their hands and their legs spread. There was now a second policeman, and the two policemen moved towards the men.

I was outraged. Really angry. The boys had done nothing, they had just walked by and minded their own business, and the policemen had gone after them for no reason.

"Why are you picking on them?" I said. "You didn't do anything wrong. There is no law that says you can't walk in the street. That's harassment."

The three men looked at me in surprise, and then one of them smiled.

"Hey, Celia," he shouted. "How you doing? You tell them, girl. We ain't done nothing, and this is police harassment."

"Please go on, mademoiselle," growled one of the policemen. "This is a police matter and I would be grateful if you would not interfere."

"This is a police matter and I would be grateful if you would not interfere." "This is a nuisance to honest citizens. It's also racial harassment."

"Miss, we have a reason to stop these men," said the policeman. "Please let us perform our duties and move on."

"The reason, Celia, is because we are black," shouted the man who called me earlier. "As you can see, there are four people on this trail, and they only caught the three black people."

"He's right," I said in a righteous rage. I can't stand racism and injustice, and this seemed like a classic example. "If you are so faithful to your duty, why didn't you make me take the position you so originally called it?

The two policemen looked at each other and seemed slightly annoyed. Then the policeman who had been talking the whole time shrugged.

"If that's what you want," he said. "Assume the position." He nodded towards the fence.

"What?" he said. That was a joke, wasn't it?

"Assume the position. You've convinced me that I have to check you out too, to prove we're not acting from a racial profiling position."

I'd said too much to back down now. I turned around and put my hands against the fence.

"Not like that," the policeman grabbed. "Take a step back and lean into your hands. Spread your legs wider apart, too. The position is such that you cannot turn against the policeman. If you even try, we can kick your feet out from under you before you can take action."

Oh, so that's why they did it this way.

The other cop started frisking the man at the end (is that the right word).

"Bingo," he said, holding something up. Next thing I know, he's handcuffing the poor man.

"I'll just put him in the car and be right back," he said.

After a minute he came back and started to check out number two. "Bingo two," he said, and another set of handcuffs was made and the man was led away.

The first policeman started to check the last man while I tried to turn around to see what he was doing. His hand came out of the man's pocket with what looked like a pair of necklaces.

"I think I got bingo too," he said with a grin, and number three was handcuffed.

"You can run them in," he said to his partner. "I'm staying with the young lady until the policewoman arrives."

I was pretty nervous now.

"What's going on here?" I asked.

"Three men have just robbed the jewellery store," said the policeman. "We had a pretty good description of them, so we stopped the three men. Guess what we found in their pockets."

I didn't have to guess. I'd seen what he'd pulled out of the man's pocket. The three of them were probably laughing morbidly at how gullible I'd been.

"I did not know. I didn "t know. I "m sorry. I feel like a fool. Can I go now?"

"Ah, I'm sorry, but no. Now that we have due process of law, we have to go by the book. You must be searched. Don't worry, I won't search them. My partner will send a policewoman to take care of it."

Oh great, I was going to let a strange woman feel me up.

"Oh. Uh, how long will it take her to get here."

"I don't know. They're only considered part of due process of law and not high priority. She'll turn up when she does, but don't worry. She shouldn't take more than an hour or so."

An hour or so, with me leaning against that fence the whole time? You gotta be kidding me.

"Oh, come on," I moaned. "You can't expect me to stay here for an hour or so."

"Hey, don't blame me. I told you to keep moving. You're the one who insisted on butting in."

"But I didn't know."

"Did you think to ask or was it just more fun to accuse the police of the wrong thing?"

It made me blush. He was right. I liked having an excuse to yell at 'em cos I knew they wouldn't do anything. Taking that position was something I hadn't expected.

"Can't you just go through my pockets or something?" I begged them.

"Hello. Me Tarzan, you Jane. What do you think of that?"

"What?"

"The police will only search suspects of the same sex.

"What, no exceptions?"

"Only if the suspect voluntarily agrees to be searched by a member of the opposite sex. Men often volunteer, women almost never."

"But they can? They can do a quick search, if I agree?"

"I could, but I'd rather not. "Women can change their minds at any time and complain later. Why should I risk it if I can take it easy for an hour or so?"

"Oh, come on. That is so unfair.

"OK, fine," the policeman grumbled. "Anything to shut you up. But don't whine to me if it makes you uncomfortable."

He advanced behind me and ran his hands along my sides and under my arms. Then his hands went around the front of me and began to stroke my breasts. I began to blush with embarrassment, but my blush jumped in full bloom when he stopped and pressed a finger on a nipple.

"What do you have in your pocket?" he asked.

"I have no pockets on my blouse," I said in a rather hoarse voice.

"Oh, right," he said, apparently realizing what he had pressed. He laughed softly, I just knew it.

He crouched behind me and his hands closed over one of my ankles. Then he rose again, his hand running up both sides of my leg. I blushed, but I honestly expected him to stop as soon as he reached my skirt, or maybe just to the bottom of my skirt. His hands just kept going up, and I gasped strangled as his hand bumped against the crotch of my panties and pressed firmly against what was on the other side of the crotch.

Did he apologize? In your dreams. He just crouched down again and his hands brushed against my other leg. He won't have to climb that high this time, I kept telling myself, because he had already looked there. Did that stop him? The hand that was pressing against my pussy told me no.

"Almost done", he said, as his hands slid over my hips, still under my skirt, mind you.

When his hands came down, my panties came down with them. One hand pushed my panties down further while his other hand started rubbing my pussy.

"What are you doing?" I was half screaming.

"I'm just making sure the last part of the search goes smoothly for you," he said.

"What are you talking about?"

"You wouldn't believe where a woman hid a switchblade yesterday," he told me. "That is why we must be very careful and very thorough in our searches. Don't worry. I can handle it."

Maybe he could, but could I? That was a very personal part of me that he wanted to search.

"Ah, maybe we should wait for the policewoman," I said, and even for me my voice sounded a little rough.

"Don't be a sissy," he mocked me gently. "I'm almost finished. Just relax and we're done."

I still said, "But," as he spread my lips and pushed his nightstick into me. And I meant his personal baton, and it felt thicker and harder and much hotter than his silly little police baton.

I said, "You can't" and "You shouldn't" and "Someone might come" and his baton kept pressing deeper and deeper. In retrospect, I guess I should have said things like "no" and "stop." Those words are so much more meaningful than insinuations that maybe this was not a good idea.

He didn't even bother to slow down, he just pushed hard until he was completely embedded in me.

"Yes", he breathed gently into my ear. "I can pretty much guarantee that you have nothing more to hide up here."

"So that means you're gonna take it out now?" I asked hopefully.

I heard a faint giggle, his warm breath blowing against my ear.

"Wouldn't it be a waste of a good start to take it out now?" he asked. "Why don't we just let things go on as they are for a while?"

Look. This is what happens when you ask questions instead of making statements. People answer the questions wrong. He started to move and slide back and forth and stir me up. To my surprise, I realized that even in the position I was in, I was able to answer and move with him. Even more to my surprise, I realized that this is what I wanted.

Slowly but surely he moved in faster and faster. At the same time my enthusiasm grew at the same pace. I gasped for breath, pressed myself urgently against him, wanted to have this cock deep inside me and enjoyed the feeling that he was rubbing against me.

The only fear I had now was the fear that he might stop before I wanted him to. I begged him, urged him to get harder, asked him not to stop. Everything piled up inside of me, stressing me, and I almost screamed, just because I knew we were outside. My former fear that someone else might come was forgotten, but that did not mean that I wanted to attract them. I just didn't want him to stop.

He gave me one last push, and I went out of the deep, trembling as my climax broke into me, and felt him moaning and writhing and shaking as he himself reached the climax.

He pulled himself away from me, we were both breathing heavily.

"I must admit that you are quite clear about me," he said. "You are free to leave."

"Thank you', I said, wondering at the same time what I wanted to thank him for.

"Just remember that in general we have a reason to stop people and racism is not one of them. If we arrest somebody for racism, we will probably be sued, and we cannot go on patrol when we take cases to court.

So I drove on my way home, chastised accordingly. I decided that I didn't like to accept this position as the police described it. It seemed to have left me with very shaky legs.

THE DOCTOR'S VISIT

It's not all sexy. But sometimes, just sometimes, you smile and go with a swagger.

Patient S. Abdominal pain. 26. F.

She was fine after surgery. But we had to monitor her for the next two days. I was on call in the post-op ward. I was just doing my post-op observation. There were four patients in this room. Miss S had just finished her meal when I consulted her chart. The usual greeting. She leaned over, squirted some hand sanitizer and rubbed her hands together.

"No, no, no, no." I said. "You must wash your hands properly. Come to the washbasin, I'll show you."

She looked a little perplexed and nodded. Pulled the sheet back and threw her legs out of the bed. The bright red nails of her toes and slender legs caught my attention. She stood up. During her night she wore a thin cotton nightgown that barely covered the tips of her thighs and was strewn with small yellow flowers. Strong breasts held the nightdress out and let it cascade over her figure. She was short, perhaps 1.2 m tall, and had long brown hair on her shoulder blades. I had to control myself to see her face. She was pretty. She gave me a sweet smile, questioning eyes, beautiful blue-grey eyes.

She went to the pool. I stood beside her and slightly behind her.

"First the soap, rub it over your hands, between your fingers, wrists, everywhere," I said as she continued to rub the greenish liquid over her delicate hands.

"Here, like this." I walked behind her and put my hands on hers.

There's something special about hands touching. No, not the way they shake hands, but the touch of the fingers touching fingers, hand on hand. As if it were a personal caress of the heart. When my hands touched hers, when I reached for her from behind, she felt it too. Her head turned upwards and looked at me with those big eyes, her mouth was slightly open.

"Let me help you," I said as my fingers slipped between hers. She spread her fingers apart and allowed me intimate access to her hands. Her skin was so soft and my own hands eclipsed hers. As I stroked her hands, I gently turned her palm upwards, my hands sliding over her palms and back between her fingers. I could hear her breathing in. I felt her body relax. I moved a little closer, my head lowered to just beside her. I could smell her hair.

"Just like this." I almost said in a whisper. "Back and forth. Back and forth between the fingers." As I spoke, I felt her body gently press into me, her neck twisting slightly as if it were an invitation.

"You have beautiful hands, Doc," she said. She turned her head, looked me in the eye and smiled.

"Thank you. Now we must wash up." I bent over to press the washstand, as I did with my own torso pressed tighter into her. I became quite aroused. Her hands were so small, so soft, and her fingers were so pleasant to feel.

Whether she felt my growing hardness, she did not say. I was sure that she could, for her body was now pressed against me. I continued to wash her hands thoroughly. I had to go away and get her a paper towel to dry.

Then she jumped back into bed.

"Much better, all nice and clean." I said.

"Doc, I have some complaints," she suddenly said.

"Oh, let me have a look." My concern for her after her operation. There could be complications. "Can you lift your gown for me so I can look?"

She reached under the sheet, pulled the hem up under her breasts. Wow, her nipples were hard. How could I have missed her before? Then she rolled down the sheet to expose her stomach. I put my hand there, two fingers squeezing in pieces to measure the pain.

"Is it uncomfortable here?" I asked.

"No. None. Actually, it's a little deeper." She said her hand rests on mine. Then she held my hand and slipped it under the sheet. I felt the soft fluff of her pubic hair, the rise of her mons pubis. Her hand kept moving mine. I heard my own breathing change. Her breath became loud and deep. She moaned very softly with my hand between her legs. Her hand on top of mine moved her up and down.

"I think she needs more attention." I breathed. I slipped my middle finger between her smooth labia. I felt the exquisite texture of her smooth skin, her inner flesh. It felt moist and warm, the delicate creases on both sides of my finger as I stroked it up and down. Her breathing and moaning was more serious. She began to lift her body from the bed, began to bend her hips and arch her back.

"God, Doc, that feels so good," she whispered. She looked at me with desire.

As her bloom opened for me, I pushed a second finger to allow me further access. Now all my fingers, my hand lovingly stroked her wet pussy in a constant rhythm. She moaned again. The heel of my palm stroked her clitoris, my fingertips searched for her entrance and inserted two while I spread my fingers apart. Now I fingered seriously and searched for her excitement until the climax.

Her breath was so deep. I could see the oven in her eyes. Her hand reached out to my ass and squeezed it hard.

"Oh, yeah, damn," she moaned. "Right there, damn." Her voice crackled with delight. Her body almost writhed under me.

"Oh fuck, oh God, I'm coming..." She almost moans a whimper. I could see and feel her trembling. Her body cramped up against my fingers deep inside her. "Oh, mmmm." The words escaped her lips as she closed her eyes and enjoyed the feeling. My hand slowed and had to stop as she squeezed her thighs.

I felt her tremble for a few more seconds before she let go of me. My hand went over her mons pubis and out of the sheets. I looked at my fingers whose tips were covered with milky juice. I put them in my mouth, sucked and licked her sperm and tasted her very sexy pussy juice.

"Thank's Doc. That feels so much better." She said. Her voice almost giggled.

"Well, I'm very well-behaved at my bedside, they tell me." I answered.

She giggled, such a sweet, sexy giggle.

"I'll come back in an hour and check on you." I said.

"Make sure you do. I think I might have a sore throat when you get back," I kept her hint as my cock popped into my pants.

And so it happened. An hour later she was sucking my dick. The next hour we fucked. She's being discharged today, someone else's shift. I'm gonna miss my patient. I just hope she still knows how to wash her hands.

MYSTERY ON THE LOWSIDE

Vasquez sat in the SUV and painted her nails red. She didn't like the color much, but it was such a slow day that she decided to paint them. After lunch she repainted her nails with white tips.

She liked the change she was in, but the novelty had long since gone. The local sheriff had given his county a reputation for keeping most troublemakers away, so she had little to do.

"Cart four, cart four!" the radio yelled, scaring Vasquez.

"Car four here, move over!" She barked at the radio.

"We have reports of a fat man pushing a motorcycle down Custer Road." The radio said. "You've got to see this."

Vasquez sighed, and when she got calls, it was always about silly things.

"Car four confirmed." She told me to put my hand back down.

Vasquez looked in the rearview mirror to check her makeup and hair. She was wearing her shoulder-length brown hair loose under the standard issue Stetson hat she was wearing.

"You're fucking sexy!" She explained throwing the gear selector into the drive.

When she arrived on the scene, she saw a man pushing a motorcycle by the side of the road, but he wasn't as fat as the reports said.

He was more out of shape than chubby, he was wearing a denim jacket with his arms exposed, Vasquez gasped when she saw how muscular those arms were. He had a thick brown beard and hair, which was best described as... as untamed.

"Where are you going?" Vasquez said out the window to the man.

The man kept pushing his bicycle, Vasquez almost thought he didn't hear them, then he spoke up.

"Third star to the left..." The rugged man said, without looking at her. "Then continue until dawn."

Vasquez laughed at this grown Peter Pan; he was as smart as he was mean, and she liked that. She pushed the gas to pull ahead of him, then cut him off and stopped to get out.

"Do you have a name?" she asked.

She asked, "Yes." He answered with a grim look.

Vasquez knew the guy, she kept silent until he spoke.

"They call me Guardrail." He grunted, and then he hit her in the eye and asked. "You have a name... Officer?"

When their eyes met, Vasquez felt a sensation she hadn't felt in a long time. It wasn't love or physical attraction... She was attracted to him, but it felt more like a spell. Whatever it was, she knew she had felt it before.

"Um..." She said, regaining her senses, "They call me Maria Lara Rodriguez Enojado Vasquez."

"Uh... right." The brute replied.

"Everyone calls me Vasquez." She said with a smile. "Well, how can we help you today?"

The biker seemed happy about it, though he wasn't smiling, but his frown seemed less sinister to Vasquez.

"I need gas, a place to sleep and some tools, I need to fix my bike," he said.

Vasquez opened her mouth and said she had a gas can and directions to a mechanic who could accommodate him for the night, but what she said instead surprised her.

"At the next intersection, keep right and keep going until you see the house with the RV in front of it, my place is next to it. I can rent you a room while you work with your bike?" she said.

"Sure." He said as if that was the only answer he could have expected.

Vasquez got back in her SUV, then made the sign of the cross. As she drove off to find a pendant for his bike, she mumbled the Saints' names in her ear. Although she was incredulous, she did exactly what he asked her to do.

An hour later she had Guardrail's bicycle in her garage and he was standing with her in her living room.

"Would you like some water, maybe a bite to eat?" She kept asking and asking herself how this man got into her house.

"No." He said if he thought about it, he said, "Get me a beer."

"Madre Dios!" She freaked out when she walked into the kitchen. "I gotta get back to work, the sheriff's gonna be mad!"

Guardrail opened his drink, then stood there staring at her while he pondered her words. She assumed that the Sheriff, who had attacked a man during the second battle of Fallujah, might have had a good reputation.

"Do you have time for a quick one?" he asked and took a sip of beer so big that he spilled his beard.

"No!" said Vasquez and turned his back on the biker.

She imagined herself getting into her SUV and then driving away, but to her own amazement she began to loosen her belt.

The biker laughed at his good luck, Vasquez was initially terrified as she pulled down her pants. She was quickly replaced by curiosity, she was not very horny, she wanted to know why she bent over a sofa.

"Do you have a rubber?" she asked, pointing at the biker with her naked ass.

"Ha!", was his gruff answer.

Vasquez heard his pants fall to the floor, followed by his heavy kicks towards her. She knew the Sheriff would be pissed off that she was wasting so much time running around and getting laid.

Her anticipation grew until he finally touched her, expecting something rough, like a slap or being pushed down. But he grabbed her Stetson hat!

His touch was not gentle, he tried to pull her top up, but with her bulletproof vest and bra he had no success.

"Shit!" he said in frustration.

Now it was Vasquez's turn to laugh.

She heard him spit into his hand, something she'd always been disgusted with. She was a woman who got wet quickly and easily, getting ready to fuck was never a problem. If those strange days came when she wasn't wet, she was ready to suck cock first.

When he pressed against her, she felt her body being pushed into the air. She did not feel well at all!

"Hijo de puta!!" She screamed: "Uh... that's my ass."

The guardrail grunted again and then slid down. This was always a moment of anticipation for Vasquez, often suggesting whether a man would be great or terrible.

She hadn't had a look at his penis, but when he pressed his head into her, followed by his shaft, she knew he was about average in size and length. Vasquez really wanted a black cock, but she was content to enjoy what he had to offer.

Oddly enough, she could tell he had foreskin. She felt the ribbed sensation that the extra flesh flap gave her. She could also hear Guardrail moaning with pleasure as he pushed himself deeper.

Though it was the strangest sexual encounter of her life, Vasquez couldn't help but notice when she arrived. What Guardrail lacked in foreplay, he made up for in thrusting. The sound of the wet slaps as their bodies collided was soon drowned out by the sound of her moaning.

She took a deep breath and filled her lungs, during sex all her senses came to life. This time she could smell many things mixed together, including his beer breath, gasoline and his body odor. It was obvious that this road traveller had not enjoyed a shower for some time.

Vasquez could feel the motorcyclist's fleshy hands pressing closer to her hips. She could also feel his growing orgasm as his grunt grew deeper and more guttural. In the past, she had let men cum quickly, but they had always kissed her first.

"Shit, you're tight!" he explained in a low tone of voice.

"Maybe it's not so bad," Vasquez thought as she smiled at the compliment.

Without warning, the man behind her quickly raised his hands along her body. She wasn't worried that if he wanted to get in trouble, he could have done so earlier.

He lifted her shirt and slid his hands underneath. Vasquez knew exactly what the heavy-built stranger in the denim vest wanted.

"They're all the same," she thought as his hands raised the underwire of her bra.

Now it was her turn to grunt as he slipped his hands into a bra that barely held her twins away. Normally she would take off her bulletproof vest and then open her bra, but this time she was content to grab the arm of the sofa.

Guardrail didn't have the biggest cock she had experienced, but his hard knocks were certainly unforgettable. The roughness he showed to her nipples was unlike any other partner she had recently.

"Uhnnnnnn..." Vasquez moaned as she came a second time.

His blows were now even fiercer and more powerful, Vasquez knowing the end was near. His grunting was louder than before, his hands squeezing her breasts even tighter.

Vasquez felt her orgasm brewing in her loins, she did not want to be cheated by this dirty biker! She pushed her hips backwards to match his forward stomping.

"Uuuuugggghhhhhh!!" Guardrail grunted as he came into her.

"Madre Dios!!" yelled Vasquez as she came too.

She felt his sperm penetrate her, it was a heavy, thick load. She assumed he'd been on the road so long he didn't have time to put the old stuff away.

Since care was not an issue for Guardrail, he took a few steps back and then pulled up his pants. Vasquez could hear him breathing heavily.

She placed a pair of pants over her crotch because she didn't want a massive

pile of semen to land on her service pants. With her pants back on, she turned around and saw Guardrail yawning and turning around as if he was trying to find something.

"What's wrong?" Vasquez asked the lost biker.

"Sleeping." was the caveman-like response.

"Lie down on the sofa." She said, "Fix her clothes. "I have to get back to work."

The Neanderthal who had banged her just before shuffled zombie-like in Vasquez's bedroom. She felt the strongest urge to pull out her service weapon to give him an extra bellybutton, a quick glance at a watch convinced her otherwise.

"¡Llego tarde! ¡Mierda! ¡Mierda!" she cried out as she ran to the door, her Peter Pan of a playmate snoring in her bed before she left the driveway.

Later, back at her speed trap, her phone rang.

"¡Mierda!" Vasquez snapped when she saw it was the sheriff.

She slipped in her seat uncomfortably.

"Hola!" she said, trying to sound happy.

"Hola-shmola!" cried the sheriff in a deep voice. "Tell your new friend to get the fuck out of my county!"

Vasquez sat back down in her seat as the Sheriff kept screaming. The Sheriff's words had not only scared her off, but she was sure that the load of semen the Guardrail was carrying inside her was beginning to run out of her!

"His bike needs fixing." She remembered what the biker had told her before.

"Yeah, he's got three days, then I'm getting a warrant to search his pig!" The sheriff droned.

Vasquez opened her mouth in response, but the Sheriff had already hung up. She was angry, but also very curious about the bike.

SPEED TRAP

The night was so humid that your shirt would be soaking wet within 10 minutes if you were outside. The deputy of the local county sheriff was sitting in his favourite speed trap. He was sweating like a whore in church.

He knew he'd catch a couple of speeders here as usual. But for some reason, this night was slow. A car hadn't passed by for over 30 minutes. When he sat down at his personal cell phone, he went through his pictures. He had stored a few of them that he had taken of a girl he had fucked a few weeks ago. She had big tits that he liked to pinch and bite. Hitting her made him hard.

Her ass was big, and when she bent perfectly round, he beat it good until it turned red. She loved him, too. It made her squeal and moan. He also spanked her fat pussy lips. It really turned him on and her on too, so she had to beg him to fuck her now!

When he thinks about it, he looks at the picture of her legs, how she spreads her pussy lips open and makes him rub his hard cock.

Giggling, he hopes that no car with his angry boner bulging in his tight uniform has driven in the meantime. But don't you know, a car speeds by. His radar showed it at 60. That was a 45 mile an hour zone.

The top of the car was down because he saw that she was cute.

So he slammed his car into the road and he raced after her. And he still had one hand on his hard cock. After he caught up with her and ran over her badge, he hit his headlights and then the siren in two short bursts.

Her music is so loud and she sings the song on the radio so intensely that she doesn't realize that she is being stopped. When she hits a sign, she sees blue reflected lights hitting the sign. She looks in her rearview mirror.

She takes her foot off the gas and slows down a little. When she hits the brakes, she stops on an old dirt road that looks like it hasn't been used for years. Weeds and grass grew wild in the middle and on the lanes.

She drove on for about a minute, moving far away from the main road so that they could not be seen by other passing motorists.

This was her intention, as she had done in the past, to get out of a parking ticket.

When she sat down, she wore a nice, tight mini skirt that reached close to her crotch and almost showed her panties. The top she was wearing was thin, almost transparent, with long, thin straps over the shoulders. Her big bouncing tits pulled on the weak straps and showed so much cleavage and tits that she might as well have been topless. When she saw this, she pulled them even further down, almost showing her brushless, hard erect nipples. Then she wiggled her seat enough to reveal her panties.

The officer gets out of his car and goes to the driver's door of her car. He hopes that she doesn't see half his erection.

Ma'am, I'm gonna need to see your license and registration, please.

Sure, officer, just one second.

He sees the tits almost popping out of her top. Then he sees her panties reaching for her purse in the passenger seat. His dick is fully erect again.

Ma'm, do you know how fast you were going?

No, sir, how fast?

60 mph, that's a 45 mph zone.

As she hands him her license and registration, she looks him intensely in the eyes and asks, "Is there anything I can do to make this go away", while she slowly pulls her top down, showing all her tits. She winks at him and looks at his cock and sees his erection.

As she reaches down she pulls up her skirt and shows her pussy hill in her white lace panties rubbing her finger on her clitoris in circular movements.

The officer knows that there will be no ticket in this case. He can't help it, she was too fucking hot!

She had long black straight hair that reached up to her big sexy ass. Beautiful big brown eyes. Beautiful face and tits that stood straight out, firm without bra.

Ma'm, please get out of the car.

She opens her door and gets up in front of him. She is taller than him in her high heels in high heels. Her tits still exposed, she pulls her skirt further up and reveals her softly tanned belly.

Ma'm, turn around and put your hands on the car, please.

She does what she's told, bending over a little more than necessary and stretching her ass towards him as if to tell him: Here it is.

He starts to frisk her from the ankles. He rubs her tanned legs to feel how soft they are, but they were tinted. He slowly works his way up to her ass, which shows both ass cheeks, because she is wearing a lace thong. He rubs her ass cheeks and squeezes them together with his hand, feeling the tanned flesh between his fingers. He slaps her pretty hard. She moans. He slaps the other one, she moans more. He reaches around her and feels her big tits. Damn, that was the best one so far, he thought. He had stopped a few times with these results, but this was the best looking one ever.

Yes, he was weak when it came to beautiful women, but what could he do? He's just a man. He's gonna fuck him real hard. And maybe it won't be the last.

He'll pinch her nipples real hard to make her squeal. He plays rough with them while he rubs his throbbing cock against her ass as he bends over her.

He tells her to turn around and squat down.

She does as she is told and grabs his zipper, pulls it down and then pulls out his throbbing cock. She licks her lips and takes her head into her hot, wet, soft mouth. No sooner does she suck on it than she tastes his foreplay, which oozes out whatever irritates him. He grabs both hands full of her beautiful black hair and moves her head closer, pushing his cock deeper into her mouth. He watches her gagging and takes everything.

Looks like you've done enough of that to know how to handle it. Suck that cock good for Daddy. Suck me dry, bitch!

The dirty talk only made her wetter and she sucked it harder. She fingers her clit and pussy with one hand while holding his dick with the other. When she looked up to him with her beautiful brown eyes, he pushed it harder and harder into her with her beautiful brown eyes and pressed her head with his hairy hands equally to counter his thrusts.

Yeah, you sucked a lot of cocks, didn't you, you little slut?

That's it baby, suck daddy's dick mmmmm fuck yeah suck it harder, I'm gonna cum all over you!

He stops her by pulling back her head and pulling out his wet cock dripping from her saliva.

He grabs her by the waist and lifts her onto the hood of her car, not caring if he's still hot from the engine. He makes her burn those luscious ass cheeks. Something for her to remember him by.

She doesn't care if the hood is hot or not. At this point, she could care less. He grabs her ankles, pushes her legs up and leans down and buries his face in her wet pussy. Damn, she smelled and tasted so good. His face was wet from her juices literally dripping from her hot pussy. He was eagerly licking it up. He started sucking on her clit, nibbling on it and sticking two fingers up her pussy and a third up her ass. She moaned loudly and wiggled her pussy on his face. Oh, daddy!! Right there!!! Suck my pussy, OMG!! He sucked her clit hard so it would come off. She moaned loudly, it echoed through the night, but nobody heard it, at least not a person. Her body shook with lust. She fucks his mouth and rubs her juices all over him while she hums.

He pulled her off the car, turned her around and pushed his cock through her pussy lips from her clitoris to her ass back and forth until she begged him to fuck her and fuck her hard. He slaps her ass cheeks alternately with each stroke. Her ass is red. He loves it!

He slaps his dick hard. He's pounding it in as hard as he can. He grunts because it feels so fucking good. He's fucking her hard and deep with every stroke so she screams and squeals. He spreads her ass cheeks wide so he can try to get in deeper.

He can feel his sperm boiling. He bangs one last time and empties his load into her as much as he can. He moans and grabs her fleshy ass cheeks and makes them redder. He lies down on her and takes a deep breath. Damn, should he have sperm in her? What if she's not using birth control? Well, she was nice and hot. She'd be even prettier if she was carrying his baby.

THE COP

It's one of those days, and I need to blow off some steam.

I get upset when I hear the siren. I sigh and look for a place to stop.

The policeman walks to the car. I roll down the window. He is amazingly handsome, with sand-blond hair, dark stubble and a strong jaw. He wears mirrored airplanes even though it's dawning.

"Good evening, miss," he paints. "I stopped you tonight to inform you that your taillight is broken. I will give you a work order to get it repaired."

"Thank you, I had no idea." I'll give him my license and registration. "I'll take care of it right away.

He goes back to his car. I look at him in my side mirror and I watch his ass as he walks away. I put my lipstick back on.

He comes back. His fat forearms bend as he hands me my papers back.

"Here you are, miss, you're ready."

"Are you sure you want nothing more from me?" I slowly lift up my skirt to reveal my white cotton panties. I caress the fabric. "Is there anything else you need from me?"

His empty expression remains motionless.

"Don't miss, you can go", he says aloud.

He turns off his body camera, goes to his cruiser and returns with more force in his step.

"Get out of the vehicle," he barks.

"Yes, officer."

I stand seductively and make sure he gets a good look at my legs. We're on a small country road with nothing but farmland as far as the eye can see.

"Turn around and put your hands on the vehicle. No sudden movements."

I obey. The policeman pats me down and roughly pats every part of me. He moves his palms along my legs and between my thighs. I open myself up for him and he probes my pussy with two fingers. A car drives by. He slides his little finger up my asshole and my knees go weak.

He drives up north and takes off my blouse. He puts his hands under my breasts and squeezes my tits. He uses his body to push me against the door. His erection is pressing on my ass.

He ties my hands behind my back and turns me over so we're facing each other. He slaps me. Hard. I gasp from the shock and the pain.

"Are you ready for what comes next?"

"Punish me," I moan.

"Get on your knees."

The cop unzips his pants and unfolds his smooth, trimmed dick.

I kneel in the gravel and take it in my mouth. I lick his frenulum and massage his head with my tongue. I taste old sperm at the tip.

It's hard to keep my balance with my hands behind my back. I almost fall into him and he presses me on his cock with both hands. He fucks me viciously in the mouth and I hear another car driving by, this one slower.

"Shit!" He pulls out his dick, and I try to catch my breath. He pulls me by my ponytail. "Get up."

He throws me on the passenger side of his cruiser and pushes me down so

I'm out of sight. He tapes my mouth shut, and we pull away and leave my car on the side of the road.

When we arrive at the old factory, it is already dark. We're about thirty miles out of town, and not a soul in sight.

The policeman cuts off the engine in the middle of the parking lot. The entire property is damaged by age and neglect. The motion-activated floodlights are so bright that I feel like I'm at a high school soccer game.

He pulls me out of the car and opens the door to the back seat. He pushes my face into the shabby upholstery. I'm ready for him.

He lifts up my skirt and roughly pulls off my underwear. He spits on my pussy, but I'm already wet. He rams his cock in and fucks me hard and furious. I scream to the gag and I press my ass into him while he takes me from behind. He pulls me back by my hair and with one hand he covers my throat. When he climaxes, he pushes my face into the seat and he slams my naked ass together.

The cop pulls me up like a rag doll and marches me to the wire fence. He takes off my handcuffs, only to have my hands zipped up in front of me. I raise my hands above my head and he ties them to the fence with another cable tie. I drip with anticipation.

He steps back and looks at me. I blink into the bright lights. He's a shadow, a silhouette.

He unbuttons my blouse, thin and white with red dots. I wear a wide white skirt, espadrille wedges and a white and gold cross around my neck. He pinches my nipples together until they are hard. He slaps me again and I fall back into the fence.

A set of headlights turns into the parking lot. It's another police car, then three more.

They're standing in a group talking, but I can't hear them. Occasionally they shoot at me and look at me. Then they stare at me openly. I turn around and grab the fence and push my ass out so they can take me in completely.

They walk towards me with strong, deliberate steps. I can't see their faces, only darkness. I spread my legs and lean on what is about to happen.

The first policeman smokes a cigarette on the hood of his car and watches the other four take turns with me. He does not say a word.

The second policeman seems ashamed and can't look me in the eye. After a few minutes he ejaculates.

The third cop is a show-off and fucks me like a porn star. He lifts me up by my hips and pushes into me while I hold on to the fence. He sucks my nipples through the wafer-thin fabric. He plays with my clitoris and hits my G-spot at the same time. I can say that he enjoys the audience.

The fourth cop is rough, almost too rough. He pulls down my skirt and whips me with his belt until my ass is red and piercing and covered with welts. He twitches my hair, slaps my tits and rips my bralette to shreds. He caresses me with his baton and knocks the chain link inches away from my body. He holds my throat with both hands while he fucks me to the end.

The fifth cop is friendlier. He peels the tape back and kisses me. I wrap my legs around his ass and crunch into him while the shackles carry my weight. I come to a climax and my screams echo.

They take turns with me for the next hour. No one speaks. My body aches and semen drips down my thighs. The glue of the tape burns my lips. My wrists are red from the stiff plastic bands. I come, over and over again.

One by one they all drive off, until only me and the first cop are left. I hang limply from the fence. My body is buzzing with excitement. He buttons my shirt, adjusts my clothes and puts my hair back in place. He slips into my shoes and ties the ribbons together with a bow.

"Let's get you to your car, miss."

He cuts the zipper that ties me to the fence, but leaves the others in place. I'm still gagged. He helps me into the back seat and ties my ankles with duct tape. All I see is the roof of the car and the mesh cage that separates us. Somebody's crackling in over the radio. We drive off into the night.

IN DEPTH INTERROGATION

In the dim light emitted by the only 60 W bulb dangling from the ceiling, her breath stirred the fine particles like dandelion seeds blown by a summer wind from the Midwest.

"...which I want you to answer as truthfully as possible. And although I cannot advise you ..." her voice went in and out as his mind followed random, incoherent thoughts. Words piled up like tree trunks that piled up in a stream, disordered and chaotic. Locked in this room, his thoughts disappeared from the walls and collided with hers. The serious tone with which she spoke referred to a circumstance as alien as the place where he was.

"Okay, so let's start slowly: Please tell me your name. Can you do that?", she asked pedantically.

After a long pause he spoke. "You already know my name. Next question," he said with a hint of anger.

"Listen, I'm trying to help you, Joey, if you could just play along, that would be great!" she flattered him.

"I am Joseph Randall, at your service," he said with false glee.

"Good boy, Joey. Now we're getting somewhere," she said as she turned around in her chair, loosened her long, muscular legs and crossed in the opposite direction. The smile on her face confirmed her deviant intention in this subtle act. "Well, do you know why you're here?"

"I don't know because I don't go to church," he offered.

"If you want me to help you, you have to stop this shit. They're making some pretty serious accusations against you," she said with sincere concern.

"What do you want from me?" he exclaimed.

"I want to know if what they say is true," she demanded.

"Well, then ask," he replied.

"It says here that you have requested various deviant sexual acts from an honourable woman," she explained.

"Requested? That's a lot of crap. I have written poems and other rubbish that no one should read," he said.

"Yes, well, someone read them," she assured him. "And these 'poems', as you call them, could be seen as a threat of violence," she explained as she looked up from her notepad, took off her glasses and put one of her arms in her mouth while she thought about what she would say next. "I must say that some of the things you have written are worrying.

"Like what?" he asked.

"You wrote, and I quote, 'I'm going to nail your arms and legs down, put my body on top of yours and remind you what it feels like to have the weight of a man on top of you,'" she said and her voice softened when she finished.

He offered a grin as the only answer.

"'I will grab your face and force you to look me in the eye as I move your body back and forth, subjecting your body to my will', she read. "That sounds like a threat, don't you think?"

"It's fantasy. I didn't threaten anyone,' he explained.

"Is it 'sticking your cock down her throat' before she can say any part of that fantasy?

"Okay, taken out of context it sounds terrible," he admitted.

"So in what context would you 'shove your cock down someone's throat' and it wouldn't be an act of violence?" she asked cautiously. Her voice was curious and her body bent inward when she asked.

"This is a fantasy. Some people like that,' he said.

"'Some people'?' she asked. "Would these people like it too... ... "um, let's see," she said as she turned over her notes. "Do they look into your eyes as they slowly take the full circumference of your cock in their mouths?"

"I think so," he said defensively.

"Has anyone ever done this for you, Joseph?" she asked.

"No. At least not yet," he said.

"And you think that the threat of holding someone will inspire him to do that?" she asked incredulously.

He sat there in silence and raised his shoulders as if to say, "I don't know.

She got up from her chair and walked around the table to which his hands were handcuffed. As she stood behind him, she grabbed the back of his chair and turned him to the side. Although his hands and feet were bound in fetters, his body was now turned to the side. Very clumsily she reached down and unbuckled his belt, his button and his zipper. "Let's see what kind of belt we're working with here," she said mockingly.

As she unzipped his trousers and pulled down his panties, she exposed his flaccid penis. As she reached into his pants, she pulled out his balls and cock for examination. "There's not much strap here, Joey," she joked. "Not sure if it would reach down to the neck, Big Shooter," she said with a laugh.

When she touched him, he started to swell up. Within fifteen seconds, he was completely erect. After watching him grow, she stood back for a moment to think. "Okay, well, this could make a difference."

On her knees, she knelt down and looked up at him after carefully inspecting his fully erect dick. "So you expect someone to put the whole thing in their mouth?" she asked, while her head was lowered. The heat of her wet tongue on the head of his cock was like an electric shock. She flicked her tongue all the way along the edge and probed briefly before accepting the head through her lips.

The saliva from her mouth covered the tip and upper part of the shaft of his cock. She stroked with her hands and spat out some of her saliva. She began to descend on his tail, taking an extra millimeter each time she descended.

"Is this what you were hoping for?" she asked sarcastically.

"I was hoping that she - or I guess you now - would go further," he said cautiously.

"Uh, I don't know how you expect me to put any more of this in my mouth," she said with a smile.

"Try again," he said and returned her smile.

As she lowered her head again, he moved his elbow over the back of her head as she put the tip in her mouth. His arm squeezed gently as she came down. When he allowed her to come up again, he pushed her head a little further down the next time and then a little further each time in succession.

As she pulled back, she looked up at him. "I'm gonna gag if you keep this up. Is that what you want?" she asked.

"Hold your breath and try again," he said with a nod.

She followed his suggestion and took a deep breath before taking his throbbing tail in her mouth. She felt the head of his cock crash into the back of her mouth and press against the opening of her throat, causing her mouth to salivate. Bouncing up and down, slowly overcoming the gag reflex, she absorbed more and more of him.

When she stood up, she wiped her mouth and picked up her clipboard again. He gave a deep sigh of frustration. "It says here that you also had fantasies of watching her undress?" she said as she began to unbutton her blouse. Within a minute she had thrown her blouse and skirt on the floor.

"And then it says here that you wanted to lean back when she sat on you?" she asked. "You wanted her to grab your cock and stick it up her hot, wet pussy?"

She spoke as she moved towards him, lifting one leg above his lap and spreading it. She grabbed his cock and looked into his eyes as she maneuvered his cock so that it floated between her dripping wet labia. "Is that what you meant?" she asked as she lowered herself onto him.

"Yes", he replied.

"And you wanted to feel her turning on you, her tits flying around in your face? Did you want to slap her? You wanted to feel her up? Squeeze her?" Her voice trembled as the pleasure began to take over. "Suck them. Suck her, Joe. Suck my tits, Joe. Bite them a little. Bite me, Joe. That's what you want, huh? Bite my nipples, Joe. "Shit, Joe," she said while she was out of breath.

"And then you wanted her... feel her..." Her voice faded as she approached her climax. "Pussy dripping on your dick and balls?"

She rocked back and forth, hard against it, up and down and in a circular motion. "Oh fuck", she screamed as she started to come. Her body twisted on top of him for another 30 seconds as she exhaled her explosive orgasm.

Standing, out of breath, she walked over, picked up her clothes and sat back down on her chair. After a few minutes of labored breathing, she was now back in her clothes and her notepad in front of her again. She was barely able to control the broad smile.

"So this is what you write about," she finally asked.

"Only you left out the part where, after you come, you get down on your knees and finish me..."

PULLED OVER BY A COP

Flashing lights become visible when you look in your rearview mirror. A pit forms in your stomach when you notice that a policeman is standing directly behind you, the lights flash and signal you to stop. Nervously you look at your speedometer, which shows 78 MPH. You slow down as you use the indicator. Slowly you come to a halt at the side of the road. You see the lights of the police car parked behind you. At night, it's almost blinding. While you think about the consequences, you ask yourself how much the ticket will cost, how much your insurance will increase? You wait for what seems like an eternity while the policeman remains in his car.

You start thinking of a way to get out of a ticket. What if you could come up with an excuse? Would he understand if you just told him the truth, that you were on that empty road late at night and that you didn't notice how fast you were driving. Maybe you could find a way out if you had the courage to flirt with him. How far could you let yourself go? When you think about the possibilities, you feel a familiar tingling sensation rush through your body. You feel a wetness growing in your pussy.

A tap on the window snaps you back to reality. When you become aware of the situation again, you shuffle in your seat to adjust your legs, a futile attempt to deal with the itching that began. You look dazed at the flashlight shining through the window as you roll it down.

"Do you know why I stopped you, miss?" You look up at him to answer and realize how cute the officer is. "Uh, I, uh..."

"Miss, have you been drinking tonight?"

"No, sir, I'm just a little tired and nervous."

"May I see your driver's licence?" You nod and explain that it's in your purse on the passenger side. He turns on his flashlight to see the handbag and asks you to take it. You unbuckle your seat belt and reach for the handbag while the light falls on it. You bend over and feel your shirt slide up your legs, knowing that your ass controls are almost exposed and the light is suddenly redirected. You begin to wonder if he's looking at your ass. You sit back and hand him your license. He shines his light on the ID. You look down at your legs to see how far up your dress has slipped, and you see that some of the light is shining directly at your exposed pussy. You now wish you had worn panties, but this exposure excites you even more. You start to wonder if he's doing it on purpose, you feel the wetness between your legs growing again. You rub your thighs together and let out a slight groan as a sharp feeling of pleasure runs up your body.

"Are you all right, miss?" You nod, "Why don't you get out of the car for me?" He reverses as you open the door. His light flashes on you as you swing one leg out of the car. He turns the light down when you try to get up. Again, you realize that your pussy is displayed for his eyes as you get out of the car.

"Why don't you lean against the hood of your car?" As you follow this and lean your ass lightly on the hood, you think again of miracles. You start fantasizing that he actually looked at your pussy.

Instinctively, you start rubbing your thighs together again and feel your skirt rise. A light flashes on your face and pulls you out of your fantasy. "Miss, get up and turn around. I'm going to check you for drugs or weapons. Do you have anything on you?"

"He instructs you to put your hands on the hood, spread your legs and relax. As his hands begin to rest on your back, they move to your breasts and cupping them while you let out a moan. Then he moves down your stomach and pulls you up against his crotch. You wonder if he did this on purpose and if you felt his hard cock or if it was something else. It was quick and then he moves his hands over your ass, suddenly you feel your skirt being pulled up. You wonder if he did it on purpose and his hands reach around your inner thighs. His fingers lightly stroke your pussy lips. You let out a steady moan of the loader.

"What was that lady? Are you all right?" You didn't answer me. You're not sure where this is going, but your silence will encourage him to decide where it will lead. Suddenly he'll pull your arms around your back and gently press your upper body against the hood. As he holds your hands together, he asks again, "Miss, you have been acting strangely, are you drunk or on drugs?

In panic, you say "No".

"Then why are you acting so strange?"

Without thinking, "Because I'm horny, my pussy's wet, and I need it touched so bad right now. When you realize what you just admitted, you wonder what's gonna happen next. Then a smooth, hard object runs down your pussy lips. Your legs shake while you expect to get what you want. As that object slides back and forth across your pussy, he asks, "Is this what you want, bitch? Do you like it when my nightstick rubs against your pussy?" Then it lightly taps the inside of your thighs, indicating that you should spread your legs wider. He pushes the end of the nightstick against your pussy. He lets go of your hands. "Do you want that inside you? Then bring it in."

They reach between your legs and guide the hard stick inwards. He pushes it in slowly as he turns it, covering the nightstick with your juices. He fucks you slowly by pulling it out and pushing it in. You pick up the pace as you breathe heavily and moan loudly and start rubbing your clitoris.

As you cum, you scream and your body presses against the hood of the car. Your legs are the only thing keeping your body from slipping. The nightstick slides out leaving an empty space, but is suddenly filled again when the policeman shoves his cock inside you. Your weakened legs begin to give way as his hand presses your body harder against the hood. You regain strength and push your body off the hood to counter his blows. He pulls at your hair and guides your body so that it presses firmly against his. His hands surround your breasts and massage them through the light material.

He pulls himself out to your disappointment. He turns you around and lets you sit on the hood. He lifts your legs over his shoulders and leads his cock back into your waiting hole. While your pussy is being fucked fast and hard, you move your hand back to your clitoris while the other one rubs your hard nipples.

You get an orgasm again and you moan. You feel your pussy winding around his cock, he stops and pulls it out. He releases your legs and lets your body slowly slide down the hood. He brings your weakened body down so that you sit on the bumper. The orgasm still affects your body, his hand grabs your face and turns you towards his cock. You open up and he pushes his cock, covered with your pussy juice, into your mouth. You are already breathing heavily, you do your best to suck him while he fucks your throat.

Easily recovering, you take his cock in your hand for the second time and stroke the smooth shaft while opening your inviting mouth. Your tongue massages the underside of his cock while your lips run up and down tightly.

He moans and you feel his sperm build up, ready to explode. Your hand, wrapped around his head with your tight lips, twitches his cock up and down, milking him of his sperm. A hot jet squirts into the back of your throat, then another one and another one. You try to keep his sperm in your mouth, but as his cock empties between your lips, something drips down your chin and onto your dress. He closes his cock back in his pants while you watch, collects the remaining sperm around your lips and swallows it.

You stand up and wait to see what comes next.

"Now, miss, I advise you not to drive horny again if it makes you go too fast. Hopefully we'll have fixed the problem by tonight. You should be able to drive now. Drive carefully."

You're sitting in your car starting the engine when the policeman drives away. You managed to get fucked and not get a ticket. Now you hope that your husband won't notice the sperm stain on your dress if you get home later than expected.

THE COP'S OFFER

I was in the heat of summer in a fallow field waiting for a buyer that I thought would be late. When I saw the team car on the dirt road, I knew it was a set-up.

It was not a well-planned operation, as there was a fast-moving irrigation canal less than 10 steps away from where I was. When the policeman arrived where I was standing, we both knew the evidence was gone. I had thrown it into the canal as soon as I saw it. By then the powder was gone, and he knew it. But that didn't stop him from arresting me. He was mad.

He was rude and made a very thorough search, even though there was no female office. He seemed terribly enthusiastic to check that I had nothing hidden in my bra. He also checked my lower level quite well - it wasn't the third base - but only a small piece of cloth away. I was not really surprised. When he tried to get on my nerves, he had no idea what kind of life I had led at home.

When I was sitting in the back seat of his car in the summer heat of over 100 degrees, the nice officer decided to have a chat. This was not a new tactic either. I was allowed to sit in the back in the oppressively hot air of the car while he stood outside and talked to me through the half-shattered windscreen. I was ready for the questions and for the heat. If that was all he had for me, I would have been all right.

The questions were so predictable. Where did I get that from? And what was it? How much did I sell it for? Did I know what the punishment was for selling drugs near the high school? Why didn't I have any ID on me? Charged questions you'd be stupid to answer, and no matter what my Miranda rights were. This was a small town, and they did things their own way.

I lost my ID, had no idea what he was talking about, and I was in that field because I had to pee. Playing dumb is easy and I was good at it.

Eventually, however, the conversation changed its course. The nice officer wanted me to know that he knew me and everything about me. He asked me by name about my boyfriend. It was hard to say that I didn't know Ronnie - we had lived together - but I just pretended not to know anything that was true in many ways.

When I didn't give in, he became insulting and asked me what it was like to use tricks at the rest stop. (I had done this, but not in a long time, because it didn't pay off well - but I had been put away for hooking before, and we both knew it). He asked me how much I was charging and if I was going to take it in the ass. I didn't take the bait and just ignored the questions. One of Ronnie's lawyers had driven this into my head.

Finally he decided to get personal - and took after my mother and father. It was a stupid move on his part. He had no idea what a monster my parents had been. But it got interesting.

"I was sorry to hear your daddy died," he said.

I'm sure he wasn't. No one in town liked my dad. His job as a payroll clerk at the local packing plant had made him an incredibly unpopular man. He was the guy who delivered the layoff slips and cut your pay if you were late, and he was an asshole to boot.

And the cop said, "Well, that's just as well. It must have been hell being married to that bitch."

I'm sure he was right about that part.

As I listened from the back seat of the police car, this policeman told me something I had suspected for years - my mother had never been completely faithful to my father. I had been mentally divorced from them for so long that it shouldn't have bothered me, but hearing the details was disturbing.

It turned out that my mother got around a lot - and her reputation was well known. She preferred uniforms - policemen, firemen and soldiers when they came through town.

She loved to ride in cars in the fields, but was even wilder when they jumped into a motel room.

She would not go home with any of them - not if they were married anyway. (She had her standards - she would not have sex in another woman's bed).

He also shared certain positions. "She likes to be on top, you know," he told me. "She probably didn't learn to sit on your daddy's face instead of his cock until after you and your sister were born, but she told me once that it was the only time old Roy actually used that mouth except to kiss his bosses' ass.

He wouldn't stop while I was roasting in the car. He talked shit about my mother. Finally, after describing in detail what kind of underwear she was wearing under her work clothes and how she probably "got hit on the chin" in the back seat of that police car, he contacted me.

If the other part had been unpleasant and my situation in the back seat hadn't been a little bit of hell, it would have been quick.

He told me they had been watching me and my friends, and at some point we would all "soon have our wings clipped". He told me that Ronnie had been in trouble before - which I knew - but that he had an amazing lawyer, which wouldn't matter this time.

"If we get him this time, everything will be by the book and airtight."

Then he started the trial.

"Will you like prison?" he asked. "Eat some carpet - be a lesbian's bitch? You think they're gonna love you in there? The lesbians will, but the blacks will stick a knife up your ass just because you're pretty." He added, "You'll be dead before your sentence is up. Probably about 20 years earlier."

Then I got the pitch - they told me there was one. They'd want me to testify as a key witness and rat on my friends, and if I did, they'd give me a light sentence. That was the usual pitch. This was gonna be a fishing expedition for the cops trying to gather evidence.

But it wasn't. Instead, I have something much easier to miss.

"You want protection? I can give it to you. Me and my friends at the station."

Then he opened the door to the back seat. Which was a good thing, because I was about to pass out from lack of air.

"You see, your mama's getting old and her tits sagging. We thought you could take her place."

So he unzipped his fly and pulled himself out. It was pretty obvious that he liked to think back to his wild times with my mother. I think he expected me to open up right away and pick him up - his dick was so close to my face I could have spit on it and hit the hole.

Just the thought of it was repulsive to me. He was an older, heavy guy, a cop, and if you believed him, he had fucked my mother. What could be less attractive?

It wasn't my first rodeo, though. When your hands are handcuffed behind you and you're in the middle of a deserted field, it's not the right time to say anything provocative. At least you'll end up resisting arrest. At worst, you'll be buried under a cornfield, probably after being fucked in the ass and strangled.

I just kept quiet and waited.

At some point, even though no words were spoken, he understood the message. His dick withered in the heat and I think he understood that I wouldn't help him - at least not voluntarily.

He gave me a few words of encouragement, telling me that the policeman's tail was the key to my freedom. I wouldn't be asked to bend in any direction that Ronnie wouldn't have bent me, and there might even be some money or a hiding place for me in it. I sensed that he had given this speech before - and I didn't believe a word of it anyway. If I relied on the men in blue to keep me free, I would be on my knees and elbows the whole time, and we both knew it.

At some point I felt his unease about how to proceed and said, "Do you intend to rape me? Because if not, maybe we should stop." It was a phrase I'd used before with men who were a little too brash. Usually I would talk some sense into them, but his cold look scared me. It was as if he was thinking about it, so I made him a peace offering.

"I'll tell you what, I know Brenda has support at the truck stop. Go to her and tell her that if she treats you well, I'll slip her something later to make her feel good.

Brenda was a hooker who worked for the truck drivers and she had told me about how she sucked a lot of cop dicks to avoid going to jail. I'd seen her more than once in the back seat of this cop car of assholes, so I assumed he liked the service.

Eventually he put his dick away, but not before I noted the size, shape and distinguishing features. (You never knew when something like that might come in handy.) He pulled out a cigarette, which he smoked with slow fury.

He frowned and asked me why he wasn't as good as all the truckers I had blown. He said he would only fuck me in the mouth anyway and maybe he would try other parts of me, but somehow I felt that his heart was not in it. It turned him on forcing women into submission, I could see that.

At some point he gave me the signal to turn around. He took off my handcuffs and let me know that it was not over yet and that I would be quite sorry that I had not swallowed my pride and his cock when I had the chance.

Because of the drugs I had to throw into the canal, I walked away about 300 dollars less. Even more devastating was the way that the cop had peeled away my dignity. I wanted to kill him for that.

Brenda told me later that day that he had been a very bad man for her and I had to get her pain pills so she could sit down. I did, and I was silently grateful that it was her and not me.

I stayed as far away from him as possible and for a long time he never got close enough to catch me doing anything else, but then we were all hit hard. It was more than a year later. Ronnie was still in prison, and the trial wasn't even over.

I woke up in a hospital after an overdose. He was there, grinning like a fucking Cheshire cat. I was handcuffed to the side rails of the bed. I could see he had a hard-on just looking at him. By then it was too late to negotiate.

13 stories: 13 Premiered Age-Proof Sex Stories:

Amira Red

Table of Contents

THE CELEBRATION

Eighty-six thousand, six hundred and twenty-one dollars.

The end result is equal to the money we raised that night. We had driven through the county and north across the state border, collecting green garbage bags with the bills locked up in self-storage facilities. The sacks were usually wrapped in an old, tattered paint sheet or hidden between similar sacks filled with used clothing of scrap dealer quality. The collected sacks filled both trunks of large American cars when it was over.

We had taken two vehicles with us - one following the other close enough to offer protection, but far enough away not to be detected. I drove with my friend Ronnie. He was the only one who knew where we were going until we got there. Both cars were equipped with handguns for each man and also a sawn-off shotgun for each man in the back seat - one in each car. It was the first time I had seen Ronnie or any of his guys with loaded guns.

It was so scary I almost peed my pants, but I wanted to be more a part of Ronnie's world, and Ronnie's world was dangerous and illegal. It was a surreal experience from start to finish. That special kick you get when you know you shouldn't do something but feel so cool that you wouldn't miss it for the world.

I didn't know whether the weapons were to protect us from a possible robbery by rival groups or from a shoot-out in case of a police intervention. I didn't want to think about what could have happened either way.

Eighty-five thousand is probably not a lot of money by today's standards, but back then it was enough to buy a very nice house even in big cities. It was more money that I thought I would ever see in one go.

That was real drug money. It was not like in the movies with crisp hundred-dollar bills nicely stacked in a leather briefcase. The bills were wrinkled and torn from the time spent in blue jeans bags - enough to get a horny boy and his girlfriend high on Friday night. A teenager was given $5 to go to the roller rink, instead they were spent to buy a few loose joints. $20 that a fast-food worker made and used to buy a gram of crank. The change from a couple of trips to the store for the mother never returned to her and instead bought some black beauties.

These were street drug money, collected over time by some of Ronnie's local distributors. It was a bunch of it. Not a single $50 bill in the stack and very few of them. It was currently lying on my bedroom floor, stacked in stacks of $100 so we could count it all.

Ronnie and I had counted and recounted the money for hours - we stopped at regular intervals to laugh, drink, draw a line and fuck occasionally. It's a pretty hackneyed scene from a B-movie these days to see a drug dealer and his girlfriend rolling around on a bed of money, but we did it loud and proud, as if we'd invented the idea. Ronnie was pretty high from his nightly score, I could see that, and he rode me pretty hard, which I had no complaints about. The sex was electrifying and fun and became more and more inventive the further we went.

It was damn hot, and I enjoyed it so much that I couldn't think straight, and I let him throw me around on the bed so he could take me the way he wanted. I wanted him to take me and make me cum all over the money, even though some of the bills smelled pretty disgusting.

I was just a little uncomfortable because I knew that four of Ronnie's friends were in the house - all wired, buzzing and armed to the teeth. The creaking bed and the unsuppressed moans and giggles were nothing they hadn't heard before, but I tried not to think about it. (It's hard to have too much privacy when you live with a drug dealer).

Every time we finished fooling around, we had to count the stacks that we hadn't tied with rubber bands yet. I sat there naked and counted some of the money, which was maybe the third time, while Ronnie admired the view. Every now and then he'd break another piece of coke or roll up another joint, and if I was embarrassed, I'd beg him to stop.

After a while Ronnie realized that it had been a while since he had looked after his boys - and with over $80,000 in the house I could tell we were a bit paranoid, even though we were having a good time. He put his pants back on and left the bedroom to check in.

I heard them talking - and again reminded myself that they could hear us too - and heard one of the boys ask Ronnie "when it was their turn". It was Mark, a big bully of a man who had been driving all night with a shotgun in the back seat of the second car.

There was no humor in his voice. That wasn't Mark just bullying Ronnie. Suddenly everyone became calm, and even from the other room I felt a certain tension. It was a problem every time a bunch of drugged up gangsters got into an argument, but for me it was twice as important, because Ronnie was the only one in the bunch who wasn't heavily armed.

After a much too long silence, Ronnie murmured: "Dude, you haven't been here long, so I'm going to excuse you this time. She is different and she is mine... "You want some pussy, we'll get you some, but let's put the fucking booty away first."

I could tell by the footsteps that Ronnie had walked away from the door after he said this - his attempt to move the conversation away from the bedroom door and my ears. Mark didn't seem happy with the answer. He muttered, "It doesn't seem right - you're having all the fun while we're sitting out here with our tails in our hands. As time went by I would find this man more and more unpleasant.

When Ronnie came back into the room, he had a couple of big old suitcases with hard side walls in which we had piled $70,000 of the money. $5,000 he stuck to the bottom of drawers he'd taken out of my bedroom dresser and nightstand. Another $8,000 he sat aside to pay the boys - he slipped this into a brown lunch bag and dropped it next to the door.

Then he turned off the light and I suspected that this meant it was time for sleep, which was a good thing, since it was perhaps 4:00 in the morning. But Ronnie wasn't finished yet, and as soon as he was lying naked in bed he manoeuvred my head down and I knew exactly what he wanted me to do. While I was serving him, he gave me instructions - Ronnie never did that before. I knew he was mocking Mark.

That kind of theatricality was just part of living with Ronnie, and I had learned to find the humor and even the power in it. But this time I became restless and I tried to withdraw and tell him to stop. He had none.

He had his hands firmly on the back of my head and I could not stop until he had finished. Ronnie almost never came in my mouth, even when I wanted him to, so I knew that this was 100% for show. He knew that Mark was probably sitting outside the door. That was Ronnie - he let people know who was in charge. I could say that it made me feel cheap - but the truth is I kind of liked the feeling that I was special enough to cause friction.

When he finished, we finally fell asleep, but around 8:30 he woke me up to give me some instructions, saying he had to go away for a while.

He told me to take his $5,000 out of the dresser over the next few days, $500 each in 10 different checking accounts we had set up around the country. Ronnie also let me know that the $621 that wasn't in the thousands piles was mine.

I knew that the other guys had been promised $2000 each for night work - but I didn't feel cheated at all. I was just a feast for the eyes - not an armed bodyguard - and would probably have gone for nothing.

Finally he told me to put my hair up, put on some make-up, then put on the nightgown behind the door and make breakfast for the boys. He and I both knew that wearing this thing was so thin that it was almost like being naked, and that was the point.

I never met Ronnie at moments like this. I did what I was told - I understood my hair and my morning swollen face as best I could. I bent over to put on some panties, but Ronnie stopped me, shoved my ass and basically threw me out of the room.

The moment I hit the hallway, four pairs of eyes were hit by the body and remained there. The gown hung on me like wet paint, and I was painfully aware of this. Although all the shades in the house were closed because we were not afraid of prying eyes, enough sunlight still came in so that they could capture my silhouette through the thin fabric.

I continued to make breakfast, flinching inside whenever I had to bend down to get a pan or open the refrigerator with its bright interior light. Ronnie was right behind me on the way out of the bedroom, so at least I knew everyone would behave - and they did - and thanked me for breakfast and even picked up their pies and put them in the sink when they were done - which they certainly didn't do at home.

Breakfast was served, Ronnie and the crew quickly packed up, and I didn't see or hear from them for almost a week. (I was worried all the time, too - I didn't even trust Ronnie's people when I knew there was $70,000 available there that they could consider their own and make with a few shots).

When I did, it was as if our lives suddenly shifted into a whole new gear. That $70,000 was used to buy us into a whole new business with higher stakes and higher payouts. I didn't know it at the time, but Ronnie had bought an area and sold his soul to a so-called cartel. They were less violent back then, but they were still people you don't know that well.

Before it was over, I would get too involved in all this, but I was young, naive, and all I knew was that we seemed ten feet tall and bulletproof. We had money, powder and power.

Until we didn't have it anymore.

THE LINE

It results from "should not" and "must not". "I can't, I don't want to". Please don't do this to me. It's a lie because every muscle in my body wants to touch me and my skin is burning to taste.

I'm going to say that he's my opposite and everything I shouldn't want and can't have. I can stand in front of him and just the sight of him makes the blood rush through me and make me throbbing. And I have no fucking idea why. But I do, of course I do. He's rough and stocky, and if I met him, I'd bounce off him. He's curvy and he's heavy and everything about him is bigger and stronger and uglier. He's my opposite, and I want him to defile my femininity. But he must not. I won't let him, because I belong with my husband.

But what if I were to...?

What if I didn't look away when I feel his eyes moving over my body? What if I leaned over the desk and allowed him a closer look at the cleavage, which I know he has spent many nights thinking about fucking. What if I whispered into his ear all the dirty things he does to me at night when I think about him.

It would be so easy to touch his chest while I do it that he would wonder if I had lost my mind or if he had finally broken my resolve. I wouldn't tell too soon - I would play flirtatiously, whisper a little "No, I can't" as he went in to kiss me.

He'd run his lips over mine as I pulled away. I can smell him; the oil of the machines he works with, the tingling of the new sweat, his breath and his body. I want the smell of him to stick to me as if he was marking me. He can see the conflict in my eyes.

I can't. I must not. But haven't I crossed the line already? Our lips met, so if I'm doomed to guilt, I should eat my fill.

In a split second of weakness, I press my lips to his. I feel the roughness of his beard, and his tongue feels strange as it enters my mouth. I am not used to being kissed like that by anyone else. I shouldn't do that. But as I cross that line, I realize again that I'm already ruined. All I can think about is the feeling of his big, rough fingers inside me.

I love that, and I'll tell him that. Nothing can save me now, because he hastily slides his hand under my skirt and I open my legs to give him access, as if I give in to his will or resign myself to it. My thoughts stray to the fact that we could be caught and there would be no covering up. Here I am, legs spread, sitting on his lap while he pushes my soaked underwear aside and the tips of his rough thick fingers probe the pink creases of my cunt. I feel ambushed as he sinks his fingers inside me, as if he is taking my second virginity. My innocence is gone; I am a fraud. It is beyond ecstasy. He knows what he is doing while waggling his fingers inside me. The pressure on my G-spot makes me squirm and whimper like a frightened animal out of control. I have spent so many nights thinking about this.

I see that his face is consumed with lust and I realize that although he is honestly excited to finger fuck me, I really want to give something back. His cock is hard through his pants, and if there is one thing I have thought about more than him finger-fucking me, it is the thought of blowing him. On my knees at his whim; the ultimate submission.

I already know he loves that. I figured it out from the subtle things he said and the way he looked at my lips. I remember once, at his request, I guiltily sent him a photo of my face. His joy at such an inexplicable image made me think...

So I kneel down, unzip and reveal the cock I had imagined for as long as I could stretch out every fuckhole I could offer. I want to show him what I can do. I spent years honing that skill on my husband. His cock is humble, and I'm grateful for that because it's easier to handle. I start with his balls, enjoy the taste he has and that unmistakable masculine smell. I like to lick and suck gently while giving a show of myself, making occasional eye contact with him. The insolence of my eye contact underlines my fall from grace. I want to be his bitch.

I lick and kiss the veins of his shaft. I look at the head of his cock glistening before coming. I like to play with him as if he were a lipstick by pulling the tip of his cock over my open lips. I can taste him. It is salty and warm and I enjoy it as if it were a delicacy. I know he's watching me, so I make sure he sees me willingly humiliating myself and my morals.

I suck gently at the tip, using mainly my lips and guiding it with my hand in my mouth. He's getting more and more urgent, so I allow him to fuck my mouth. The feeling he has in my mouth is satisfyingly uncomfortable. It's almost a sadomasochistic kick that I get. The elation brings my mind to bliss. I'm wet and throbbing between my legs. I want him to lick and fuck me until orgasm, but when his dick head presses into the back of my throat, it brings my orgasm mentally closer. I try to open my throat for him, but it makes me choke. He ignores this and I enjoy the kick that comes with it, disregarding my right to comfort.

My orgasm becomes more pronounced, and I doubt it takes much to push me over the edge. When he starts masturbating on my face, I rub myself and bring the orgasm to a ticklish climax where "before" meets "after" and "I must not" becomes "I did it". This rush to my head makes my muscles weaken and for those few seconds I ride my orgasm and nothing else exists anymore. My body contracts rhythmically and I scream. I feel his sperm hitting my skin, first hot and then quickly cooling off.

And then it dawns on me - I am a cheater and he has made me his little whore.

THE CEOS WIFE

A colleague of mine was a strange guy with a lot of strange stories from the old days in the steel mill. He had even published a book about life in the steelworks, mostly a book with lots of black and white pictures.

One day we visited a plumbing shop. Some students had a great idea, probably trying to be funny, so they poured cement into the sink on Friday afternoon, and of course the sink had to be replaced.

We went over to the desk to place an order. Behind the desk sat a nice woman in her early fifties. Pretty fit and hot. I could well imagine that she was very hot ten years ago.

Back in the car my colleague was laughing. He said he had seen how I looked at her as if I was a dog and she was a bitch in heat. He laughed at his own remark.

He told me that she was married to the big boss, the CEO, as they call it today, of the old steelworks. The plant where I used to work. She divorced him, five guys, myself included, got fired. I looked at him, he smiled. We fucked her, the big boss found the proof, she divorced him and we got fired.

I looked at him and I laughed. Without saying a word, he started the car and we drove back to our school and the cemented sink.

The next day after lunch he showed me a thick envelope. His hand moved it across the table towards me. He blinked.

I opened it and found a photo album. On the front was a big yellow flashing smiley face. He said these were the unpublished pictures of life in the steel mill.

Page one, a picture of her... a black and white picture. She was dressed nice and neat. Classic skirt and blouse. Just like a secretary. She was hot, she had a beautiful smile, and she had this thing. I find it hard to describe, some women have "sex" written all over them.

He told me that in her younger days she was, and still is, the hottest girl in town. Of course she married the big man at the mill. Rich, big house, but a really boring economist. His humour was as dry as the Sahara, and he could drive a person crazy with boredom after a five minute conversation. But he was good at running the mill.

His wife worked as a coordinator at the mill, booking meetings, fixing conference rooms and so on. She was the opposite of her husband. She flirted, laughed, was happy and sexy.

I turned to the next page in the album. Next picture, also black and white. Her in the middle, light-gray skirt, short tight, white blouse. And two dirty guys in helmets, coveralls and safety shoes. She was laughing, her whole face was laughing.

He went on talking while I looked at the picture, describing how things developed over the years. How her little flirt with the boys evolved from little hints and blinks to more boldness, and how the boys' comments evolved from little comments about her beauty to more direct comments about her body.

Again I opened a new page. In this picture she was standing in front of a desk, leaning forward and holding a pen in her hand. A normal position in an office. Except that her head was turned back and she was smiling, she looked directly into the camera and blinked.

When I looked at the pictures, my colleague told me that he had a good relationship with her. How he was a talented photographer back then and how she enjoyed his attention with the camera and that all the pictures were taken with her permission.

I turned to the next page, I was quite excited. On this page there were two pictures. She was in a mechanical workshop. On the first picture she held a grease gun in one of her hands. She had a devilish smile and a spoonful of grease in the other hand. On the other picture she sent the photographer a teasing smile as she rubbed the grease with her fingers.

When I looked at the pictures, he explained to me how things had developed over the years. How her flirting had become rougher and rougher and how the boys, like in these pictures, introduced her to different things in the workshop. Like the grease gun. How they told her that day before the picture was taken that the fat was Vaseline. And how they responded to her more direct flirting, she responded to her sexual attention. A mutual pleasure is the right words.

I turned to a new page and was curious about the next picture. It was in a break room where the boys were eating their lunch. She was sitting at the table with the boys. I noticed that it was the same boys in all the pictures. Four boys and the photographer. She was holding a banana in her hand and the tip in her mouth.

My assistant continued the conversation, but I didn't listen much.

I quickly turned to a new page. I'm not sure what I expected, but I was not disappointed. There were four pictures, artistic style, and like all pictures in black and white. No colours. The first picture, a dark room, the flash of the camera made her white shirt look very white, a dirty industrial worker hands her the tit. She smiled and looked into the camera. Second picture, another hand on the other tit. Other hand, bigger. Third picture, both hands removed, but her white shirt was not so white anymore. Two dirty handprints on her tits. In the fourth picture, a guy kissed her neck and three others stroked her.

The contrast between her beautiful white and grey clothes and her dirty hands and overalls was fantastic.

My colleague said that this was her game, she was in full control and then he left the room.

I stared at the pictures. I remembered the nice woman in the plumber's workshop. Her smile, nice and polite.

Again I looked at the fourth picture. Her eyes were closed, she leaned with her back against the man who was kissing her neck. Her face was turned upwards towards the ceiling. Her mouth was half open.

On the next page, a picture, it was the workshop. A dirty mattress on the floor. She was on her knees. Still dressed, but not as clean. Four guys around her. She smiled into the camera.

I turned the page. Almost the same picture, but all four had erect penises, and she was holding two in her hand and sucking on one. She wasn't looking into the camera right now.

On the next page, the fourth guy was sitting behind her. He had pulled her skirt up around her waist. His hand was between her legs from behind.

New picture, close to her face. A cock in her mouth, eyes half open, animal lust. The angle of the photo was good, and I could see the fourth guy smiling, and I imagined his fingers deep in her holes.

I closed my eyes. My dick was rock hard. These pictures were much better than a modern digital HD home train.

I flipped to a new page. She was standing, skirt around the waist, shirt around the waist. A hand pulled up her black panties, they were enclosed by her pussy panties. Some other hands pulled her tits and squeezed her nipples.

One hand pulled her head back after her hair, and a finger was in her mouth. I imagined a hard time for her.

In the next picture, scissors cut off her panties and bra. Skirt and shirt still around her waist. She was still held by many hands and because of the view of her nipples they were not tender. She looked down. Whether she was looking at the scissors, the nipples or at what I could not make out. But one thing I could say. She was horny. Her eyes and her mouth could not lie.

I looked at the picture for a long time. Every detail. Her white skin had traces of her dirty hands. Tits red stains from pinching.

My hand turned to a new page. It was lifted by three men. One on each side and one holding her head. It was nice to see how they treated her with care and not at the same time. The fourth man sat between her legs. The face was buried in her crotch. Her nipples were stiff, and the expression on her face made her groan.

New page, new picture. Her pussy, close up. She was glistening. Swollen pussy lips, a swollen clitoris. A dark, hairy finger stuck halfway inside her. Or it was on its way out. glistening from her white, creamy juices.

Next page. She was still held between the fingers. She pulled her hair, raised her head up and looked down herself. The fourth guy was between her legs. He showed her the grease gun and a big grease spot, or Vaseline, on his finger.

I quickly turned to the next page. A picture from a good angle. It shows a knuckle deep in the butt and face. I couldn't remember ever seeing a woman with a hornier expression on her face.

From here it was a series of pictures of her basically getting fucked in every direction, in every hole. They changed positions here, on all fours, on her stomach, riding, on her back. Fucked in the pussy, fucked in the ass, fucked in the mouth, DPed. Certainly sucking the cock that had fucked her in the ass. And cumshots in pussy, ass and mouth. And a really red ass with a distinct handprint.

The last picture was of her lying on the mattress. Exhausted. She was glistening with sweat, semen and salvia. Smiling in a tired, happy way.

I closed the album. Surely I would never be as horny as I am now.

My co-worker entered the room. He smiled. She told me that somehow her husband found out about it, and that was the end of the marriage and our work. These pictures are the only copies, and you're the only one who saw them.

Maybe we should go to the store and visit her one day. He winked at me and smiled.

NEW OFFICE

Despite the various restrictions imposed by the corona virus, I was able to start my new job on Monday, and it had been a hell of a week. I had just finished my last scheduled session on Friday and was thinking about lunch when my phone rang.

"Amy!" I answered happily. "What are you up to?"

"Well, it's been a long time since we've had lunch, and I was curious if you'd like to eat," she said.

"Sure. Where are you?"

"I'm down in your building. After you told me the good news, I thought I'd come out and surprise you."

"Fantastic. I'll be right down," I said, hanging up, grabbing my coat from the back of the door, then walking through the empty office space to the elevator.

I got off the elevator and saw Amy. She was wearing leggings and a sweatshirt with a zipper. Based on past experiences, I could clearly remember the busty figure she was hiding under her humble clothes. Despite the social distance, I gave her a big hug and felt her face and chest pressing against my torso.

"It's good to see you! You look fantastic, as always," I said.

"Thank you," she blushed slightly. "You look good too. All dressed up like a boss," she said, flicking her tie.

"You know me, I'd rather be in a T-shirt and cargo pants. But you gotta do what you gotta do, right? Besides, Lisa likes it," I said in allusion to my wife.

"I bet she does," she said as we headed for the parking garage.

"Where are the children?"

"At home with Sean. I said I needed a ride after being cooped up for so long."

I opened the door for her, and then I put myself in the driver's seat. My dick twitched, remembering the times we fucked in the same car over the years.

We swung by a local gyroscopic joint and we were able to drive off, because all the seats were closed. Since we had nowhere else to go, I suggested we eat in my office. Amy agreed it was the only option that made sense.

We laughed as we remembered it and caught up. Most of our interactions in those days took place through social media where we checked each other out.

"Nice office," she said, looking out of the floor at the windows on the ceiling as I pulled a chair up to the desk and cleared some space for us to eat.

"Yes," I smiled proudly, "it's all right."

We sat and ate and laughed, and the stress of the week disappeared from our minds. Our knees shook a few times, and when she leaned over to steal one of my fries, I stole a peek into her shirt to get a glimpse of her ample cleavage. Once, when she bent down to speak, her hand rested on my thigh just above my knee.

When we finished eating, I leaned back and said, "What a pity we didn't get dessert."

"Maybe we can think of something else," she said, moving her face closer to mine and turning her chair towards me.

"Perhaps..." I leaned towards her repeatedly in silence, my hands sliding up her thighs to her hips and then to her waist.

She wrapped her arms around my neck and our lips met.

I had neglected to kiss Amy. She was such a passionate lover, and it makes cheating, which was true for both of us at the time, even hotter.

Without breaking the kiss, I took one hand and pushed the leftovers of lunch onto the desk, then grabbed them by the hips, picked them up and lifted them up to put them on the desk.

She giggled playfully and pulled me towards her while I pressed my body against her.

To waste no time, I kissed down her neck and my hands moved up her chest, over her sweatshirt that covered her voluptuous bosom. She moaned as I touched her, expressing the same lust that had swollen inside me.

I leaned back and pulled the zipper of her shirt down, revealing her tits covered with a black bra.

"That's so hot, baby," I said and bent over to kiss her cleavage while I held her tits in my hands.

She took off her jacket behind her and then felt her bra loosen as she must have opened it from behind. I let it fall from my hands as I kissed up to one nipple, sucked and nibbled at her and then went to the other, her fingers running through my hair.

I withdrew to kiss her again, our mouths opened, our tongues danced. My hands pulled my tie apart when I felt her hands finding my belt. As I unbuttoned my shirt I felt my zipper come down and then my boxers were pulled down so she could grab my stiff cock.

She stroked me before pushing me back and slipping from the desk to the floor. When she started kissing and licking my naked cock, I took off my shirts and threw them on the floor with the growing pile of clothes.

I moaned loudly as she began to take me in her mouth. My hands rested in her hair and held it out of the way as she started to bob.

"I missed your mouth," I said, my eyes closed and my head tilted back as she teetered and sucked and licked me.

There was a popping sound as she pulled her head off my cock.

"I missed sucking you," she said, and then went back to him.

As much as I wanted her to go on for hours, I knew our time was running out, so I pulled her up and turned her over to the desk. I grabbed her leggings and panties and pulled her down by her shapely legs while she looked at me hungrily over her shoulder.

I laid my cock at the entrance of her already soaked pussy and pressed my head inside. Amy moaned loudly as she laid her head on the desk.

I slowly rocked into her, enjoying the feeling of her pussy, which was intensified by the sound of her squeaking and moaning. In a short time I was deeply buried with my balls and enjoyed a pussy I had not had for years.

"Baby, you feel so good," I said as I picked up speed.

"Moooooorrrreee", she moaned as she came on my cock.

I pulled it out, turned it around, put it on the desk and dived back into it.

Her tits bounced and giggled on her chest as I stomped off.

"Sperm, please," she moaned. "I need it in me."

The feeling was so incredible I wanted to fuck her against the window, but I couldn't deny her what she wanted.

"Ahhhhh," I moaned loudly as I came in her spurt after spurt, my hands holding her hips.

"My God", I said, my head tilted back, my cock still stuck in her pussy.

"I missed you," she said, "but I really missed that."

I pulled back and sat in the chair.

"Do you want to clean me up?" I asked with a grin.

Moaning, she fell back on her knees in front of me and took my soft cock in her mouth, sucked it carefully and licked it clean.

"I wanted to fuck you against the mirror."

"I wanted that too," Amy replied. "Maybe next lunch," she said before putting me back in her mouth.

NEW CAR

Jasmine and I left the restaurant laughing.

Jasmine: I have a new car.

Me: You got rid of the Subaru?

Jasmine held up the keys: Yes, since my mother-in-law lives with us and romps around with the kids, I needed something bigger. It's a Volvo. It's nice.

Me: Better than the Subaru?

Jasmine, laugh: I hated the Subaru.

Me, reaching for the keys: Let me see.

She gives them to me as we walk over. I unlock and look inside: Spacious. You could take a nap in here. (We laugh.) How does she handle it?

With Jasmine: She's fine. I like her.

Me: Can I take it for a quick spin?

Jasmin: Jasmin: Do you have time?

Me, looking at my watch and smiling: It will be alright.

Jasmine: It will be all right.

I climb into the driver's seat while Jasmine gets in on the passenger side. I take the opportunity to look at her legs and feel myself getting stiff.

I start the car and put the SUV in reverse. The Volvo drives gently out of the curve. I start the car and leave the parking lot.

Me: That's nice. How much is it?

Jasmine: 43

Me: Not bad.

I'm walking straight down the street where our old office used to be.

Me: You rented out the old room. It's now the headquarters of some bank.

Jasmine: Cool.

Me: There's our old place. Should I stop over there?

Jasmine: You are so bad.

Me: Well, you were wearing a dress...

I put my hand on her thigh and press her hem slightly upwards.

Jasmine: I was wondering when you were going to say something about that.

Her eye blinks as her mischievous grin grows.

I turn into the parking lot where we park after work and walk towards the shady spot.

Jasmine: I can't. You have to go to work and I have to go home.

Me: Just for a minute?

Jasmine (grinning and biting her lip): Just for one minute?

I'll park the car and leave it running.

Me: (winking): Yeah, just for a minute.

I lean forward as she leans in, our lips kiss. No sooner was the contact established than she grabs me and pulls me towards her. My hand continues to slide up her thigh and my other hand grabs her hip. She pushes herself towards me and pulls me closer to her over the centre console.

I (breaks our kiss): Let's see how big her back is.

Jasmine, her breath ripping, moans approvingly and climbs over the centre console and into my back. I take off my suit jacket and climb back following her.

Without any loss of time she immediately climbs onto my lap and kisses me. My hands grab her ass and pull her further on me. Her double-Ds are pressed against me.

My dick is pressed against my pants.

My hands move up her sides and find their way to her chest. She moans into my mouth.

Jasmine: I dream of it.

Me: Me too.

One of my hands is rubbing her nipple through her dress, while the other is returning to her thigh and pushing her dress up on the way to her panties.

She's rubbing up against me.

Me: You're rubbing my pants.

Jasmine: I'm sorry, Jasmine. (She continues to crunch.)

Me: Let me help.

I kiss her deep and then move her from my lap. I reach down to loosen my belt, but she is already grabbing my zipper. As I undo my button, she reaches into my boxers and grabs my cock.

Jasmine: I missed that...

She starts to caress me.

I pull down my pants and she lets go of me for a moment. As soon as my pants are down, I lean back and she bends over to suck me into her mouth.

Me, by my moaning: I missed your mouth.

My left hand rests on her head as she bounces and sucks while my right hand reaches around to caress her chest.

Without removing her mouth, she climbs up and puts her knees on the seat. My right hand pulls up her dress and I put my hand on her panty-covered ass and squeeze her.

Me: This is so good...

I pull down her panties on her thighs and put my hand on her dripping pussy.

She's shaking and pulling her mouth away from me to moan.

Me: Come here.

I pull her up and kiss her. She slides closer to me.

Me: Climb up.

I: Jasmine: Please...

She sits on me and lowers herself down on my cock. My hands are on her hips under her dress, while I make sure she doesn't go too fast and enjoys every inch as she slides down.

Jasmine (begging): Please...

I pull her down and fill her up.

Jasmine: Thank you. I needed this so much.

She swayed her hips as she snuggled against me.

Jasmine: So good, so good...

Me: You feel incredible.

I push into her while she rocks against me. I hear her breathing faster and then she hums.

Her body trembles as she pauses for a moment while I am buried deep inside her.

Jasmin: That was amazing!

Me: More?

Jasmine: Jasmine: You cannot come inside me.

Me: Okay.

I turn us around and lay her down and climb on her. I hammer my only regret into her that we don't have time to take off her dress and let me fuck her tits.

Jasmine, moans quickly as she builds to another climax. She shudders at me again as I look further inside her.

Me: I'm going to cum. Where to?

Jasmine: In my mouth.

She presses herself against me and while I lean back, she climbs back on her knees and lifts her butt up into the air. She devours me while I put my finger in her dripping pussy.

As she keeps sucking and bobbing, I push myself up to meet her here. My hands move to the back of her head and help to guide her in an original way.

Me: Here I come.

My back arches and she intensifies her sucking while my tail stutters. She continues sucking until I lean back and take my hands off her head. She swallows my semen while I breathe.

Jasmine: I have to go now.

Me, looking at my watch: I have to go too.

We adjust ourselves and climb forward again.

I, while we are retreating, put my hand on her thigh: That was great. Thank you.

Jasmin: Thank you. I needed that so much.

Me: So, can you have lunch again next week?

Jasmine, grinning: Maybe.

BED REVIEW

I took a photo of the pendant on the bed and sent it to you with the message: "Your wife said she loves my bed".

You would understand it as the picking up boys do to each other all the time, if you would just perceive it in such a way that I am referring to the time when she had slept there, when she lived with her sister and we were all out and about, or when you both had slept there while you were babysitting for my wife and me. You have no idea that we had collapsed in a pile of wrapped limbs on top of each other after we'd been fucking hard for a morning or an afternoon.

But we hadn't just shagged in my bed. We used every opportunity to steal a quick fuck. We'd done it once, when we went to get everyone coffee. And every time we had lunch together, now that our offices were within walking distance, we'd wet my cock. Your bed was best when you were downstairs with her family and we had put our respective children to sleep.

Sometimes these were quick naps where I would take him deep and fast and leave her with a pussy full of cum. Another time we took our time and I enjoyed every inch of her petite body.

And I know you don't make her blow you because she thinks it's not right for a man and a woman to do it, but I do. We're already doing so much wrong that I make her suck my dick like she's drowning and it's full of air. She's a natural. I took it from her bubbly personality that she'll be a donor, and I've not been disappointed.

And these secrets we share, like the fact that you cheated on her once in the lounge or the secret trips to the strip club? Well, she knows, and let me tell you, kid, she fucks well when she wants revenge.

She wanted to confront you, but I knew a better way for her to get back at you, and that clearly had something to do with her setting me up. But I couldn't just tell her that. I had to convince her myself.

So over several days, over lunch and text messages, I led her down a trail of crumbs. We talked about how you were the only man she'd been with, and that you were probably who you always were, and that you wouldn't change. We talked about the effects of divorce on the children and how upset her parents would be. We talked about how she was just trying to get over it, and that no matter how much time passed, every time she looked at you, she would still see your infidelity. We talked about revenge, but how nothing she did to you would ever equal that.

That's when I told her it was really about how she felt. If she agreed to get over it, it would only affect her, just like if she didn't. So I told her to do what would make her feel better, even if she was the only one who knew.

At the end of this lunch she gave me a big, tight hug, the first time she really pressed her body against me and let me feel her breasts bouncing against me. She thanked me and we planned to have lunch tomorrow.

The next day she seemed nervous and a little awkward. At first she said that everything was fine, but when I pushed her, she finally decided that she had decided what to do, but she needed my help. I told her that I would do whatever I had to do because I just wanted her to be happy.

She kept telling me that she had never been with anyone else but you and that she had never seen anyone else, she hesitated to see her naked before. She decided that she wanted to take revenge, even if you never knew, because it was about how she felt about it, as I had said. So she looked at her phone and then back at me and told me she was ready.

My phone beeped, and I noticed that I received a series of messages. When I looked, I saw that they were pictures of her from her bathroom at home. As I flipped through the pictures, she had less and less to see in each one, so she absorbed the digital striptease she was playing to me.

I let my excitement and attraction show on my face when I finally looked at her nude photo. I tried to burn every inch of her sexy body into my memory, from her shaved hill to her sassy tits to her aroused nipples. I was careful to bite my lip when I looked up from my phone. As I looked up from my phone, my eyes slowly moved up her body, clearly undressing her before me.

She was crimson, and I knew that in this situation I had to strengthen her self-confidence. I began by telling her how beautiful she was, how amazing her body was and how amazingly brave she was to take this step. I laid my hand on hers when I told her how much it meant to me that she trusted me and decided that I could be trusted too.

She relaxed and held my hand and thanked me again for all the help I gave her and my support. We ended the lunch with many flirtatious looks from her and I made it clear that I was taking a close look at her. After we finished our lunch, I took her back to her office as usual, only that I took every opportunity to finally check her out openly.

The next day we met again and again for lunch, and again and again she sent me a set of pictures, this time in sexy lingerie, with her undressing. The next day it was the same and this time in different underwear. And every day more cleavage was shown, so that I could see with my own two eyes what I could only see on pictures before. Every day I made sure that I let her know how beautiful and brave she was.

On Friday, after another series of lingerie strip photos and a flirtatious lunch, she took me back to her office by a different route. When we arrived at a place where nobody was around, she hugged me again and then leaned over for a kiss. That was our first kiss, deep and passionate, and I finally had the opportunity to grab her ass and squeeze it while we kissed.

When my wife and I came to your house this weekend, we both pretended that nothing was going on and nobody seemed to notice, especially you.

On Monday at lunch she took me to her car instead of our regular place. As soon as we entered the elevator of the parking garage, I couldn't help but wrap my arms around her. We kissed angrily, both of us persisting in our hunger and passion for the other. Only when the elevator door closed after we reached our floor did we stop our kiss, although no one got out. We pressed the button to go back, but it was too late, our elevator had been called to another floor. We did our best not to laugh so much when the other person got in and the three of us returned to their floor.

After we got off, she led us to her cabin, stealing an occasional kiss and I grabbed her waist or butt. When we arrived at the car, I lifted her onto the hood, wrapped her in my arms and made out with her, pulling me against her with her legs and arms, hitting me with as much of her body as possible.

She broke our embrace and told me we should get in the car. I gladly did her the favor of letting her climb into the back seat and pat her butt as she continued to crawl in front of me. I climbed in and sat down next to her but before I even sat down we were hugged again. My hands were finally really free to stroke her body.

My hands found a way under her shirts, touched her naked skin for the first time and I could hear her breathing. I pushed my hands up, felt her flat stomach and rubbed her back. We had leaned closer together, practically over each other.

I pulled her onto my lap, and because of her petite size she had some headroom. My hard cock was now pressed against her pussy, closer than ever, despite our pants and underwear. I twitched it against her and heard her moaning again.

I pulled her shirts up and she forced me to let her take them off. I took a moment to feast on her white bra-clad breast before kissing, licking and massaging her. You are a lucky man.

She undid her bra and dropped it when she bumped into me. She must have been so aroused because it only took a few minutes before she played with her tits, kissed and crunched them. It was a pleasant surprise, especially how overwhelmed she seemed by the experience. Later I learned from her that this was her first orgasm. Of course it was not her last.

After she had come, she insisted on taking care of me as well, so she slipped off my lap and sat down next to me. I let her unduly drop my pants and helped her to let them slide down. I was rock hard and she couldn't help mentioning that I was taller than you.

She started to caress me and when I encouraged her to take it in her mouth, she apologized that she was no good because she only did it a few times. It's really your loss.

I've had girls in the past who were never that good, and here she rocks my world. And to top it off, when I blew my load, she didn't even pause. She swallowed that shit. I complimented her on her skill, which made her blush. It was just the first of many blowjobs she gave me, either as her main event or as a prelude.

We finally did it a few days later. We both called in sick and got a hotel room instead. She really dressed up for the event, with her make-up and lingerie, a new set she had bought just for me.

I fucked here in every position imaginable, which was an experience for her, considering she told me that you only do a few punches and a grunt. She loves to drive, which works well, considering how many times we've done it in cars.

She also loves the puppy, which also worked to our advantage, because she is adventurous and has the potential to get caught in public. We have banged in parks, parking garages, family bathrooms and even a few times in the woods. The craziest ones were of course in one of our houses, in the middle of the night, when we sneak into the kitchen or living room and do a quickie.

Anyway, that first day really set the bar. I must have injected into her five or six times, and one of them was in her mouth. I remember that because she came when I came in her mouth. Unbelievable.

We only snuck away a couple of times for a whole day, I'd like to do more, but we only have so much time. And I think we should do it soon, considering you've been talking about having another baby. While it's exciting to think about getting her pregnant, I'm sure that everyone would realize that it's my child.

Anyway, I look forward to fucking her in your new bed.

THE NEW ADMIN

WOW a new girl in the office. I am speechless.

"Hello" is all I can do with a little smile.

Man, it's hot in here, it must be me. She is hot. Slim, petite, with a nice smile. Small, perfect tits, hot legs. Uhhhhh... what did I come here for? Oh right, I need to speak to your boss. With one last smile on the new girl and she goes back to the shop to fix more equipment. The rest of the day I'm locked in a daydream dreaming about seducing this beautiful woman, but I noticed a ring. I'm not a cheater, but damn it, I could cheat with her!

My daydream is a distraction because it goes on every time I see her. The seduction would be so sweet. For the past few days, I can't even remember her name. Her boss is an ass and doesn't formally introduce new employees. Finally I find out that her name is Nat. Natalie.

The daydream grows more vivid as we talk over the next few weeks. I wonder if she caught me staring at her in a daze. Hey, pumpkin, get a grip. You don't have a chance, you're both involved with other people. Days go by, but my imagination of her seduction doesn't fade. I learn more about her and her life. She may not seem like a cheating girl, but a boy can dream.

It would begin at a place we both agreed upon...

Hot kisses and caresses. I lead her into the shower, our hands gliding over each other's bodies as I sensually pull off her skirt and low-cut blouse while the hot water in the bathroom rises steaming. I fiddle with my clothes while she undresses them hungrily. I turn her around and bring my hands around her neck to her shoulders and down the sides to her hips and pull her close to me. She raises her arms and wraps her hands around my head and neck. I kiss her just below the ear and pull kisses down to the shoulders while taking the bra strap first from one shoulder and then from the other. I put my hands around her sides and clasp her beautiful breasts tightly. She pants and emits a small groan while I pull her towards me and pinch her neck together. She lowers her hands to my sides and pulls my hips closer to my hips, rubbing her butt against my erection. Now it's my turn to moan.

One sharp inhale: "Natalie."

"Mmm, I like the way you say my name. You make it sound so sexy. Say it again."

And then a muffled whisper. Natalie.

She turns to me without breaking off contact. I brush her hair back and wrap my fingers around her with one hand, the other holding her tight little back against me. I lead her face upwards, exposing her neck, leaning in for a kiss just below her jawbone and moving slowly towards her collarbone. I bite gently while opening her bra and throwing it to the side.

We move into the waiting hot water and let it pour over us. She puts her hands around my head and pulls me to her chest to get the attention I need. Slowly I lick her nipple and take it in my mouth. Natalie moans a little and I feel her tremble. I move to the other nipple and she trembles again, pressing my mouth even harder into her breast.

"You're driving me crazy," she moans.

"Well, you've been driving me crazy for weeks, and now I finally have you. I guess a little payback is in order."

I start hauling kisses into her navel. Natalie writhes and lets out a little giggle. She pulls me back to eye level to show me the desire in her eyes. We pour the hot water over each other as we explore each other with our hands. I grab some soap and quickly lather up something to make us nice and slippery. I press her against the shower wall and attack her neck again. She lifts her leg around my hip to drag her smooth hill against my throbbing cock. The feeling she has against me is electric and I am ready to come from the heat of our passion to orgasm. I need more. My desire to hear this beautiful woman in orgasm is overwhelming. I pull her tightly against me and start kissing and licking me to her navy as I pour the hot water over us. I put her leg over my shoulder and get a first glimpse of her most private area. I put a kiss just over her hill and slowly pull my lips towards her beautiful clitoris. I split her swollen lips to expose her clitoris. She pants and pushes her fingers into my hair and leads me to where she needs more attention. I lick her clitoris and close my lips around the delicious little bud and suck gently.

"AHHHH Fuck". No more quips. I want you."

"Not yet." I tell her while I slip two fingers inside her pussy and roll her up to rub her G-spot.

"Ahh." She gasps. "I need to feel you."

"MMM. "No, I want you to come for me first." As I continue to rub her G-spot and put my mouth back on her clit and twirl my tongue around and start sucking on that delicious little nub.

"Please!" She's begging me. "I'll be right there."

I look up at her with a smile. "Come for me, Natalie. I want you to come just for me."

I come back to lick her nectar. Her body cramps as her pussy squeezes my fingers and I feel a warm flood wash into my waiting mouth.

"MMMMMM FUCK, I want you so much," she screams.

She pulls my hair and tears me from the beautiful pussy that gave me pleasure. She lifts me up until our eyes meet.

"Take me to bed" while she wraps both legs around my waist and her arms around my neck and holds me tight. She pulls my head back and nibbles my neck, and the electricity of her touch weakens my knees as I fiddle with the shower door to carry her to the waiting bed. I sit her down on the corner and gently lay her feet on the floor. She loosens her grip, but tries to pull me close to her.

I tear myself away from the hot kisses she demands and slide down her hot body, kisses after, until I stare at her beautiful pussy again. I put her hot little feet on my shoulders and expose her all over me. I kiss the tender spot where her thigh meets her body.

Natalie moans." God, you make me so aroused. I want your cock inside me. I need you now."

"I'm sorry, Natalie. I want to see you cum. I want to taste your sweet nectar when you come for me.

"Mmm, I like the way you say my name. That is so sexy. I don't usually use my full name, but it gives me goose bumps when you say it."

"Mmmm... Natalie."

I moan in her beautiful pussy and slide my tongue from her entrance to the top of her hill. She breathes in small breaths through clenched teeth as I use my fingers to spread the hood around her swollen clit and wrap my mouth around it. I nibble at her, taking care not to bite too hard. Her fingers are intertwined in the sheets as she screams

"Ahh FUCK... Enough!"

She pushes me away with her feet until I'm on the ground, and then she slams on top of me and pushes me down. She pulls my nails into my chest as she spreads my hips.

"Now it's my turn to tease her." She tells me so, a smile on her face, her eyes burning with desire.

She slides her fingernails across my chest and then down my arms. Our fingers entwine as she scratches her pussy on my cock. She glides along without allowing me to reach her entrance. Her touch is electric as I feel the heat of her gorgeous pussy almost making me let go.

"Ahh... Natalie, you're making me cum."

A wicked grin spreads across her beautiful face.

"Not so funny when we tease, is it? Now it's my turn to get what I want."

Natalie rolls her hips and bends over to guide my cock into her pussy. She slowly descends on me. Now it's my turn to gasp and shake.

"Oh my God, you're so perfect." I moan. "Tease me. Please me. Use me. Use me."

She leans over and bites my earlobe.

"I need you deep inside me. I want to feel you coming."

Natalie starts rubbing up against me and I can feel her cervix pressing against the tip of my dick.

"Ahh... you're so deep. I want you so much."

She moves forward until only the tip of my dick is left in her, then she pushes her pussy back and pushes our pubes together. The pace accelerates with long, full blows. Our breathing comes panting and moaning as our hunger increases. I adapt to her blows. She digs her nails into my chest.

The excitement with which she takes control is electric as I place my hands on her breasts to gently press her nipples between my fingers and apply pressure until she moans. She slides her hands up my chest and bends forward, crossing her arms behind my head and holding my hands on her nipples. I lift my hips according to her strokes and let the pressure build. I can feel her excitement. The pressure is almost unbearable.

"Mmm. Natalie, I'll be right there."

"Oh, yeah... come inside me. I want to cum with you. I wanna feel you.

I push hard in her pussy and I rub my cock deep, my pubic bone against hers. I can feel her pussy tightening and I'm swaying my hips.

"Oh YES", she screams.

I can't hold myself back any longer because this familiar rush goes right through me.

"Ahh Natalie." I scream as I try to pull her hips even closer to mine.

She makes a deep groan and trembles as I let go deep inside her. She leans back and digs her fingers into my hair and pulls my head against her breasts. I move my hands to bite her nipple and she screams as her pussy contracts and milk every drop of me.

We break down with her on my writhing chest and let her hair fall around us and wrap ourselves in a hot, sweaty cocoon.

"Wow," she says and whispers hoarsely, "How about an encore?"

CHEATING YOUNG GIRLFRIEND

Ever since we met in college, I've been warning myself about what other people would say about my girlfriend. As a nineteen-year-old sophomore, Annabelle was the girl who seemed innocent until you met her. I had known her since the late freshman year of high school and had witnessed her blossoming within two or three years from a clumsy young petite blonde with no sexual experience to an extremely sexually mature young petite blonde.

When I started courting Annabelle in my last year of school, she was a virgin with little appetite for sex. After I had seen her for about two years, she had transformed into an unprecedented level of sexual appetite and fervour. As a strapping, young, petite blonde, Annabelle had limited herself, and I knew it. My craving for porn and erotic stories finally made me succumb and attracted her. At first it started quite innocently, with my own subconscious urging us to play different scenarios. We started with the most obvious scenarios, such as the messenger and the bored housewife. After some basic nudges, Annabelle started to enter these role-plays each time with an extremely wet center. I started testing her sexual boundaries with my hands and fist until I could no longer nudge her with my fingers or penis alone. However, her favorite role-playing game took place towards the end of her climax and involved a hypothetical large penis penetrating her and killing her.

On a whim, I used a debit card that my grandmother had given me for Christmas to buy a toy for Annabelle and me to play with as we rang in the New Year. My mistake was ordering her toy while I blacked out drunk at a Christmas party. The party had caused me to miss the 22nd with Annabelle and my family. Annabelle added to my frustration by sending me a picture of her in red underwear and matching bra, fucking the fake Christmas tree we bought. When I looked at this photo and drank a bottle of liquor at my desk, I suddenly had a tendency to order sexual toys. A few clicks further on I realized that her "present" had no chance to arrive until Christmas and still ordered the most realistic but inconspicuous dildo I could find in a drunken stupor. In my drunken state I thought I had ordered a soft looking pink dildo that Annabelle could play with in front of me.

Instead I had somehow ordered a realistic black cyberskin dildo. Amazon only made me aware of the difference in memory when the package arrived. Ashamed, I checked my phone on Christmas Eve and saw the recent delivery. I checked my drunk purchase and was ashamed. Hoping to return it, I created a return option since I had finished work for the day. Without my knowledge at the time, my girlfriend had knocked on the door half-naked and signed for the box. Without thinking, my girlfriend took the box into her bedroom and opened it, thinking the contents were a BLU Ray or Xbox controller. Instead, the plastic lining of the cyberskin dildos revealed itself, and without thinking, she tore open the box. With little interest, but much remorseful horniness, Annabelle spent the next few hours exploring the inside of the packaging on her own. Towards the end of the working day I checked my account again and saw that the package had been delivered. I clicked on the product details and saw first hand my drunken mistake. The sexual toy I had ordered for my young girlfriend and me to experiment with was 9" long and simulated the size of a real BBC. I checked the shipping details and was shocked to learn that it had been updated to show that it had been delivered to the front door.

Instead of dealing head-on with the impending "delivery", I let the problem resolve itself naturally. Without the actual dildo product, I naturally assumed that the "misdirected" toy had been delivered to the wrong address, and I continued with my normal life when I received my credit note in early

January. During a fairly routine dive into the issues of the year, I saw the delivery of the toy. As Annabelle went into the store, I rummaged through the walk-in closet, expecting to find nothing but curiosity. After looking around briefly, I found the black cyberskin dildo. I suspected it had been lost, but inspected it more deeply, found it smelling of sexual fluids and stowed it away.

I decided to ignore the find and let the toy walk around the bedroom apparently without my knowledge. This went on for 2-3 months until my girlfriend used my laptop for a project and forgot to log off. Not only did she forget to log out of the course website, but Annabelle also forgot to log out of her Apple ID and the media and the following photos were synchronized. Knowing that the deadline was tight, I searched her computer while she was using the toilet. In just a few minutes I had logged into her website and checked the results. Not only did Annabelle have an Adult Friend Finder account that filled automatically, but several other dating sites showed up. Curiously, I checked each address in her browsing history and loaded the associated websites.

Nineteen-year-old Annabelle not only had pictures sent to her by other people, but she also had sexually suggestive pictures on each of the profiles I flipped through. Strangely enough, my penis hardened when I looked through my girlfriend's robust search history and remained erect the whole time. Never before had I been fascinated by the thought that my girlfriend's vagina had been "misplaced" and enjoyed by someone else. But the thought crossed my mind as I poked around on my laptop. Finally I could no longer hold the thought back when I found the 9 inch cyberskin dildo in Annabelle's panty drawer. I got into the panty drawer almost immediately. I came almost immediately after discovering it, but hid it from myself. I now saw the length and circumference that only a toy of this size could have. I continued to place the big dildo in the usual place and was amazed every time I could secretly pick it up and insert it into Annabelle while we were having normal sex.

Almost three months after Griffin began to notice that Annabelle was coming home with an increasingly less tight interior, he became surprisingly wise. And yet, as the relationship between Annabelle and Griffin changed, no one spoke directly about the difference. That is, until the discovery that would change their deep and painstakingly managed relationship forever. One afternoon, I came back early and parked my car in the driveway. I walked from the garage into the living room and heard the unmistakable sound of moaning. Instead of feeling my blood boiling and my face glowing red all by itself, I held on to that feeling and continued to listen to the muffled moaning and screaming. Instead of attacking the source of the animal noises I stood in the entrance and listened apparently forever.

Finally I was overwhelmed by the source of the noises and I crept quietly up to the master bedroom. When I reached the top of the stairs, I was struck by the depth and extent of the infidelity that was occurring at that moment. My typically shy girlfriend was lying splayed on my desk when a tall black gentleman stood between her legs and kept pushing forward.

I watched in shock as every second at least seven centimetres of hard black penis rammed into my young white girlfriend. I could see Annabelle's face from my vantage point and it was clear that she was contributing to most of the satisfying sounds. Instead of interrupting the action, I hid and tugged at my penis when my little friend finally came and pulled out the black cock and shot across Annabelle's face and mouth for almost a full minute. Watching the thick ropes of cum cloud my sweet girlfriend's face proved to be too much for me, and I soon lost my short blows. In no time at all I was left standing onmy side while my girlfriend went to a restaurant to eat with the big black man while she was covered with his sperm and did not respond to my own text messages.

ETERNITY IN A MOMENT

Alli chatted with Nick for a few weeks. They had had a social conversation the Sunday before, and she was a little surprised that she wanted to meet him. More surprised that after seeing her, he seemed more attracted to her than ever. She had called him "Sir" a few times and knew that he loved that - he called her "Kitten" by now - partly because her screen name contained "Cat", but also because of the Snapchat filter photos she had sent him, which always had cat ears on them.

She had been reading his stories for weeks and was so incredibly turned on by them - now she was just turned on talking to him and had found herself incredibly horny after their conversation on Sunday. They were both married but frustrated - she thought she was practically a virgin - she had only ever been with her husband, had only ever felt touched by one person and longed to explore. He was naughty, perverse and had an evil side that excited her.

In the beginning she had only chatted and sent stories and occasionally a teasing photo that she had sent him. But lately she had found out that he had given her some orders and she enjoyed obeying him. Then he had asked for a hug and told her how much he had longed to kiss her. She was conflicted - she had never cheated on him, but with Nick she was tempted and excited. They were in the same boat, eyes open and not out to fall in love - just explore some naughty fun together. She decided to meet him for a talk and a hug and see how things went. They had agreed that if she called him sir while she was with him, he could kiss her.

The morning of the meeting dawned bright and clear - she was curled up in bed when Sir's "good morning" message arrived. He again said cheeky and nice things that made her smile, then he sent a photo of "what she had done to him". Fucking - his dick looked thick... she felt the wetness start between her legs, announcing the need to be fucked. She flirted a little, then finally got up and moved. He sent her some stories to start her day off. She hurried around knowing that she had to leave soon, half of her clothes were packed when she suddenly noticed that she didn't wear panties - it wouldn't be the first time she went without, so she put on the pink bra she liked, her black dress and leggings and headed off to work.

The next few hours seemed to drag on, she felt horny and nervous and insecure at the same time. Both were working, so there was little news. She tried to concentrate on her work, but was distracted again and again as she checked her phone, remembered the look on his tail, how wicked his imagination was and wondered how far she was ready to go this afternoon. Lunch arrived and they talked, he sent more stories she hadn't read just yet - she was horny enough already. But his words calmed her down - she knew he wouldn't pressure her, so she was looking forward to seeing him. She mentioned the missing panties to him, and his predictable reaction almost made her giggle.

Back to work for another hour or two, and then it was time. She made her way downstairs - full of doubts and some nagging insecurities - did he really like her as much as he said? Could she go through with it? When she came home from work, he told her where to go and she walked around the building to the little side street where she could see his car. Slowly she walked to the car and remained determined as she reached the car, opened the door and slipped in next to him. He smiled cheerfully and greeted her cheerfully with the words she learned to love... "Hello, kittens."

Hello", she managed to get out - she felt the nerves and horniness fighting inside her - he asked her if she wanted a hug and she decided that this was exactly what she needed at that moment. She leaned over to him and felt his arms hug her. She was protective and at the same time comforting and arousing. She began to relax a little. She smiled at his remark that she smelled good. His fingers caressed her arm and back through the material of her top. She wasn't sure, but she thought she felt him almost kissing her crown and then pulling back. They talked briefly about their work and the chaos there after some outside visitors. Then he asked about the stories - she explained that she hadn't read any of today's yet, and he suggested - quite firmly - that she read one of them now.

She felt her shyness pressing to the fore, but decided to obey him. She turned away so that she would not look at him while reading, opened one of his stories on the phone and started reading. As she did so, she felt his fingers gently on her neck - stroking in slow, gentle circles. When he asked her if it was okay, she sighed in agreement - it felt good on her neck after the stress and chaos of the last few days - but it distracted her and didn't help her horniness at all. She started to read and felt that the low throbbing excitement turned into a fire. She squeezed her legs together and wondered if he had noticed her deeper breathing and the changes she was trying to mask as she felt the need burning inside her. She wanted to kiss him. Shit - she wanted to do more than kiss him, but would she be able to handle it afterwards?

She decided not to read the second story just then - she couldn't really concentrate on it anyway. She slipped into his arms, rolled against him while he held her - the two thoughts arguing back and forth in her head. His soft words in her ear reassured her that there was no pressure, that they could just do what they were doing and that he would be happy. He could be, but would she be? The conversation revolved around his stories and the

adjustment he had made to the previous meeting - where he had turned a friendly encounter into something evil, and she had loved it. He whispered softly in her ear what he would write about today's meeting, and she moaned softly - the fantasy sounded so good - but would reality be any better?

He asked if she was really not wearing panties, and with a cheeky grin she pulled down the edge of her leggings to show her bare hips and waist. This time it was his turn to moan - the word "fuck" slipped gently from between his lips. When she said she was also wearing the pink bra she knew he loved the photo, and he said, "Prove it," she smiled with a slightly cheeky grin and pulled her dress all the way up to show the gorgeous bra and breasts she knew he loved.

Now she could see the lust burning in his eyes and she was so aroused. They talked - cautiously above expectations - it wasn't about love or about hurting anyone - it was two people who were inquiring and trying to do it in a safe way. She looked at him, his eyes, his smile, the gentle firmness with which he had encouraged her, while at the same time taking care not to be pushed or pressured. "Yes, sir..." she whispered. His arms slid around her and his lips met hers. She was soft, searching... the first time she had kissed anyone but her husband. It tasted different, but good. Her lips met and explored, his hand slipped over her soft skin - it felt like an eternity to her, but there was no dramatic outcry in her head. Just the desire to go on - to explore more.

Nick slowly pulled away and smiled at her - she knew how much he wanted it. His gentle words telling her she was a great kisser made her smile. He bent over again and she kissed him eagerly once more. They stayed like that for a while - ignoring the two or three cars that passed them. This time, when he broke the kiss, he undoubtedly knew how to turn her on. His soft voice reminded her that she had to be back at work soon. Then he asked a question she didn't dare answer.

"Is there anything else you'd like me to do before you leave Kitten?"

Fuuuuuck... there was so much she wished for - but she shouldn't go so quickly - should she? In a deep and shy voice she asked him to play with her breasts.

His hand quickly slipped up her dress and lifted it. His deft hands scooped her breast from the cup of the bra - his fingers teasing and pinching her nipples. Her need was now almost too great. She did not think beyond how amazing it felt. Then she felt his fingers caressing her legg-covered pussy and his apology. She didn't want his apology - she wanted his fingers. He had said he wouldn't go that far today, but she needed him to do it, and the way her body reacted to him, she knew he knew it too. So when his whispered voice asked him if she wanted his fingers on her clitoris, she answered immediately with the "Yes Sir", which she knew he would like to hear.

They were with her in a moment, slipped between her soaking wet pussy and found her clitoris in seconds. He knew what he was doing and in a few moments she had her first orgasm. She came, on the fingers of another man, in his car, in the middle of the day in a side street in the city. That was the naughtiest thing she had done in her life. She exploded to a second orgasm. She could have squirted further and further, but Nick suddenly pointed out the time - he didn't want her to get into trouble - and if she was any later, she would be. He pulled his fingers back and held her gently in his arms as she came down. She couldn't believe what she had done, but she didn't regret it. It had been amazing - and she felt that it was only the beginning.

CARRYING ANOTHER MANS SEED

It starts in my bedroom. It's a weekday morning and you've been there for two hours. You've already come inside me twice.

Now you sit on the edge of the bed and I kneel between your legs and I use my mouth and tongue for your cock, balls, stains and asshole.

For 20 minutes now I've been using my tongue and mouth to make your semi hard cock hard enough so you can try again to get what's left in your balls into my pussy. I'm starting to feel your frustration with my inability to get you hard again by seeing how you started grabbing my head and saying the things you started to say. You're also deeply frustrated that I'm not carrying your baby yet.

We were screwing for about 10 weeks at this point. We managed to meet a few times at my apartment, one night at a hotel and surprisingly many times in bathrooms and changing rooms. All together you managed to come inside me over 30 times, but it didn't work out.

The situation has worsened as we have moved forward. Originally, we both injected so violently within minutes, but given the sheer amount of sex in such a short time and the danger and risk, we both really increased what we were both willing to do.

Even this morning, when I opened the door, instead of telling me something, you just grabbed me, squeezed me over the back of my couch and stuck your cock inside me. I had learned by then not to bother me with underwear because it would just get torn off my body, or with your frustration when I wasn't wearing a dress or skirt in those bathrooms. You come into me quickly and roughly from behind.

Your cock continues to pulsate and you push deeper into me to make sure that you fill me as much as possible. You have wrapped my hair around your fist and still haven't let go.

Finally you pull back and tell me to get ready for the next round. Put on the white underwear and white stockings and prepare myself for a time that will not come easily.

In the last weeks the physicality of our relationship has really started to intensify. It took more than a month, but you have finally found and exceeded my limits and boundaries. The first time you managed to do this was in our night at the W-Hotel in the city centre, where you brought me to the ground by the combination of belt and riding whip and I said our safe word.

You were very happy at that moment and quickly climbed up and got inside me while I was lying helplessly on the bed. Your only concern that night was that my screams before you gagged me would cause someone to call the reception or that the marks you left on my body would arouse suspicion in my husband.

Today it would be no different, and after you had roughly taken off your underwear and left only your stockings, you tied me to the bed face down with my bottom in the air. At first you slowly use the leather whip we bought weeks ago on my ass, pussy and legs. You can still see some of your semen when it comes out of my insides.

In the beginning I only move my body away from the whip, but in the end, when I break and can't anymore, you use all your power on me.

This time there is no gag and you are happy about my squeaking and screaming. Of course, that made you rock hard, and you quickly mount me from behind. My moaning and pleading for you to put a baby in me makes you even harder. You tell me that you make me "scream louder now than in 9 months when the baby suckles". You stop deep down inside when your whole weight is on me.

It takes you a few minutes to recover and remove your now soft cock from my pussy filled with semen. You look down at your handiwork and see your sperm coming out of my pussy and the welts you left on my ass and legs. You think maybe you went too far this time, because these wounds are slow to heal.

This concern doesn't last too long and you tell me that if my body would only carry your child, you wouldn't have to fuck me so much. That once my belly starts to swell and my breasts fill with milk, you probably wouldn't have to use the belt and whip to get hard anymore.

You spend some time catching up on work, but you won't let me take a shower because you think you might give me a charge before you have to leave. You tell me to get between your legs and make you hard again.

Since you are still not quite hard and time is running out, I tell you to do whatever you need to do to get there.

You pull me up by my hair and hit me hard in the face out of frustration, the sound of the slap and the shock in my face seem to excite you. Four more times you bring your hand back and the slaps sound. This has had the desired effect on you and you throw me on the bed.

You hold my legs against your shoulders and kick me, push your now hard cock into my wet pussy ... My stocking-clad legs are pushed further back while you try to fuck your cock even deeper into me ... You squeeze the soles of my feet together and work on getting my feet almost completely behind my head ...

Almost completely bent in half, you have full control over my body and I feel you coming closer as you start to move faster. You start to give me some really dirty names and suddenly you punch me in the face for more time and tell me to tell you what you need to hear. I'm asking you to stick your semen inside me, fuck a baby in my stomach.

When you come closer, you put a hand around my neck and start pressing while your orgasm builds up. I feel you start to let go inside me while you call me a dirty cunt and your baby factory. Your hand tightens at my throat as you shoot into me and I get reckless and start to see stars. Finally you stop humming inside me and let your hand out of my throat.

Finally you pull your cock out of my pussy and hold my legs up to make sure your sperm stays in it. You tell me you're not sure what else you can do to put a baby inside me, but you emptied everything you have into me.

You take a shower to get back to your office... You come back into the room in a towel, staring at my body, and even though you have nothing left, you still want to fuck me.

You take out your phone and start taking some photos and videos and move my body into the positions that show your cum inside me or the marks you left on my body.

You grab my chin and kiss me passionately and deeply while your hand gently caresses my belly, hoping that this time it finally worked.

FUCKING THE FIANCÉE

It was well after midnight, and Leo was in a great mood. It was the first night of an amazing festival, and he had stayed out late to watch the last set. Now he wandered back to his tent and the rest of his friends in tears, slightly confused by the flag system, but sure that he would arrive eventually.

As he stopped to fill his bottle from the petrol pump, a small, incredibly drunk guy staggered towards him.

"Yoodude, whatsupp!! He slipped, his arm drifted up and hit his fist.

'Hey man', Leo replied. "I'm a bit lost!

'Ohh, that's, uh,' the guy opened his mouth unsteadily and staggered to the ground. Reflexively, Leo caught him before he struck. Then the guy threw up. Most of it missed, but some of it dripped onto the guy's shirt.

Damn it, Leo thought.

"Sorry, sorry," mumbled the drunk.

"Come on, man, where are you? I'll get you back', Leo said resignedly. He wasn't the most caring, but leaving this guy lying in barf just didn't sit right.

After a few minutes of slow stumbling they reached one of the smaller tents. The man had fallen into a kind of dizziness, but when he saw that the tent brought some energy, he came back to himself.

Katie, hey! Katie!," he groaned as he crawled unsuccessfully for the zipper of the tent. There was a pause, and it was reversed from the inside out.

Ricky', cried a girl from inside. The tent flap fell away, and Leo caught a glimpse of pale arms reaching for the drunk, presumably Ricky. "Shit, what the hell," she exclaimed and smelled the vomit.

'It's okay, I just need sleep, it's okay,' mumbled Ricky, pushed himself past her and collapsed on the tent floor. Leo crouched down to the entrance.

"Hello," he shouted, "I am Leo. I am Leo. I accompanied him from the pump. Ricky waved one arm in Leo's direction.

He saved me, babe, we owe him.

'Oh! Thanks,' said Katie, giving him a quick smile before turning back to Ricky. Leo got an impression of big, innocent eyes and friendly features the second she faced him. It was hard to look at her properly in this light, but she seemed to be petite. Katie bent over to knock Ricky down and Leo caught a glimpse of a perfect peach-colored butt.

'Hey, let me help you,' said Leo and crawled into the tent. Together, they laid Ricky on the front and put a bowl under his mouth. Almost as soon as they sat down, Ricky started snoring.

Any excuse,' Katie said with a sinister look.

Happens a lot, doesn't it?

Every other week, always the same. "The way he grew up," Katie flicked angrily at a mud wrench. He said he'd change once we got married, but who knows when that will be.

"Wow, you are...

-Committed, yeah. Katie reached out a hand, the glimmer of a ring just visible. "He's wonderfully sober, but that's just...

"Too much?" Leo offered.

"Too much?" offered Leo. There was a brief pause. "So, are you camping around here?" Katie said.

'I have no idea,' Leo replied laughing. Red Zone, wherever that is.

'Oh shit', Katie replied, moving away from him and opening a map. 'Yes, it's about an hour's walk from here'.

'Seriously?' replied Katie. Leo looked over at the map. He had been walking in the opposite direction since the set was over.

"Urgh. He raised his hands in desperation.

'Oh, sorry,' said Katie and gave him a quick hug. You did a good thing tonight, fate will make it up to you. Leo felt her breasts pressing against him. As they parted, he carefully weighed his words.

I'm really tired and don't want to go back. So can I sleep here tonight?

"Uh..." he could feel that Katie was torn. Sure, why not? I guess we owe you one,' she said and showed him another smile.

She closed the tent and made room for him on the mattress by wrapping her sleeping bag around her. They lay there for a minute before Leo mentioned the obvious and asked her to share it with him. It was only a small sleeping bag, so they were squeezed together at the end, her hair in his face and her bottom against his crotch.

Time dragged on, and it was clear that neither of them were asleep. Leo turned the situation in his head and made his move. An arm around her stomach, ready to be pulled away when she said something. Not a word. He moved his hand to her chest, gently grabbed a handful and let it slide free. He felt her ass bump against him and she sighed.

They continued as it felt, forever, the question and the answer were obvious to both. One hand gradually became two and her top fell off. Katie had been rubbing against his erection the whole time, and when Leo's hand finally passed her panties, he noticed it was dripping.

His fingers slipped in gently, and the slightest caress of her clitoris left her breathless. Leo teased both her clitoris and her pussy, brought her close to orgasm and disappeared just before. He wanted her to be as horny as he could make her.

At the climax of a near orgasm, he pulled his pants down to her knees and maneuvered his cock between her legs. He slid up behind her and enjoyed the wetness of her cheating pussy.

Suddenly her hand grabbed his head and pulled him towards her. She kissed him hard on the cheek and whispered in his ear.

"I want you to cum inside me.

Leo fucked her slowly, with a little more force at the end of each stroke. It was for her, but also to prolong it. It was a raw thrill to fuck someone's fiancee while she was passed out next to you. It took everything he had not to fill her up right away.

He played for time, changed his position and rolled her over. Every stroke pushed her into the mattress. Out of an impulse, he wiggled his hand under her and reached for her chest, pressing her almost painfully.

His thrusts became fast but steady and he squeezed again. Katie gasped in time and Leo felt her pussy cramping up. He managed one more push, then a hard one came. His balls pumped to the rhythm of her pussy as he flowed in towards her. Both had tried hard to come quietly and it seemed to be enough. Ricky's snoring continued.

As they put their clothes back on, Leo smiled at the thought of his sperm warm inside her. Then he saw Katie leaning over Ricky and whispering something to his sleeping body. Leo thought Ricky was awake for a second, but he was definitely asleep. That's weird.

"What was that?" he whispered. Katie turned to Leo, and her face was surprisingly serious.

I said, "This is for you.

For the rest of the festival, they were a group. Katie was friendly but never flirted while Ricky was awake, picking up one load after another of Leo's sperm as Ricky fainted.

After each night, she whispered the same thing to Ricky, "This is for you.

Three months after the festival, Leo was surprised and happy to be invited to their wedding. It seemed as if something had pushed Ricky to turn the corner. Leo thought of his sperm seeping out of Katie on the last night of the festival and smiled as he clicked on "Present".

THE CABIN

I know how I got here; I just don't know what to do about it. Many of you will think I am a disgusting bitch who doesn't care about herself or others, and to tell you the truth, you are right. If you'd met me two years ago, you'd think I was a prude. You'd never believe that I've had sex with more than 10 different men in the last month. I don't even know most of their names. Still, I crave it. That's how it all started.

To tell you a little bit about me: I'm a small, fit redhead blessed (or sometimes cursed) with firm D-cup breasts. You tend to pay a lot of attention to me. At the same time I often wear clothes that play down their importance. I am a very active person, my husband calls me the Energizer Bunny. I do not go out often and we tend not to talk. Our circle of close friends is small. I work in the financial sector. My job is very demanding and stressful, but I am very well compensated. I guess other people would describe me as classy but friendly. Only recently I have developed a preference for quickies. My husband is more than willing to help me whenever I want. I had started to masturbate, sometimes with toys, when he was away on business.

We have two grown boys who don't live with us. One is in college, the other is working in the world of work. My husband is a good-looking man with a great job. We have a big house in the country. We love camping, going to concerts and doing all the normal things that people do.

There's one thing most people would never believe about me. I love sex, with strangers, outside. How I got to be like this is a pretty long story. Some people like the details, some people don't. I'm the former. This story will be detailed and you will understand how I felt at every step of this experience.

As I said before, I am active. I love a good run in the morning and often find myself hiking or kayaking, anything that takes me outside and into nature. I have always been like this. Last year, during my lunch break from work, I did some hiking on trails that are about 5 minutes away from my work by car. It is a kind of nature reserve, no vehicles are allowed. I drive there, put on my hiking boots and go for a little hike. The parking lot is not very big and there are rarely other cars there. Sometimes, when my husband is away on business, I drive there in the evening. We live in a small town and it is very safe.

The road system is quite complicated. In winter it is used as a cross-country skiing track, and in summer people go by bike, walk their dogs and hike there. The tracks have a fairly large outer loop, with quite a lot of forks and inner loops. I had taken the same route because I need just enough time to get around during my lunch break. On one occasion, last year, I decided to take another fork and follow one of the inner loops. I came across a small clearing and found a hut that is obviously used by skiers in winter. I got curious and went inside.

What I saw in the hut shocked me at first. There were indications that people had sex there. I found used condoms, wrappers etc. and even a pair of ladies' panties. At first I was quite disgusted and left. I thought, "What kind of slut would have sex in there and leave her panties behind? The next few days I started thinking about who would have sex in there. It seemed to me that it would most likely be people, probably married people, who would go there to cheat on their spouses. I told one of my long-time girlfriends what I had found in the woods and she told me that she and her current boyfriend were out there "grim". I'm not very familiar with the deviant sex vocabulary, so I had to get her to explain what she meant. Most of you know what it means, but she told me that her boyfriend loved going out into the woods with her and having sex there, sometimes in front of other people. I had no idea that was "a thing." I just couldn't figure out what kind of payoff it was for her, but she said it was very exciting and they didn't do it often.

In the following weeks I still hiked there, but avoided the hut. Apart from that I am a very curious woman and the train to the hut was always present. Every time I hiked, I found myself thinking about going back to the hut, not knowing exactly why, but it definitely occurred to me. I remember having the opportunity for an early lunch on a

Wednesday and deciding to hike again. When I arrived at the parking lot, I noticed a very shiny new Lexus parked there. I ventured down the path. When I reached the fork in the road leading to the hut, the bait was too big; my curiosity forced me to do so. When I approached it, it seemed deserted. When I entered, I was shocked, repulsed and yet petrified. There was a middle-aged man, tall, obese, well-dressed. His fly was open and he was masturbating. I froze. Every fibre in my being told me to get out, but I couldn't move. He didn't stop, he just smiled at me and went on.

I still remember his look and his cock. He was focused on what he was doing, beads of sweat on his forehead. His cock was thick and long. His fleshy hands wrapped around it as he pumped it. He muttered a few words and persuaded me to "help". I shook my head negatively, but stayed there, feet away from him. He said something like, "Suit yourself, I don't mind if you watch." He went on for a few moments and then emitted a deep groan as huge streams of semen erupted from him. They flew so far that I had to lift my foot so he wouldn't splash it. He silently closed the zipper and slid past me on his way out. I was still in shock when I looked at his sperm on the floor. I couldn't believe how much it was.

When I came out of my stupor, I realized where I was and I was afraid of getting caught. I rushed out of the booth and back to my car. I returned to work and had 20 minutes left for lunch. Once there, I had calmed down sufficiently and realized that I was highly excited. I was so wet that I was afraid that employees and customers might recognize my state of arousal, so I made a decision as a manager. I went down the stairs to the floor below my office, found the handicapped washroom, went inside, locked the door and masturbated until orgasm. I came so hard that I was surprised that nobody heard me. Not only did I rub myself, but I put several fingers inside me and squirted quite a lot, so much that I had to clean the toilet I was sitting on.

I went back to my office and was quite ashamed, but I could NOT get the image of him masturbating out of my head. Luckily my husband was away on business, so I didn't have to worry about him feeling anything else about me. After work I got into my car. It was like a dream, I was in a haze, and when I came to, I realized that I was in the parking lot of the hiking trails. I was trembling, excited and felt a little sick. Nevertheless, I got out of the car and walked down the paths towards the hut. To this day I don't know what I expected, but I found myself in the hut, sitting on the bench with my fingers in my pussy. I came, hard, and made up my panties and skirt. When I calmed down, I left the cabin. When I arrived at the beginning of the path, I saw a young couple with a blanket under their arms entering the path. I was horrified that they could see the wet stains on my skirt.

I got into my car and drove home. I was confused and frightened. I wondered what would have happened if I had been caught there. I fell asleep. The next morning I woke up and got ready for work. I thought about what kind of clothes I would have to wear to reduce the risk of my clothes being smeared with LOL. The only thing I could think of was to take a towel or blanket and when I went back, take off my underpants/panties and put them back on again. It was as if my subconscious had taken over, and when I wanted to leave I threw a small towel in the back of the car. When I got to work, I got my laptop and lunch from the back seat. I saw the towel I had put there and felt a little shame and disgust, but I quickly let that go out of my head.

This morning at work was LONG. I was restless and fidgety. I tried not to think about the cabin, but it kept popping into my mind. At lunch it was as if I was on autopilot. I found myself back in the cabin, naked from the waist down, sitting on my towel and fingered myself like crazy to get out as quickly as possible. Every little rustle that the wind made scared me, but finally I reached orgasm and hurried back to work. This routine lasted for several weeks until one day I was near my orgasm and a dog stuck his head in the cabin. I didn't hear him approaching and that really scared me. He didn't come into the cabin, his owner, a male dog, called him over and he ran away. My orgasm hit so violently that I literally splashed across the whole width of the room. I was so startled that I did not go back into the cabin for a few weeks.

In those few weeks my head was buzzing. Every time I was alone, I masturbated thinking about what would have happened if I had been caught. I had no preconceived ideas about what I would do, only the image of a stranger coming in the doorway while I was in the middle of orgasm made me cum hard. I squirted a lot and had masturbated on the floor of the washroom or in the bathtub to make it easier to clean up afterwards.

When I finally had the courage to return to the cabin, the season was almost over. I went there almost daily until it got too cold. It took longer and longer until I reached orgasm. I am now convinced that I deliberately slowed down to increase the chance that someone else would come in with me. That winter, I even convinced my husband to start cross-country skiing. We went to the hut a few times and even had a quickie there. The hut had been cleaned up by the skiers, the graffiti had been painted over and the floors had been well cleaned. Someone even installed a small wood stove on a big brick block outside, and more than once we found the hut to warm up.

Spring could not have come earlier for me. I seemed too anxious to return to the hut. The first hike did not go well. It was wet and muddy, and I turned back before I got there. I waited another week and masturbated at every opportunity. When I got back, it was dry enough to make it there. I masturbated slowly; I barely made it back to work in time. This routine continued for about a week. I still remember the day the routine changed. It was a Thursday, I had masturbated there at noon, and since my husband was not there, I went back in the evening. I got out of my car, grabbed my towel and headed for the hiking trail. When I entered the path, I looked back and saw another car entering the parking lot. A man got out. My heart was racing. He was alone. I noticed he was tall and thin, but I couldn't see him clearly. He definitely saw me, and as I walked along the path, he followed me, but kept his distance. I was wearing yoga pants, a tank top and a sweater.

When I came to the fork in the path leading to the cabin, my mind screamed that I should swerve, but my body had other ideas. I walked along the path. When I got to the cabin, I didn't know if he was still following me. I sat down on the bench and waited. My heart was racing. I didn't dare touch myself, although I was overexcited. In fact, I could hear him approaching. He stopped before he entered. I was paralyzed with fear. I was breathing very heavily. When he finally entered the cabin, he was about three feet in front of me. We didn't say anything, just stared at each other. Finally, I took the strength to ask him, "What do you want?" He answered, "I don't know," and he walked a few steps towards me. He was wearing nylon running trousers, including a sweatshirt and a muscle shirt. I looked at him, and he adjusted his stride. To this day I don't know what got into me, but I reached out my hand and felt his step. He was semi-erect and wasn't wearing any underpants.

Again it was like a dream. I stroked him a few times, then I rolled my fingers under the elastic waistband and pulled on him. His cock jumped free and then he was in my mouth. I sucked it eagerly. It wasn't huge, I had no problem taking the whole length. When he was about to cum, I thought about what I wanted to do, take him out and jerk him off? No, too risky, he might jerk off on me. He tried to pull away, but I held him there as his sperm shot out of his cock. I swallowed it. I remember thinking it wasn't as bad as I thought it was gonna be, swallowing. It tasted salty, earthy. When he pulled away from me, he pulled up his pants in silence and left. No thanks, it was good or something. He just walked away. I sat there, vibrating, ashamed and at the same time extremely aroused. I thought about leaving, but I didn't want to run into him again on the paths. I decided to drop myself off.

I took off my yoga pants and sat down on the bench again. It felt cold, but I started to touch myself. The mixed emotions stirred up my desire and soon I was completely gone. I realized that I was not determined to have a quick orgasm. I played with my lips and clitoris and enjoyed the sensations. Then I heard another sound. I froze. It sounded as if someone was approaching again. I sat there, half-naked on the bench, legs spread, hand on my sex, and my mind was moving at a million miles a minute. It felt like an eternity. I tormented myself putting my pants back on, but for some reason I didn't. When he entered the cabin, I immediately recognized him as the man I had walked into the season before. He smiled confidently and without a word, pulled his cock out. Before I knew it, I had his thick flesh in my hand and was stroking him. All I could think of was: "Holy shit, what am I doing, I just cheated on my husband with a complete stranger and now it's going to happen again".

I put it in my mouth. It tasted like sweat, very revolting, but I kept sucking. It erected in my mouth and it was too much for me. I gagged him, mainly because of the size, but partly also because of the smell. I felt sick to my stomach, but I kept on sucking. I just wanted to get rid of him and get out of there. He had other ideas. He seemed a little frustrated with my attempts to stick him in the throat. I gagged a lot. Eventually, he pulled it out of my mouth. He raised his hand in front of me and took out a condom. Almost robotically I took it off him, opened it and pushed it on him. He lifted me into a standing position and then told me to turn around. I hesitated and he took my elbow and led me. He is a whole lot bigger than me, so I knelt down on the bench voluntarily and I felt him touching my pussy. It was like electricity shooting through me. He pushed it against my hole. He adjusted my position and pushed it into me. My body literally exploded in orgasm.

He fucked me hard, holding me up with one arm around my waist. It was animalistic, and I was having orgasms all the time. He fucked me like a dog in heat. I could see he was about to orgasm, but he pulled the condom out and took it off. I was terribly afraid that he had put it back in me, but again he led me and turned me around and put the condom back in my face, twitching. Before I could react, he erupted in my face. His sperm was hot and thick and some of it ended up in my mouth, most of it was on my face and some of it ended up on my shirt and sweater. I realized that I was on my knees in front of him. I grabbed my towel and tried to clean up. At that point the light was very dim. He said a few words to me; I could not say which ones they were.

He closed the zipper and left. I sat down on the bench again and sobbed. Not only had I been very sloppy, but it was the first time I had cheated on my husband with two different men. I did not know their names. I cleaned up as much as I could. I put on my pants, but by then it was already dark. I left the cabin, and only when I came home did I realize that I had left my pants there. Now I was the bitch who fucks in the cabin.

CPSIA information can be obtained
at www.ICGtesting.com
Printed in the USA
LVHW061447020421
683319LV00004B/359